The House *at* Helygen

Victoria Hawthorne lives with her partner, two wild Golden Retrievers, and an even wilder cat. As Vikki Patis, she is the bestselling author of psychological thrillers. *The House at Helygen* is her debut historical suspense novel.

The House at Helygen

Victoria HAWTHORNE

QUERCUS

First published in Great Britain in 2022 by

QUERCUS

Quercus Editions Ltd
Carmelite House
50 Victoria Embankment
London EC4Y 0DZ

An Hachette UK company

A CIP catalogue record for this book is available
from the British Library

HB ISBN 978 1 52941 915 3

10 9 8 7 6 5 4 3 2 1

Typeset by Jouve (UK), Milton Keynes

Printed and bound in Great Britain by Clays Ltd, Elcograf S.p.A.

Papers used by Quercus are from well-managed forests and other responsible sources.

In memory of Ruby

ONE

JOSIE

2019

I watch my shadow disappear into the darkness as Helygen House blocks out the low winter sun. Leaves crunch underfoot as I make my way across the gravel, the wind whipping my hair into my face. The promise of winter is in the air, clouds the colour of slate drifting across the sky, and the breeze sends goosebumps rippling across my skin. I'd only grabbed a light jacket for my trip into town earlier, but now a shiver runs through me. I pull my scarf tighter and walk on through the shadow of the house.

My phone buzzes in my pocket. I pull it out and smile as I swipe the screen to answer it. 'I'm almost there, Flick,' I say without preamble. 'You're early.'

'You're late,' comes the reply and I laugh. My friend could never be accused of being too subtle.

'I'll meet you by the willow tree,' I say and hang up,

tucking my hands into my pockets and lowering my head against the wind. It is fierce here, in the clearing between the house and the woods, and I try to move as fast as my bump will allow. The baby is heavy, sitting low against my pelvis, telling me that she is almost ready to make her entrance into the world. *Not yet, little one*, I tell her silently. *You've got another six weeks to go.*

I round the corner by the old stables and finally find shelter from the wind. I can't help but glance up at the building beside me, with its decaying roof and wide weatherworn doors, which will be turned into accommodation to sleep up to eight people. I can almost see it now, and excitement fills me as I picture what it will be like. The bright, airy rooms, the four-poster beds and the beautiful bathroom suite I loved so much, Henry had it installed in our own bathroom too. We only moved into Helygen House a year ago, as we'd had to wait for the renovations to be completed on what is now our apartment, but it was worth the wait. My husband's ancestral home still takes my breath away.

'I could get lost here,' I said on my first visit to meet his mother, not long before our wedding. I remember being astounded by the high ceilings and stunning architecture, and all of it surrounded by such beautiful grounds. There are more rooms than I can count, with hidden staircases and a library bigger than the flat I grew up in on the outskirts of Bodmin, which contains more books than I could ever read in a lifetime. 'Why did you move away?' I asked Henry. He only glanced at me, a wry smile on his lips, and said nothing.

I can't imagine what it must have been like, growing up here, but our daughter will. Helygen House will be her home, her inheritance, and I know it will outlast all of us.

Although it still needs a lot of work – particularly the west wing, which was destroyed by a fire a long time ago – I am utterly in love with this house. Henry had made plans to carve out a separate living space in the east wing, turning it into an apartment which is almost entirely independent from the rest of the house, with its own front and back doors. I'd like to say I had an influence on the design, but it is Henry who has the grand ideas, and we have both enjoyed seeing his vision come to life in our new home. I love sitting at the breakfast bar or out on the patio with a cup of tea, watching the lake glisten in the distance, the willow tree standing guard over the water. I've never felt more at peace than I do here, which I found odd at first. I'd never expected an estate like this to feel like home, but we are happy here, and our daughter will be too.

We wanted to think of a name for it, our apartment, to separate it from the rest of the house. We tried a few things but everything sounded like an Amazon TV show. Nothing seemed to fit. 'Little Hely,' I suggested jokingly when we were curled up on the sofa together, my feet tucked beneath Henry's legs, the detritus of moving day still strewn around the living room.

'Little Hel,' he responded with a grin, and it stuck, though not in Alice's hearing. Henry's mother lives in the main part of the building, which I have to admit I'm quite glad about. I'm not sure we could actually live together, though in reality she is only a stone's throw away. If I had to describe Alice in one word, it would probably be *prickly*. She still employs a cook and a maid, and was unimpressed by our refusal to make use of her 'staff'. The idea of having people cook and clean for me is so beyond anything I could ever feel comfortable with, and although Henry was slightly more used to such things, having grown up here, he agreed with me. Sometimes it feels as if Alice is from another time entirely; she doesn't seem to live in the modern world at all.

The sun breaks through the clouds just as the lake comes into view, turning the water to diamonds. I can see Flick standing beneath the willow tree, her arms lifted towards the sky, bare despite the chill. Her blonde hair is pulled up into a high ponytail, her arms and bare feet still tanned from the summer. I watch with awe as she lifts one leg, bringing her foot up to rest against the opposite knee. She doesn't even wobble.

'You'll catch your death out here,' I say as I approach, lifting an eyebrow as she swivels her head to look at me without moving her body. 'Show-off.'

Flick sticks out her tongue as she drops her leg and turns, slipping into her shoes and bending to pick up her rucksack in one fluid movement. 'Just showing you the talent.'

'Is that what you're calling yourself these days?' I lean against the trunk of the willow tree, my legs aching from my walk. 'I feel like a sack of potatoes.' I indicate my bump and grimace. 'And my back is killing me. Who knew carrying another human would be such hard work?'

'I've got some stretches for that,' Flick says, opening her bag and pulling out a folder.

I smile. 'You've got stretches for everything.'

She hands me a sheet of paper with a flourish. 'You can thank me later.' I glance at it, noting how much smaller the illustration's bump is than mine, before she hands me another sheet. 'Here's the list of classes,' she says. I run my eye down it. There are a few types of yoga – vinyasa, hatha, hot – and Pilates, all broken down by levels and intensity. Just looking at it makes me feel exhausted. 'And this is what I'll need. Mostly mats, resistance bands and some blocks.'

'How many people per class?' I ask, reading through the list.

'No more than eight, I'd say.'

'So The Hut would be big enough?' I gesture towards the small building on the edge of the lake, the water reflected in the large window.

'Definitely.' Flick nods. 'Did you bring the keys?'

I roll my eyes at her. 'You are talking to a professional here.'

She snorts. 'No, I'm talking to my friend who used to think a pasta bake was a gourmet dish.'

I shove her with my shoulder as we walk towards The Hut. 'Can you swim as well as you can stretch?' I tease. 'That lake is deeper than it looks.'

'Is that any way to speak to your best friend in the world?' She grins. 'Until the little one comes along, that is.'

'Then you'll be my bestest friend *and* my bestest

babysitter,' I say. Flick pulls a face, and I feel a rush of guilt at my light tone. I open my mouth to apologise but she waves me away, flashing me a bright smile that tells me to drop it. As happy as she is for me and Henry, Flick still finds these conversations difficult. I need to be more mindful of that.

We step inside The Hut and I reach out to switch on the light. It flickers once before illuminating the room. 'I think we'll need to put in new flooring,' I say, looking down at the scuffed floorboards. 'And some brighter lights. Do you know what colour you want to paint it?'

'White,' she says decisively. 'Boring, I know, but it's calming. Though I might do a feature wall, maybe something to tie in with the willow tree.'

I smile, picturing it. Flick is an incredible artist, and at first I wondered why she decided to become a yoga instructor when we graduated from university, but she has a real passion for it, particularly for helping people with chronic pain. This is probably the most exciting part of our project to revamp Helygen House. Once it's been spruced up, Flick is going to be running yoga and Pilates classes from The Hut, plus some two-day retreats with accommodation in the yurts we're going to erect in the clearing beyond. I remember Alice's face when we told her, the way her lips pinched together when she said the word *yurts*. She isn't a fan of some of our plans, but this is Henry's house, and besides, he needs the money. *We* need the money. Renovating and running an estate of this size isn't cheap, and these ventures will start to make Helygen House pay for itself.

'Sounds amazing,' I tell her as she wanders around the space. 'Whatever you want.'

'This may need a bit of updating too,' she says, poking her head into the small bathroom. 'Maybe some lockers and changing benches. Oh, and parking. Will there be access? You know some of my clients can't walk too far.'

I nod. 'We're going to put a gate in up there.' I point out of the window. 'There's already a dirt track leading down from the road, we just need to create a small parking area, probably on that end.' My finger follows the track down towards a clearing beneath a cluster of trees to the right. The road must have been used for deliveries in the past, or anything else the owners of the house didn't want coming to the front door. Sometimes it strikes me that this house is so full of history, with such a vibrant past. There's so much still to discover.

'Great!' Flick says excitedly. 'I can't believe this is happening, Jose. It's going to look *amazing*.' She twirls around in the middle of the room and I laugh. 'When do we start?'

I run through my mental checklist. The yurts are on order – we've gone for three to begin with, which can sleep up to four people each – and I need to check on when the gate is being installed, but there's no reason why Flick can't start working on The Hut now. 'Whenever,' I tell her. 'Send me a list of what you need later and I'll order it.'

'Who'd have thought it?' she says, still grinning. 'Felicity Daniels and Josephine Corbyn, kick-arse businesswomen.' I laugh. 'Oh, sorry, Josephine *Fox*,' she adds with a mischievous twinkle in her eyes.

'You *know* I didn't change my name.' I shove her play-fully, remembering Alice's horror when we told her that I wouldn't be taking Henry's surname, her hand fluttering to her throat as if we had just delivered a shocking piece of news. I suppose we had, to her. She didn't understand how two people, so different on paper, could be together.

'Have you thought of a name yet?' I ask Flick as we leave. 'For the classes?' I pull the door shut behind me and twist the key in the lock before holding it out to her.

She takes it with a smile. 'How about *Relax with Flick*?' she suggests, then shakes her head. 'I'm no good at names.'

'I'm sure you'll come up with something *fabulous*,' I say with a wink.

'*Feel Fabulous with Flick*? I like it.' She rolls her eyes then glances at me. 'What about you?'

It takes a second before it clicks and I place a hand on my stomach. 'We're torn between Louisa and Beatrix.' I wrinkle my nose. 'You can guess which one Alice wants.'

Flick snorts. 'Who cares what *Alice* wants?'

I smile, knowing Flick doesn't understand the tenuous relationship I have with my mother-in-law. I like her, for the most part, but there are so many things we don't agree on. Sometimes it feels like they're all stacked up between us, keeping us from getting closer. The one thing we really have in common is Henry, and our love for him.

The sun is brighter now, casting a slight warmth across my face. Flick holds out a hand and touches the willow tree as we pass as if she is saying goodbye. I notice the scratches on her arm, the tell-tale sign of her recurring anxiety. Has she been worrying about this new venture? Or is something else bothering her?

'What about Willow?' she says, turning to me before I can ask questions. 'Willow Louisa Fox. Or even Beatrix as the middle name. It has a ring to it, and Alice couldn't complain either.'

I pause, considering. It *does* have a ring to it. I smile at my friend. 'I think you've just chosen my baby's name,' I say, linking my arm through hers as we make our way back towards the house. 'But it'll be Corbyn-Fox. Willow Beatrix Corbyn-Fox.'

She grins. 'A name fit for a princess.'

'And for my daughter too.'

I wave Flick off, watching as she turns her car around and drives out of the gate, gravel skittering beneath her tyres. The sun is once again hidden behind a cloud as I turn and walk back towards the house. I check my watch and decide there's just enough time to grab a late lunch before Henry's due home from his meeting. I can't wait to tell him about Flick's ideas for the studio. I remember when I first mentioned the idea of yoga and meditation retreats to him, and he tilted his head in that way he does when he's considering something but isn't quite convinced. It didn't take much for him to agree, though. Flick had already drawn up sketches of the yurts, The Hut in the background and the lake spread out like a blanket. She has a way of bringing things to life, and I could tell that Henry saw it as I did. But Alice took a bit more persuading. She has lived here since her brother died back in the eighties and she's used to being in charge. Henry inherited the estate when he was just four years old, which is when Alice moved into Helygen House with two small children in tow. 'Why didn't your mum inherit? Why you, when you were so young?' I'd asked when Henry told me his uncle had died without a spouse or children, and he almost looked ashamed when he told me the history of the estate.

I press a hand against my stomach, smiling at the memory of Henry changing the order of succession, as we jokingly called it. We both made a will when I fell pregnant, mainly driven by Henry's confession that, historically, only male heirs could inherit Helygen House. The idea of all the Fox girls – Henry's older sister India, and even his mother – being passed over in favour of their male relatives left an impression on me, and so we made a will to change things. To ensure our child, no matter the sex, would inherit Helygen House.

'Do you think your dad will like your new name?' I murmur as I push open the front door to Little Hel, my hand still on my stomach. As I wipe my feet on the mat and hang my jacket up on a hook behind the door, the tumble dryer in the small utility room to my right emits a beep, the lights flashing to show the cycle has ended. I open the door and breathe in the burst of warm air and the scent of fresh towels before moving into the hallway. I hear a skitter of claws on tiles and smile as Ivy bounds out of the kitchen, her tail wagging as she prepares to jump up at me. She's started doing that more as my pregnancy has progressed, as if she can smell the child inside me and is desperate for her to come out and play.

'Ivy and Willow,' I say as I lift my hand to tell her to sit and scratch behind her ears. 'It's got a nice ring to it. Are you ready to be a big sister?'

She suddenly turns and bounds a few feet away before stopping and cocking her head at me. She does this when she wants me to see something, to make sure I'm following her, and I frown. 'If you've brought something in again . . .' I murmur, remembering the time she dragged a rabbit onto the patio a few weeks ago. It was still alive and apparently unhurt, thanks to her gentle golden retriever mouth, but utterly petrified. It didn't seem to understand that Ivy just wanted a friend to play with.

She barks, the sound too loud in the quiet house, and I feel my pulse quicken. 'All right, I'm coming.' I follow the dog through the hall and into the kitchen, watching her disappear behind the breakfast bar. I open my mouth to call her name then stop, my legs suddenly full of lead as I take in the scene before me.

Blood is splattered across the tiles, droplets splashed against the wall. There are red pawprints too, from where Ivy must have walked through it to greet me. I look behind me and notice faint marks on the floor tiles and along the hallway. When I turn back, it feels as if time has slowed down, my pulse pounding in my ears, my brain unable to make sense of what my eyes are seeing. Ivy's head pops around the breakfast bar and she gives a low impatient woof, but my eyes have found what is lying on the floor beside her and suddenly I can't breathe. The air leaves my lungs as I drop to my knees, blood rushing in my ears. There, just visible behind the breakfast bar, is a hand coated in blood. Henry's hand.

My husband is dead.

TWO

I'm so cold.

My teeth chatter as I watch several uniformed officers sweep into the house, their heavy boots leaving mud on the floors. *I only cleaned them yesterday,* I think, and then I remember what else is staining the tiles and nausea rises again.

Alice is beside me, quiet for once, her face pale and drawn. Usually she would be taking charge, barking orders in her posh voice, but I am grateful for her silent presence now. I used to tease Henry about his accent, and how, for a Cornishman, he sounded remarkably like someone from the Home Counties. 'Boarding school beat the Cornish out of me,' he would say with a wink. Pain hits me in the guts at the memory and I double over, gasping for breath. Henry. Henry is *dead*.

I feel a hand on my back, then something being draped over my shoulders. 'That's it,' a voice says, warm and comforting and as Cornish as my own. 'Take some deep breaths.' After a few moments, when the world has stopped spinning, I look up and see the face of a paramedic, her bright pink hair pulled into a messy bun on top of her head. She has a tattoo of a rose on her forearm, a name written beneath that I cannot read. A child? A parent? A husband or wife? Someone special enough to be inked on her skin forever, a part of her. She smiles at me. 'All right, maid. You'm all right,' she says, and I want to wrap myself in her words, to believe that everything *is* all right, that my husband isn't lying dead in our kitchen, half of his face missing from a gunshot wound.

I will never be able to scrub that image from my mind. I can never unsee it, the mess of Henry's beautiful face, the way his body is lying unnaturally against the tiles, one arm flung out, his wedding ring glinting in the light.

Hot tears spill down my cheeks. I taste salt in my mouth and gag, imagining it is blood, *his* blood. I drop my head down again and sob into my bump, whispering an apology to our daughter who will now never get to meet her father, who will never sit on his shoulders to see over a crowd, or feel his gentle fingers putting a plaster over her grazed knee. She will never listen to him read her a story, will never giggle at the silly voices he would have put on for her. She will never look for him in the audience at a school play, relief flooding through her when she spots his smiling face, full of pride. She will never feel his love, his warm, all-consuming love that promised to give her the world, and that would never have let her down, ever.

Henry is gone, and my daughter no longer has a father, and I feel myself crack down the middle, a splinter that will never heal.

★

'Mrs Fox?'

I lift my head to find two men standing before me. They are not wearing uniform, but I can tell they are police officers. Detectives, perhaps, as this is a crime scene. The thought fills me with hope. A crime has been committed here, and someone needs to pay for it. I realise I am rubbing my hands together, skin chafing, and clamp them between my knees.

'Yes.'

I turn to see Alice standing, her hands smoothing down her long skirt. The men exchange a glance and one clears his throat. Alice is the only Mrs Fox here, but it is me they will want to speak to.

'I'm Henry's wife,' I say, instead of explaining. My stomach lurches at the tense but I do not correct myself. I cannot think of him in the past, not yet. Not ever. 'I'm Josie.' I clench my fingers together, my bump heavy and uncomfortable, the baby wriggling around inside me as if she knows what is happening. She can feel my emotions, my grief pouring into her, and I feel a wave of guilt. *I'm so sorry,* I tell her in my head. *I'm so, so sorry.*

'Josie,' one of the men says, taking a seat opposite me. Alice sits back down, her forehead wrinkled. 'I'm DS Fergus, and this is DC Jones.' The other man sits beside him and pulls out a notepad. 'Please accept our sincere condolences for your loss.'

The words hit me like a blow, for they describe so perfectly what this feels like. What this is. A loss. I have lost my husband, lost the future we dreamed of together, the years of laughter and arguments and pride and love, all gone. The picture of us as a family of three, our daughter growing from baby to toddler to teenager to adult, standing between us in family photos, my hair greying, his thinning, our faces showing the signs of a life well lived. All of that has been snatched from us, wrenched from between my fingers and thrown to the wind.

I see Alice's lips grow thinner as she watches the men, waiting for them to speak, to tell us something of note. Their silence is deafening. We will not like what they have to say. 'What is it?' I ask finally, my voice stronger than I expected. I see the men straighten, their eyes widening as they take me in, this grieving widow. This heavily pregnant, grieving widow. They don't know how to deal with me. *I* don't know how to deal with me.

'Josie,' DS Fergus says gently. 'We need to ask . . . Was your husband suffering from depression?'

I sit back, his words forcing the breath from my body. 'Depression?' I echo. I try to swallow but my throat is too dry; it aches with unshed tears. 'No, no. He wasn't suffering from depression.'

'He *was* under a lot of pressure,' Alice says, her voice high and clear. I stare at her, my mouth open, my mind struggling to catch up.

'And your name is . . .?' DC Jones asks.

'Alice Fox, Henry's mother,' she answers primly, as if he should have known.

He scribbles down her name. 'What do you mean by "under a lot of pressure"?'

'Precisely that. He was always so busy, what with the running of the estate and his newfangled plans.' She sniffs. 'He was running himself into the ground.'

'So would you say he had been . . . troubled, lately?' DS Fergus asks.

'No,' I snap as Alice nods. I grasp her arm, feeling the scratchy wool of her cardigan beneath my fingers. 'No. What are you talking about, Alice?'

She doesn't look at me as she shifts away, and my hand falls from her arm. 'As you can see,' she says stiffly, 'my daughter-in-law is due to give birth very soon. Preparing for a new baby is stressful, and perhaps he . . . Well. Perhaps Henry wasn't ready.'

I am stunned. I always suspected that Alice had never truly warmed to me, unable to see past my council house and state school upbringing, and it's true that we rarely see eye to eye on anything – from the future of the estate, to politics, to breastfeeding – but I am still stunned by her words and her tone. My husband, her son, is lying dead in the kitchen just a few feet away from us, and she is telling the police that he had been depressed, inferring that he may have . . . hurt himself, in such a matter-of-fact way that she could be talking about the weather.

'Mrs Fox,' DS Fergus says, looking at me.

'It's Corbyn,' I say automatically. 'Josie Corbyn. I kept my surname.' Alice wrinkles her nose. Even now, *even now,* she finds it within herself to show her distaste at my choices. I force myself to ignore her. 'My mother-in-law is mistaken,' I continue with gritted teeth. 'Henry was not depressed. He was busy, yes, perhaps a little stressed. We all are. But he was happy. He was excited for the arrival of our daughter.' My hand finds its way to my stomach again and I feel her kick against me, the pain sharp beneath my fingers, a reminder that she is still alive, that she needs me. 'He was happy,' I repeat. '*We* were happy.' DS Fergus nods while DC Jones writes something on his pad. I can't read his scrawls upside down. What is he writing about us, about Henry? 'Why are you asking me these questions?' I demand. 'You should be looking for whoever did this. Someone came into our house and . . .' I trail off, my throat closing over the words that I can barely allow myself to think, let alone say. *Murdered my husband.*

DS Fergus looks at me with pity in his eyes. I clench my fists, fingernails digging into the palms of my hand as anger sweeps through me. *I don't need pity*, I want to scream. *I need you to do your fucking job and find whoever did this.*

Alice lays a hand on my wrist, her fingers cold against my skin. I fight the urge to pull away. 'Josie is distraught,' she says. 'She needs to rest. She has the baby to think of.'

'No,' I say again, my jaw clenched. 'What I *need* is to find out what happened to my husband.' I turn back to the police and catch sight of the camera sitting above the back door. 'There's CCTV on both entrances, and dotted around the estate. You can find out if someone came in. If someone . . .'

I choke back a sob as I contemplate what that someone did while they were in the house, how terrified Henry must have been. Who could have done such a thing? Was it a burglary gone wrong? I hadn't thought to check if anything was missing. But who brings a shotgun to a burglary? I drop my head again, trying to breathe through the pain in my chest.

'Josie needs to rest,' Alice repeats, her fingers tightening on my arm.

'Of course,' DS Fergus replies, something like relief crossing his face as he stands. 'We'll be in touch again soon.'

The officers almost bow to Alice as they take their leave, and if it were under any other circumstances, I might laugh. I *would* laugh, and Henry would laugh too, the kind of giggle you try to keep quiet, smothered by a hand, until your whole body shakes and tears leak out of your eyes. We often laughed like that, Henry and I, our sides hurting, struggling to catch our breath as we threw our heads back in hysterics.

Right now, as I watch two women lift a stretcher up the steps and into the kitchen, I don't think I'll ever laugh again.

THREE

ELIZA

1881

The autumn leaves skittered beneath her feet as she got out of the carriage, her carefully polished boots clicking against the stone steps as she climbed up one, two, three. Her eyes were focused on the building before her, so grand and beautiful it almost took her breath away. The windows were dark, reflecting the heavy grey sky back at her, and she felt a shiver of something – excitement? Fear? – and reached out to take the arm of the man beside her.

Her husband. She could still hardly believe it. She looked up at his profile, taking in his straight nose and dark eyebrows, one icy blue eye flicking towards her, the edges of his lips tugging upwards into a smile as he realised she was watching him.

'Is everything all right, dear?' Cassius asked in his honeyed voice.

Eliza smiled. 'Everything is perfect.' And it was. She was captivated by him, this man who had asked for her hand, who looked at her in a way that made her breathless. Their wedding day had been beautiful, the air full of the scent of fresh flowers and happiness. He had picked petals from her hair as they were whisked away to their honeymoon suite, his fingers leaving a line of fire as they brushed against her skin. She was mesmerised by him, and she intended to be the wife he deserved.

The large front doors opened and she pulled her gaze away from Cassius to see five people, two men and three women, file out to stand before them. There were fewer servants than she had expected for a house of this size, especially now she was here and could see it in all its glory. She thought then of the one poor maid she'd had at home, who'd had to do everything from fetching the water to helping her dress. *At least she will have less to do now, with me gone*, she thought. She felt a tug at the thought of home – her parents' house, she reminded herself. This was her home now. She shook the memories from her mind and focused on the people in front of her as she made her way across the gravel, her hand tucked firmly into the crook of her husband's arm.

'Welcome home, sir,' the butler said, stepping forward and offering Cassius a bow. He turned to Eliza next. 'And welcome to Helygen House, madam.'

She inclined her head, giving him a warm smile. *Hel-ee-gan*, she thought, trying to commit the pronunciation to memory. *Hel-ee-gan House.*

'Is my mother home, Thomas?' Cassius asked the butler as he and the other male servant stepped forward to remove their bags from the carriage.

Thomas cleared his throat. 'Yes, sir. In the drawing room, I believe.'

Cassius nodded and squeezed Eliza's hand. 'We'll get settled in first. I trust a fire has been laid in our rooms?'

'Of course, sir.'

Eliza smiled at the remaining servants as they passed. One was an older woman with a ruddy complexion and her hair neatly tucked beneath a cap, who offered Eliza a curtsey. The cook, Eliza surmised. They all looked the same to her, every cook in every house seemingly bred from the same stock, with large hands and a no-nonsense approach. She'd always liked the cook her family had employed ever since Eliza was a child, who would sneak her a biscuit before dinner and let her lick the bowl when she was baking, and missed her when she'd had to leave. Standing next to the cook were two girls dressed in the uniform of maids. One of them caught her eye, her bright red curls escaping their pins and tumbling down her back. She looked so young to Eliza, barely thirteen if she was a day, with pale skin and bright spots of colour on her cheeks. She bowed her head as they passed, and for a moment, Eliza could swear she'd met the girl before.

She felt a tug on her arm and turned away, her attention suddenly captured by the beauty of the house once again. They stepped over the threshold and Eliza admired the tiles beneath their feet, white with a black motif, scrubbed clean and sparkling in the low autumn light. A grand staircase opened up before them and as they moved towards it, Eliza saw panelled walls on either side, leading to more rooms.

So much to discover, she thought as she began to climb the stairs after her husband, one gloved hand on the smooth railing. *I could get lost here.*

Several doors led off the first-floor landing, some closed, and there was another staircase beyond a smaller corridor. Cassius turned left and led her towards the last door, taking out a key and unlocking it. 'Welcome home,' he said with a grin, throwing open the door with a flourish.

Eliza gazed around as she stepped into the room, relishing the warmth from the crackling fire. Her lips curved into a smile as she took in the huge bed with heavy curtains neatly tied to the posts, the large dressing table by the window lined with glass bottles twinkling in the sunlight and the grand wardrobes standing against the wall. She touched a finger to a small bird on the wallpaper, marvelling at the intricacies. 'It is beautiful,' she said, turning to smile at her husband. She walked through the open archway beside the window to find another small room, one wall lined with shelves and a comfortable-looking chair in the corner. She could imagine herself curling up in that chair, a book on her lap, a cat purring at her feet. She turned to see Cassius watching her, a smile on his lips. 'My own library?' she asked, hardly daring to believe it. Her mother had always told her that reading was not for girls, that she should be focusing on learning French and the piano and other more suitable, ladylike pursuits, but her father had indulged her, bringing back books from his travels to London, and it seemed that her husband would be the same.

'You haven't seen the best bit yet,' he said, striding forward and taking her hand. She fought the urge to giggle as he pulled her across the room towards another door. *You are a woman now, a wife, no longer a giggling schoolgirl*, she reminded herself, but her excitement was palpable as Cassius pushed open the door and they stepped inside.

The first thing she saw was a large white bath on cast-iron feet standing beside the fireplace. Cassius made his way over to it and began to turn the taps. 'Come,' he said, and she did, allowing him to remove the glove from her left hand and bring it under the running water.

Eliza looked at him, her eyes wide with surprise. 'It's hot!'

He grinned. 'Only the best for my love.'

She felt her cheeks flush as he turned off the tap and passed her a towel to dry her hand. She looked around the room, taking in the dark green tiles on the walls and the lavatory in the corner beside a white sink with glistening chrome taps. She remembered how the maid used to haul buckets of hot water up to Eliza's room from the kitchen, her face and hands red, to pour into the bath in front of the fire. *How modern this house is in comparison*, she thought, *how luxurious*.

'I am the luckiest woman in the world,' she said, pressing a hand to her husband's cheek. He brought it to his lips and kissed the soft curve of her palm.

'It is I who is the lucky one,' he said with a wolfish grin, sending a jolt of electricity through her. He took a step back and glanced down at his clothes, splattered with mud. 'I will get changed, I think. Mother would not approve of me wearing a soiled suit to tea.' He winked, then moved past Eliza back into the bedroom. She followed, her hand trailing along the surface of the dressing table – *her* dressing table. She peered at the bottles; there were so many, so much choice. 'I didn't know which scent you wore,' he said, noticing. 'So I bought them all.'

She caught his eye in the mirror and smiled, deciding not to tell him that she had not worn perfume for years, that she had made do with lavender water which always made her nose itch. She lifted one and brought it close to her nose, inhaling the sweet fragrance. When she looked up, she saw Cassius was opening the bedroom door. 'I thought you were getting changed, husband?' she asked, bemused.

'I am. My room is next door.'

Eliza's smile faltered. 'Next door? But I thought . . .' She trailed off, unable to put her feelings into words. She had believed – hoped, really – that they would share a bedroom, like her parents always had. As an only child she had spent most of her life in isolation, loneliness breeding boredom and discontent. She had longed for a sibling, then for a companion, and then for a husband, someone she would go to sleep with each night, wrapping herself in their warmth.

'My clothes are in there,' Cassius said, his expression

unreadable as he backed out of the room. 'I'll be back in a moment.' And then he was gone, and she was left alone in her new bedroom.

She glanced down at her dress, which was wrinkled but clean. Eliza, unlike her husband, had not had to assist in pushing the carriage out of the mud somewhere in Devon, but she suddenly wondered if she should change too. This would be her first time meeting her husband's mother – unusually, she had chosen not to attend their wedding in London, and had declined Eliza's parents' invitations to dinner. 'She doesn't like to leave Cornwall,' Cassius had told her parents. 'Her health is often poor.' Eliza's mother, who too suffered from a weak constitution, had smiled in sympathy, and the matter had been dropped so as not to offend Eliza's suitor. There was so much at stake for them, after all.

Cassius appeared in the doorway then, breaking her out of her reverie. 'Shall we go down?'

'Will I do?' she asked nervously.

'You look marvellous,' he said, his eyes glittering, and she felt herself simultaneously relax and brighten beneath his gaze. A memory of their wedding night flitted through her mind and she felt her cheeks redden, hoping her husband would not notice as he held out his hand. He would still visit her, of course, even if he did not share her bed all the time. She followed him out of the room and back down the hallway, marvelling at the architecture as they descended the stairs, admiring the beautiful furniture positioned just so and the portraits hung artfully on the walls. *So much history*, she thought, *so many people to learn about*. She realised she knew very little about her husband's family and resolved to ask her new mother-in-law. Her own mother loved nothing more than to speak of her ancestors, the men who'd built the family name and reputation, and Eliza supposed that Cassius's mother would be the same.

Cassius led her through a corridor with panelled walls and yellow wallpaper covered in delicate flowers. The windows were shut tight against the October air and Eliza felt sweat prickling beneath her armpits as they entered the drawing room. She could feel the strength of the fire from the doorway, hear the crackle of the wood in the grate. 'Mother,' Cassius said, and Eliza suddenly noticed the woman sitting on the couch beside the fire, her white hair pulled back into a tight bun. She was wearing all black, and as she stood to greet them, Eliza saw the long train of her skirts and the shape of the crinoline beneath. She smoothed down her own skirts, surprised to see her mother-in-law in such an outdated fashion. Cassius moved into the room, Eliza on his arm as his mother extended a hand. He dropped a kiss onto it before speaking. 'Mother, I am pleased to present to you Elizabeth Jane Fox, née Atkins, my beautiful wife.' He turned to Eliza with a smile. 'Eliza, meet Harriet Fox, my mother.'

'It is a pleasure to meet you, madam,' Eliza said, dropping her eyes demurely. 'I have heard so much about you.'

Harriet made a noise in the back of her throat, and Eliza looked up to see her turning away. She glided back to the couch, carefully arranging her skirts as she sat down. Cassius ushered Eliza over to the seat opposite, not seeming to notice the shift in atmosphere, and she sat with her hands folded in her lap, trying to appear calm despite the nerves bubbling in her stomach.

'A drink,' he said, clapping his hands together. 'A toast, to our new family.' He rang a bell and Thomas hurried in. 'Three brandies, my good man,' Cassius said with a grin.

'Sir,' the servant said, moving over to the cart against the wall. He poured a measure into three crystal glasses and arranged them on a tray.

'Ladies first,' Cassius said, and Thomas moved to Harriet, bending slightly at the waist as he offered her the tray. She took a glass, and Eliza noticed that her hand was shaking. *Is she as nervous as I am?* she wondered as she took her own drink. *Perhaps she just needs some time to get used to having a new daughter.*

Cassius lifted his glass into the air while the servant scurried out of the room. 'A toast,' he repeated, 'to my new wife, and my beloved mother. May we all be the best of friends.'

As Eliza lifted her own glass to her lips, she fancied she saw something flash across her mother-in-law's face. A shadow, barely there before it was gone, but it filled her with a sudden dread.

FOUR

JOSIE

2019

I stare into the mirror, the room behind me unfamiliar. I have been staying in the main house since it happened two weeks ago, unable to face going back to the apartment, but still I cannot feel at home here. I miss the apartment, and the life Henry and I had built together. At least Ivy is with me, her head resting on her front paws, her eyes watching me as I pull my hair back into a bun. I no longer recognise the woman looking back at me either, in her too-small black dress, her hair lank and greasy, her eyes ringed with purple. Who is this woman? I have found myself thrust into the role of grieving widow and I can no longer see myself in her.

It is his funeral today. The police have released Henry's body, after informing us that they are not treating his death as suspicious. The gun found beside him had been his own shotgun, usually carefully locked away and rarely used, so it is unlikely somebody broke in and used it against him, they said. I absorbed this news like a sponge absorbs water, taking it into myself and making the grief a part of me. I will never be free from this pain. It is heavy, weighing down my limbs as I descend the stairs, my hand gripping the railing to steady myself. Despite everything, I still have my daughter to think of. She is the only thing keeping me going.

The front door is wide open, letting the cold October air inside. As I reach the bottom of the stairs, I see the hearse is outside, Henry's name spelled out by flowers. I cannot think of him being in there, cannot imagine my husband's body locked inside that wooden box. I have let Alice take charge of the arrangements, choosing the flowers and the music, buying the food for the wake which will take place here later, in the house Henry grew up in. She even chose my dress, her maid Marie letting it out at the waist to make room for my bump, though it is still too tight. I cannot find it in myself to care about any of it.

'There you are.' Alice appears from behind me, dressed in a flowing black dress that somehow feels inappropriate. It looks more suited to an occasion, a black-tie event to raise money for underprivileged children while the attendees drink expensive champagne from crystal glasses. I say nothing. I sit on the bottom step to put on my boots, but my ankles are swollen and the zip won't move. I feel tears of frustration spring to my eyes and close them, taking a deep, shuddering breath. I haven't worn anything except trainers or wellies for months, anything I could easily slip my feet into, since my ankles started swelling and my bump grew too large for me to reach my feet without difficulty. I remember the stilettos I bought for an event with Henry, back when we were in the first flush of love and I wanted to impress him, wanted to look as if I belonged by his side. He laughed when I came out of the bedroom, the high heels making me unsteady, and pointed at his own feet, which were encased in smart but comfortable trainers.

How did he do it? How did he manage to sail through life so easily, doing whatever he wanted, not caring how it might be viewed, how he might be judged by others? Flick is the same, in a way. Perhaps that's why they always got on. I remember her surprise when I told her about his career in politics, how he had started as an aide to a Tory cabinet minister, but she softened when I told her about how we met. Henry had just started working for one of the Labour party leader contenders after the Conservative prime minister said Britain should not take in more refugees, and I was standing outside Westminster with a sign held above my head that said 'Will Trade Racists for Refugees'. Rather clever, though I couldn't take the credit for it: I had come unprepared and a fellow protester had given me his spare sign. Henry smiled when he read it and opened his jacket to reveal a badge with the same words printed in red capitals. The thing about Henry, I soon discovered, was that he wasn't afraid to change his mind, or to speak it.

'Really, Henry. Why must you make everything about politics?' Alice asked once when we visited Helygen House for the weekend. It was shortly before we got married and when work on Little Hel was just about to start, and we were sitting in the large dining room, the three of us clustered at the end of a table big enough to seat eighteen. Henry had started talking animatedly about the EU referendum and how there had been a recent rise in racist attacks, and I remember the look in his eyes when she'd said that. And when he spoke, his voice was heavy with disappointment.

'Everything is political, Mother.'

He was right. Everything *is* political. If we hold racist views, we are less likely to support the politicians who pledge assistance for refugees or feel angry when a black man is shot dead by the police. If we look down on the working class, we are less likely to believe in socialism and the even distribution of wealth. Our beliefs fuel our votes, and our votes reaffirm our beliefs. And we find friends and lovers amongst those who align with us, for the most part; with those who believe in and fight for the same things we do. People who truly get us, at the deepest level. Like Henry and me.

'Josie?'

I look up, surprised to find myself still sitting on the bottom step, my face wet with tears. Flick is in the doorway, her face creased with worry.

'I couldn't put my shoes on,' I say lamely, and she rushes forward, crouching before me.

'Oh, sweetie.' She pulls a packet of tissues from her pocket and hands me one. 'Here, let me.'

She gently wrestles my feet into the boots and zips them up while I stare up at the ceiling, the grand chandelier glinting in the morning light. It is breathtaking, this house. Although I only moved in properly a year ago, I feel as if I belong here, as if it is where I was always supposed to be. Will I have to leave now? The thought sends a shiver through me. Where would I go? I have no family left, no real money of my own. I gave up my job when we moved back to Cornwall, excited to start working on our renovation plans. What will happen next?

Flick holds out a hand and helps me to my feet. 'I'll be with you,' she says, wrapping an arm around my shoulders. 'Every step of the way.'

I cling to her, desperate for her support, knowing it will not be enough. I remember my father's funeral, the small crematorium with dark wooden seats and a leak in the roof. I remember watching the droplets fall behind the celebrant, counting them as they splashed against the floor, trying not to think of my dead father lying in his coffin before me, his life cut cruelly short by an illness he had battled for over a decade.

I lean on Flick as we make our way outside. The wind is wild today, whipping my hair into my eyes, my tears blocking my view of the hearse. I am grateful for it. I cannot stand the sight of that coffin, knowing what lies inside, what I have lost. Flick helps me into the first car where Alice already sits, straight-backed and dry-eyed, and I feel myself begin to tremble. Flick squeezes my hand and I close my eyes, trying to centre myself. My mind is full of memories, my heart desperate to remember Henry as he was, and the love we had for one another. I try to grasp that love as I hold Flick's hand in mine. I try to keep it in my heart to ease the ache, but I can feel it slipping from me, like water running through my fingers.

FIVE

I do not give a reading. I do not listen to the words of the vicar, a man I have never met before. Henry was not religious; we'd married in a registry office in London, a small, intimate event with just a few close friends. I remember Alice's distaste when we told her about our plans, and the sour face she wore as we vowed to love one another in our own, true way. I know that this is all her doing. The hymns, the prayers, the invoking of the Lord's name. But I cannot find it in myself to care. Henry is gone. Despite what the vicar says, he is not looking down on us, he is not walking through the Pearly Gates to the tune of harps and singing angels. He is lying in that coffin before us, awaiting his final journey back to the earth in the family cemetery in the grounds of Helygen House. Did he even want to be cremated? Had we ever talked about it? I can't remember. Do people in their thirties contemplate death in such a precise way? We'd made our wills, put our affairs in order to ensure there would be no confusion should the worst happen, but had we ever gone so far as to envision our own funerals? Or had we ignored that part of dying, not wanting to look it in the eye just yet?

I sit silently in the front pew, letting the words wash over me. The vicar stands aside and one of Henry's university friends gives a speech full of anecdotes I don't understand, before Alice reads a poem. None of it matters. None of it is Henry, truly. Yes, he was a son, a friend, a husband, a soon-to-be father, but none of this captures the essence of him. The way his eyes crinkled when he smiled; the way he would always pet a dog if one came near him, his fingers twitching if it was a service dog and he knew he wasn't allowed; the way he stood by the patio doors with his morning coffee, looking out over the grounds. The scent of him, how it would linger in the bedsheets and on my clothes, surprising me when he wasn't around. The feel of his arms around me, his hands soft and warm against my skin. He was kind, loving, all of the adjectives one can use to describe a lost loved one, but they are empty, hollow. He is gone, and all of that has gone with him.

Finally it is over, and we are standing, Flick's hand on my arm as she guides me towards the exit. Alice pauses to speak to the vicar but I keep walking, not wanting to look at the coffin, not wanting to be anywhere near it. We burst out of the door and I take a deep, ragged breath, staring up at the slate sky. The sun has not made an appearance today, as if it dare not shine on the darkest day of my life.

People begin to file out behind us and I move, shifting to the side to let them pass. I feel their eyes upon me, radiating sympathy for the poor, grieving widow, and eight months pregnant too. *Gosh, what a tragedy.* I breathe in again, a breath that catches in my throat. I need a drink. I need a cigarette. I need something to cling on to, to pretend it is helping me cope with this new life. I glance down at my bump and guilt floods through me, but I cannot pretend that my daughter will be that life raft. She will have Henry's eyes, I think, perhaps his fair hair and a dimple in her right cheek, like he did, and every time I look at her I will see him, and it will be another pinprick of pain.

Flick shifts beside me. 'Shall we go?' she murmurs. I look up to see people crowding around, laying flowers and speaking in low tones. I nod. I do not want to be accosted here. I do not want to listen to their words of condolence, see their masks of pity as they press my hand in theirs. No. I suddenly want to go home, desperate for the home Henry and I made together, the familiarity of it. I long for the comforting scent of him. It is too cold here, too impersonal, and he feels too far away. I need to hold him close, if only for a little while longer.

We move through the crowd, Flick leading the way. I see Alice standing in a small group, inclining her head as another woman speaks, but I do not try to catch her eye. She will be loving this, all of the attention on her.

I shake my head at my cruelty. Whose thoughts are these? Alice is grieving too. I know how much she loved her son, how close they were, despite their differences. Despite the wedge I seemed to drive between them, simply by being present. By marrying above my station. But she softened when she discovered I was pregnant. In fact, it was Alice who suggested I do a test. Having a baby hadn't been on our radar, not yet anyway, and my periods have never been regular, but after a few days of feeling unwell I told her I was thinking of booking an appointment with the doctor.

'Is there any chance you might be in the family way?' she asked, looking pointedly at my stomach. I shook my head. I'd felt nauseous and thrown up a few times, but never in the morning. It was always after lunch that the nausea struck. She smiled when I said that. 'My morning sickness happened in the afternoon too, with both Henry and India.'

She went out and bought me a test, then waited outside the downstairs toilet while I tried not to pee on my hand. For those three minutes, I was convinced she was wrong. I would know if I was pregnant, wouldn't I? I would know if something so huge was happening inside my own body. But it was me who was wrong. Two lines appeared and I felt that moment stretch out, the life I'd envisioned swiftly morphing into something else.

Alice was thrilled. It wouldn't be her first grandchild – India has two young girls aged four and seven – but it would be the first grandchild who would be living with her, with whom she could forge a real relationship. India rarely visits Helygen House or even the UK, as her husband travels the globe for work and she goes with him, documenting their adventures on her Instagram page. I don't know how she keeps two children occupied and happy trekking around the world, but it seems to work for her. Though perhaps the reality is quite different to what her Instagram page shows. She isn't coming today, after all, and I remember how Alice had brushed me off when I'd asked why.

I get into the car, unscrew a bottle of water and drink noisily, wishing it was vodka. Flick sits beside me, checking her phone before guiltily shoving it into her pocket.

'It's just Jaz,' she says when I give her an enquiring look.

'How is she?' I realise I haven't asked after Flick's girl-friend in a while, though in truth, I've never really warmed to her. There's something in the way she treats Flick, always taking charge and speaking for – and over – Flick that has never sat well with me. My friend has her demons, that much is true, but Jaz doesn't seem to think she's capable of making her own decisions.

'She's fine,' Flick says, flashing me a smile which doesn't quite meet her eyes.

'Working hard?'

'Or hardly working,' she cracks, but her words fall flat. We sit in silence, the plastic bottle crackling between my fingers as I clutch it, my mind drifting like a boat untethered. It feels like forever until Alice arrives, sliding into the seat beside me.

'Perhaps you should go and lie down,' she says once the car starts moving. 'When we get home. Today was clearly too much for you. You need to keep your strength up.' She glances at my stomach before looking away.

I bristle at her words. As if I do not know what is best for me and for my child. As if I should not attend my own husband's wake, though of course it is the last place on earth I want to be. 'Thank you, Alice,' I say icily. 'But I will join you. I just needed a moment.'

She sniffs, staring out at the countryside rushing past outside. This county is truly beautiful, and although I escaped to London as soon as I could, I always knew I would return to the place of my birth. There's something about Cornwall that gets under your skin, and I know I could never leave Helygen House.

I head straight for Little Hel, leaving Flick to contend with my mother-in-law while I get changed, and have to choke back a sob when I realise that this has become precisely that, my own little hell. Ivy greets me at the door, her tail wagging, her eyes flicking behind me like they always do, searching for Henry. The sight brings fresh tears to my eyes and I put a hand against the wall to steady myself, trying to breathe through the pain. Ivy sniffs around my legs, nudging her nose against my bump, and I reach down to pat her head.

'Poor pup,' I whisper as she stares up at me. 'You don't understand what's happening, do you? Well, neither do I.'

The breath catches in my throat as I stand there, memories playing through my mind. Henry's coat is hanging on a hook beside me and I turn towards it, burying my nose in his scent, the fabric bunching between my fingers as tears stream down my face. I realise suddenly that this is what I have been longing for, to be reminded of him. To feel close to him, no matter how much it hurts.

Exhaling loudly, I feel something bumpy beneath my fingers and reach into the pocket to pull it out. Henry's keys. I smile as I turn them over, rubbing a thumb over the keyring Flick brought back from Majorca. She's forever jetting off on a last-minute holiday, cheap flights and hotels booked on a whim, and never fails to bring us back a memento. A silly hat that will never see the light of day, a fridge magnet, a keyring. Henry and I rarely travelled. We spent a long weekend in Paris after we got married, and we did a few day trips to cities and the seaside on the train when we lived in London, but we never really got to see the world together. Another regret to add to the list.

I slip the keys into my handbag which is hanging up beside his coat and take another deep breath. My eyes find the place where I last saw him, the stool tipped over, the tiles splattered with crimson, and I close my eyes, trying to push the image aside. Instead, I think of the bed I shared with Henry for so many years, waiting for me upstairs. The bed we'd foolishly tried to manoeuvre down the narrow stairs from our old flat into the moving van without dismantling it, knocking a hole into the wall and chipping one of the legs before admitting defeat and having to find an Allen key in one of the packed boxes. We'd laughed so much I'd almost slipped down the stairs as we carried it back up to the flat.

Ivy follows me upstairs and into the bedroom, where I

kick off the wretched boots and throw them into a corner. I fall onto the bed and stare up at the ceiling, remembering the day we moved in here, the pieces of the dismantled bed laid out on the floor before us, the Allen key safely in a back pocket, ready to do battle again. Every night for the past year, I have looked at this ceiling before I fell asleep, watching the branches outside make shadows across the walls as I admired the shapes and swirls of the cornice and the rose from which the light fitting hangs. Every morning I have woken to the same view, the summer sun casting a glow across the room, bathing us in golden light, or the dark winter sky turning the room blue. How many pairs of eyes have stared up at this ceiling? The apartment used to comprise much of the east wing, which had been built centuries before and had no doubt hosted a number of people over the years. Henry made sure that as many of the original features as possible were retained, and so I often picture another woman lying where I am now, looking up at the ceiling. What was she like? Was she the lady of the house, or a visitor? Was she happy? Or was she grieving and alone, like I am?

Henry hadn't known what this room was used for other than that it had been a bedroom, and a grand one at that. The en-suite, which had been put in at some point in the nineteenth century, is huge, with a large clawfoot bath and beautiful dark green tiles, and there is a smaller room through an archway opposite the bed, which we use as a walk-in wardrobe. I go there now, desperate to get out of these clothes. The dress is particularly tight across my bump, the fabric sticking to me like a second skin. Of all days, I deserve to be comfortable today, if only in my clothing. I wriggle out of the dress and pull on a pair of black maternity trousers, breathing a sigh of relief as the soft material touches my skin. I don't have any blouses that fit, but I find a black long-sleeved top that will do. I have a wild urge to put on something bright – the dress Flick bought me for my birthday last year, a beautiful navy blue covered in little foxes – something which Henry would have enjoyed. He always said he loved the little pops of colour I brought into the otherwise mostly monochrome apartment: a bright yellow cushion, a blue vase, a dusky pink bath mat. I glance at the dried wildflowers in a vase on the windowsill, remembering the way Henry's eyes lit up when he noticed them. 'It's the little things you do,' he said, wrapping an arm around my waist, 'that make this place a home.'

Ivy nudges my foot and I turn towards her, a thought swimming up from the murky depths of my mind. When we'd left for the funeral, Ivy had been in the spare room in the main house, but now she is here. Halka must have let her in. I know she has a soft spot for Ivy and has been taking care of her when I couldn't, feeding her strips of ham and pieces of cod between meals. 'I hope you've not become spoiled,' I whisper, reaching down to scratch behind her ear. I bend to kiss the top of her head, but as I'm straightening I feel a twinge in my back and gasp. The baby shifts inside me, a foot or an elbow digging into my ribs, and I rub a hand over my bump, trying to breathe through the pain. 'I know, little one. I know,' I murmur, waiting for the feeling to subside.

I pause at the dressing table on my way back into the bedroom, taking in my sallow skin, my unruly hair escaping its bun. I'd tutted whenever Henry said I was glowing, but, despite the swollen ankles and late-night heartburn attacks, pregnancy seemed to suit me. Until now. Now, not even Henry could say I am glowing. Now, I look like a ghost.

I glance out of the window to see it has started to rain. I watch a droplet trickle down the glass and reach out to touch it. It's freezing cold and I snatch my hand back as if burned. Ivy makes a noise, the short *a-woo* sound she makes when she's trying to get our attention, and I turn to her. 'What's the matter?' I ask as if she can answer, reaching out to cup her face. She leans into my hand, staring up at me with her large, trusting eyes. 'Come on, you,' I say, stroking her chin. 'You have to keep me company today, I'm afraid.'

I decide to go through the internal door instead of outside into the rain. It was something I wasn't keen on at first, keeping a door in Little Hel which leads directly into the main house, but Henry won that particular argument. 'We'll keep it locked,' he assured me, showing me the bolts he'd bought for our side of the door, and the key only we had access to. 'No surprise visitors.' But I still don't understand why he wanted to keep it. Easy access to his mother, I suppose, though she is hardly elderly or in need of care. Perhaps he had been worried about the baby, concerned he might need Alice in the middle of the night. He always was a worrier, though he tried to hide it.

I pause, my hand on the doorknob. The bolts are open, and when I try to turn the key, it doesn't budge. The door is unlocked. How long has it been like this? I try to think back through the haze of days since Henry died. Did I check it? I know I didn't use it while I stayed with Alice, but was it unlocked the whole time? Had it been unlocked when Henry was in here alone?

My throat constricts and I close my eyes, taking a deep breath in and holding it. I need to speak to the police, see if they've reviewed the CCTV footage yet. It might have been Henry's shotgun, but it doesn't mean he pulled the trigger. I haven't heard anything in a while, though I assume Alice has been taking control of things, shielding me from the worst of it. But she cannot shield me from this. I open my eyes and, taking another breath, I square my shoulders and pull open the door.

SIX

HARRIET

4th September 1847

The Lord giveth, and the Lord taketh away. How true this is. Today we lost our dear Edgar, our firstborn son, who turned one only last week. How cruel this life can be.

And yet I must abide. Though their brother is gone, the child that grows inside me still depends on me. I feel it is a girl. I *fear* it is a girl, for Edmund must have a son to take over the family business, especially now Edgar is gone, but I cannot bear the thought of having more children. More children to love and to lose. But I must prepare myself. This child will be born in less than three months. I feel her stirring inside me, something which gave me comfort when I first realised I was with child, but which now brings only anxiety. Edgar's birth was a hard one. I am not permitted to speak of it to anyone, not even to my dear sister Alexandrina, but perhaps my diary can be one exception. For who reads it but I?

I had been present when Alex gave birth to her two daughters, but my sister had borne the pain with such strength, such might, that it hardly seemed to affect her at all. But then she is the elder daughter; she is used to bearing hardships. I became Alex's burden after Mother died, yet she never once showed me impatience. She is a wonderful sister, and an equally wonderful mother, and I thank God every day that I was blessed with her. But the inclement weather stopped her from attending Edgar's birth, and Edmund has discouraged me from speaking of it, for he says it makes me sound ungrateful for the blessing of children, but now the worst has happened and I must find a way to cope.

I must confess that I was not prepared for the birth. I lost count of the number of hours I was abed after the pains came upon me. I know that I felt the first pangs of labour on a Thursday and came back to myself enough to ask the day on a Sunday, but whether three days or several weeks had passed I did not know. Time seemed to elongate, stretching out until each second was a minute, each minute an hour, and each hour an entire day. The pain was fierce, unlike anything I had ever felt before and, I hope, anything I will ever feel again. It felt as if I was on fire, and no amount of washcloths dipped in water and laid over my forehead would put out the flames. And the blood . . . I'd truly wondered if I was dying. I cannot say how much blood I lost, but I fear poor Sara will have had to wash the sheets several times to remove the stains – though I suspect she simply burned them.

Perhaps Edmund is right, that Edgar did feel my emotions whenever I held him in those first weeks, my exhaustion seeping through my fingers and into his heart. The truth is that I felt drained after Edgar was born, so tired that my arms could barely hold my beloved son. For he truly was beloved, and I can only pray he knew how much we adored him. Despite everything.

I feel tears pricking my eyes as I write these words. How short my son's life was, how cruelly short. But I must trust in God's plan. Edgar was simply too good for this world. Perhaps he was given to me so I could learn how to be a mother, learn how to bear the unimaginable pain of bringing a child into this world and then losing them after such a short space of time. I must be stronger for the next child. I *will* be stronger. I will give Edmund the son he needs, the boy who will continue the family name. Helygen House has been in my husband's family for generations, passed down from father to son, the elder content that the younger would do him proud. Our son will do that. Our son will be our pride and joy, and I will be the mother he deserves.

SEVEN

JOSIE

2019

Locking the door behind me, I follow the narrow corridor into Helygen House, Ivy on my heels. I have a sudden memory of her as a puppy, when one of her best tricks was to trip you over when you walked anywhere. She was always underfoot, particularly if you were carrying a hot cup of tea, but now she walks slightly behind me, like a protective shadow, her claws clicking against the wooden floor as we navigate our way towards the drawing room and the people waiting there.

I think of all the feet that have walked along these corridors over the years. They were mostly used by the servants scurrying through the house, out of sight but never out of earshot. How many private conversations did they overhear, the voices of their employers echoing through the walls? I can hear the low rumble of voices now, the tinkle of silver spoons on china cups as the mourners stir sugar into their tea. I suddenly feel removed from it all, from everyone gathered here and the reason why. How many of these people knew Henry as I knew him? Some of his friends are here, and Flick and Alice of course, but how many of them could say, hand on heart, that they knew every inch of the man I loved? Even I only knew this version of him, the most recent rendition which had been built by all the years before. I hadn't known him as a child or as a student. I hadn't known him as a first lover or a son. We had been together for four years, married for two, and it had felt like both a lifetime and no time at all.

I feel another twinge in my lower back and pause, one hand pressed against the panelled wall. I can hear snatches of conversation now, a laugh cut short and turned into a cough. I smile despite myself, picturing Henry's face as if he'd heard it too. *Putting the fun in funeral*, he says inside my head.

'Josie!' I look up to see Alice walking towards me, her brows knitted together. 'There you are. I was about to send out a search party.'

The smile drops from my face, Henry drowned out by his mother. 'I had to get changed,' I say, waving a hand at my outfit. Alice looks me up and down, frowns.

'Did you have to bring the *dog*?' she asks in a lowered voice.

'She was lonely. I think she misses Henry too.' The sadness of it suddenly threatens to overwhelm me and I reach down to pat Ivy's head to hide my tears.

Alice tuts. 'Very well. Come through, there are lots of people who want to speak to you.'

I swallow, and consider running back through the corridor and into Little Hel, back into the safety of our home, but no. I can do this. I have to do this, for Henry.

I follow Alice into the drawing room and try not to notice the silence that descends as we enter. *Hold your farts*, Henry whispers in my ear and I try not to laugh. Am I mad? Is it normal to hear my dead husband's words on the day of his funeral?

Would you rather I disappeared?

No. Not that. Never that.

Chin up, Corbs. You've been through worse.

Have I?

Our wedding, for one. That was excruciating.

I shake my head. *Not excruciating. I got to marry you, after all.*

You'll never get rid of me now, darling. I'm inside your head.

I glance up and my eyes instantly land on one of our wedding photos hung on the wall. I'm wearing the long, dark blue dress I'd found in a charity shop, and he's in black jeans and a crisp white shirt with a tie to match my dress. We were both wearing comfortable shoes, though mine were hidden beneath the dress. I remember how he'd helped me curl my hair that morning, burning his fingers on the curling iron, and can't help but smile. We were late to the registry office, having missed our stop on the Tube, and arrived hot and sweaty after the twenty-minute walk in the hot July air. And then the ceremony had been a disaster.

They'd somehow lost the music I'd provided the week before and so we walked in to 'Cotton Eye Joe' instead, my cheeks burning with embarrassment as I met Alice's icy stare. Henry stood on my train and caused a small tear in the fabric – *good job it only cost thirty quid*, he said later when we found it, sticking his thumb through it and making it bigger – and the room which had looked so quaint and historical on the website in reality was, as my father would have said, 'as dark as a sack', and smelled faintly of sick covered up by bleach. But then I remember catching Flick's eye over Henry's shoulder as we said our vows and had to stifle the urge to giggle. Suddenly we were eighteen again, wide-eyed freshers bonding over a shared love of pineapple on pizza and Jason Momoa, not women in our late twenties hovering on the edge of marriage and mortgages and children, and all those other things only adults are supposed to do. *How did we get here?* I wanted to ask her then. *How did we get old enough?*

I sobered up enough to say my vows, and was touched to see a tear in Henry's eye as he slipped the ring onto my finger. All of it was worth it, then, the sweaty faces and torn dress and vomit-covered carpet and Alice's disapproval. All of it was worth it to see the look on Henry's face as we cemented our partnership.

I had no bouquet to toss as I'd scoffed at the tradition, so we took some photos and chatted with our friends while we waited to be handed our marriage certificate. 'Always keep your wife on your left,' the registrar said as he gave it to

Henry with a wink, 'because it's closer to your heart. And your wallet.'

You could have heard a pin drop in the silence that followed. Flick half stood, as if she'd expected me to fly at the man, but I was too surprised to do anything but gape at him. Even Alice looked surprised, her lips pursed into a tight line. It was Henry who slapped him down.

'And what if I had a husband?' he asked in the chummy, overly posh voice he used whenever he was annoyed. 'Would we go around and around in circles until we died?' And I'd almost choked on my laughter.

That was the thing with Henry. He could turn anything into a joke, something to laugh at instead of cry over. I had never spent any time as a child dreaming up my wedding, had never really thought about getting married, but that day would have been ruined if it weren't for Henry. If he hadn't been standing by my side; if the room hadn't been filled with our love for each other. If he wasn't who he was, the kind of person to put a positive spin on anything.

Try now, I tell him in my head. *Try putting a positive spin on this*. But any response is interrupted by Camilla, one of Henry's university friends, whose sympathetic face fills my vision as she takes hold of my shoulders.

'Darling,' she says, kissing me on both cheeks, bathing me in her noxious perfume. 'How *are* you?'

'Well,' I begin, and she seems to take that as a response.

'I know, I *know*. How dreadful for you.' She sighs dramatically. 'Do let me and Teddy know if there's *anything* we can do. Anything. You name it.' She puts a hand on my arm and I fight the urge to bat it away. 'We're here for you, darling.'

'Does she call me *darling* because she's forgotten my name?' I'd asked Henry at our wedding reception, the first time I'd met Camilla and Teddy, a banker's son who was her childhood sweetheart. He'd grinned, his eyes twinkling, and I'd known I was right.

'Thank you,' I say, shaking the memory away. I cannot seem to escape them today, those rose-tinted days when Henry and I had our whole lives ahead of us. If I had known what lay ahead, would I have done anything differently?

Tell me you didn't do it, I plead with him. *Tell me your mother is wrong.* But he is silent.

I find a corner to sit in, a cup of tea going cold in my hands, trying to avoid catching anyone's eye. I am exhausted already, and it hasn't even been an hour since everyone arrived. Ivy lies down beside me as if she is keeping watch, guarding me from more of the sympathetic expressions and recycled words. *I'm so sorry. How are you doing? Our sincere condolences.* I have thrown every single *With Sympathy* card away, ripping them into little pieces and stuffing them into the bin. What makes people think I want to be reminded of what I have lost? Why do they insist on regurgitating the same rubbish over and over again? None of it matters. None of it makes a difference.

'Penny for them,' Flick says, sitting down beside me. Ivy

lifts her head then drops it again, letting out a sigh when Flick scratches behind her ears. 'It's bloody awful, isn't it?'

I glance at her, hearing the wobble in her voice just before I smell the alcohol on her breath. 'Have you—'

'Only one,' she says quickly, flashing me a smile. 'Okay, two.'

I try to keep my face impassive. Flick hasn't had a drop of alcohol in over two years, since she almost lost herself at the bottom of a vodka bottle. 'Flick,' I say, but she shakes her head.

'I know. It's okay. Today is about you anyway.' She puts a hand on my arm. 'I bet you wish you could have a drink.'

I exhale loudly. 'You could say that.' I turn to her, put my hand over hers. 'It was selfish of me to ask you to come today.'

She gives a small smile. 'How could I not come?'

'But it's too much for you. After . . .' I trail off, unable to speak of the thing that drove Flick to the very edge, even after all this time.

Flick is still shaking her head. 'It's been three years, Jose. I can't avoid funerals forever. Besides, I'm here for you. I have to be here for you. It's what friends do.'

I squeeze her hand. I'd thought she was coping, that Jaz had been keeping Flick on the straight and narrow. They'd met at an AA meeting to which Henry and I had practically frogmarched Flick after she had tried to jump off Waterloo Bridge, out of her mind with grief and a concoction of vodka and sleeping pills. Thankfully a good Samaritan walking past had grabbed hold of Flick's arm and pulled her back to safety just in time, then kept her talking until the emergency services arrived.

She gives me a watery smile. 'I'm going to go back. To counselling. I need to . . .' She inhales, her fingers tight in mine. 'I need to learn how to remember her without wanting to crawl into a dark hole. She was a part of me. I need to stop hiding from her.'

I nod, releasing her hand to wrap my arms around her. 'I'll be there, every step of the way. Jaz too.'

'Jaz has left me.'

'What?' I say, too loud in the hushed room. I lower my voice, trying to ignore the stares. 'What happened? Why didn't you say?'

Flick blows out a breath. 'It was a few weeks ago, just before I came down to see The Hut. The day when . . . Well, everything happened and there wasn't a good time.' Her eyes fill with tears and suddenly everything makes sense. The drinking, the nervous scratching at her arms. The same compulsions I feel, my fingers moving in my lap, trying to touch in a certain way to satisfy an illogical need. I developed severe OCD when my father's illness got worse and I became solely responsible for the cleanliness of the flat. For a time, I believed that if I could arrange the mugs just right in the cupboard, my dad would get better. If I washed my hands for twenty seconds and touched every crevice just so, my dad would be able to get out of bed. If I stepped on every crack in the kitchen floor with both feet, my dad wouldn't die. After years of counselling and some antidepressants, it only resurfaces when I'm stressed or anxious. It's no wonder it's happening again now.

'Oh, Flick.' I pull her in again. 'I'm so sorry.'

'You've got enough to worry about,' she says, wiping her eyes. 'You don't need me adding to it.'

'Don't be stupid,' I tell her. 'You're my best friend. We're in this together.' I pull away and look into her face. 'Do you need somewhere to stay?'

Flick shakes her head. 'I've gone back to Mum's. Hence the booze.' She gives a watery smile. 'Joking. It's fine. We're getting on better these days. And besides, I'll be down here soon, working on The Hut.' She pauses then, the smile dropping from her face. 'Oh, God, sorry. I just assumed . . . I didn't even think if that was . . .'

'It'll still go ahead,' I say, sounding more confident than I feel. We may need to wait for probate, and what if there are things I don't know about, things which might put a stop to our plans? What if Henry really was under too much pressure, or there had been an issue with money he'd kept from me? I exhale shakily, the cloak of grief settling once more around my shoulders. I'd managed to forget about it for a moment, managed to focus on Flick and her worries and forget all about mine, but now it's back, heavier than ever. 'I'll let you know,' I finish lamely, trying to smile.

'About what?' I look up at the sound of Alice's voice. She looks disapprovingly at Flick while she blows her nose, as if it is inappropriate for someone to be crying at a wake. I frown at my mother-in-law and say nothing. 'Can I borrow you for a moment, Josie?' she asks after a beat.

I nod and haul myself to my feet. I have trouble getting out of chairs these days, and the ones Alice insists on having in the drawing room are so low it's almost impossible to get up without help. My lower back twinges again and I gasp. Flick shoots me a concerned look and I shake my head, waiting a beat until the pain passes before trying to get up again. The baby is heavy, pressing down on my bladder and making my movements sluggish. I suddenly wish I could disappear into Little Hel and crawl into bed, wrap myself around Henry's pillow and sink into happier memories.

'I was going to do a speech,' Alice says as I follow her across the room, one hand on my back. It is aching now, a low thrum that makes my movements stiff. 'To thank everyone for being here today.'

I know by the way she's dragged me away from Flick that it's me she wants to give the speech. 'I don't think so, Alice,' I say, glancing around nervously. I don't know many people here, not really. I recognise a few faces, Camilla of course, and some of Henry's old friends and colleagues, but it's almost as if we separated ourselves from that part of our life when we moved back to Cornwall. Most of our friends stayed in London, and not many of them have visited us in the past year. Besides, we've been so busy with the renovations and preparing for the baby, I suppose we'd almost cut ourselves off, spurning dinner parties and functions for early morning site visits with the builders and evenings on the sofa. How I regret that now. How I wish I had more people around me, people I can trust.

'We must say *something*,' Alice protests. 'It's only right.' I sigh and she smiles, a small flicker of a smile that tells me she knows she's won. She picks up an empty glass and taps her wedding ring against it. The room quietens, all eyes turning towards us, and I try to swallow down my nerves as Alice begins to speak. 'Thank you all for coming,' she says, her voice high and tinkling and tinged with just the right amount of sadness. 'Josie and I are so grateful for your support. It is touching to see just how loved Henry was.' She gives me a small nod and I clear my throat.

'Thank you,' I repeat, my voice too quiet, catching on the words. 'Henry was —' I stop suddenly, feeling a wetness spreading down my legs. I hear a collective gasp as I look down and see that my waters have broken.

EIGHT

I thought this kind of thing only happened on TV, I tell Henry as hands grip my upper arms, half dragging me towards the chairs lined up against the wall.

And the award for most dramatic scene goes to . . . he says, laughing, and I am relieved to hear his voice again. I thought he'd left me.

'We need to get you to the hospital,' Flick says urgently, dragging me out of my thoughts. 'I'll drive. My car isn't parked far away.'

'Where's my hospital bag?' I ask, then realise I haven't packed it yet. How could I have left it so late? But my baby isn't due for another three or four weeks yet, and isn't the first baby often overdue? I seem to remember reading that somewhere. But this isn't like me. I should have packed a bag. I should have been more prepared.

A wave of pain washes over me and I feel my knees buckle, dragging Flick down to the floor beside me. 'Josie?' she asks, her forehead creased with worry. 'Josie, are you okay?'

I shake my head as a low moan fills my ears, and I'm

surprised to find it's coming from me. 'I think she's coming,' I gasp during the brief respite between contractions. I try to count the space between them, but they're too fast now, too powerful. Does it usually happen so quickly? This doesn't feel right. Something isn't right.

'Fuck,' Flick says, and Henry echoes the word inside my head as I try not to scream.

'Breathe deeply,' Alice says from my other side, her hand on my back. 'That's it, breathe, Josie. You can do this.'

Flick nods encouragingly, but I can see the fear in her eyes and it seems to be contagious. I didn't want a home birth. I wanted to be in the hospital with all the experts and drugs and machines. I wanted Henry beside me, his hand gripping mine, his eyes wet as our daughter was delivered. I didn't want to be a widow, still raw with grief, giving birth in the drawing room of Helygen House.

'Excuse me,' a voice says. I turn to see that the mourners have clustered around us, trying to catch a glimpse of the action. 'Excuse me,' the voice says again, impatient now, and the crowd parts for a short woman with grey hair pinned up on top of her head. She drops down before me, holding out a hand for me to shake. I grasp it like it is a life-line, a piece of driftwood in the middle of the ocean. 'Hi, Josie. I'm Lorna. I worked with Henry back when he was on the blue side.' She winks. 'I won't hold it against you if you don't hold it against me. I used to be a midwife. Can I help?'

Relief washes over me as another contraction grips me

and I squeeze her hand. To her credit, she doesn't wince. 'Yes,' I manage to croak when the pain abates. 'Please.'

'Let's have some privacy, shall we?' Lorna looks up at the crowd behind us, clapping her hands together and raising her voice. 'Can we all move into another room, please? This lady is about to give birth, and I think she'd rather do so without all of you gawping at her. Off you pop.' I don't turn around to see the impact of her words, but I hear the shuffle of footsteps and low murmurs moving further away, and try to smile my thanks, but another wave of pain hits me and it turns into a grimace. She helps me perch on the edge of a long settee. 'Not quite what you were expecting, I daresay, but it'll do,' she says with a smile. 'Gravity tends to help.'

'Can I do anything?' I look up to see Flick hovering behind Lorna, her expression worried.

'Towels and warm water, please. And perhaps we should call your midwife, Josie. I'm no longer practising and I don't fancy a spell in prison, not even for the Fox heir.'

Flick hurries out of the room while Alice rubs my back. 'Corbyn-Fox,' I say between gritted teeth as another contraction hits me.

Lorna makes a face. 'Even worse,' she says, winking again, and I think I might be in love with her. How some people can be so calm and even downright jolly in situations like these I don't know. I can feel my heart pounding in my chest, anxiety threatening to swallow me whole. Lorna squeezes my hand as if she can read my mind. 'You'll be fine, Josie. Everything will be fine. Just breathe with me, that's it.'

'Midwife is coming, but she's about half an hour away,' Flick says, returning with a load of towels. 'She asked about dilation.' She shoots me a look so uncomfortable, I might consider laughing in other circumstances.

'Yes, I rather think we're at that stage now,' Lorna says. 'I'm going to need to have a look, Josie.'

I nod, gritting my teeth, trying not to scream as the pain rips through me. My vision blurs and I feel Flick slip her arm around me, her fingers clenched in mine, while Lorna eases my trousers down. I should have kept that sodding dress on.

'You can do this,' Flick says. 'I'm here. I'm here.'

But Henry isn't, I think as the tears start to flow. *I need Henry. I need my husband not to be dead. I need to not have my baby in this house.* This last thought is so clear, so violent that it takes my breath away, but I have no time to consider where it has come from. The world turns red as the pain fills me, until there is no room left for anything else.

I am lost in a sea of blue.

Flashing lights, a wailing siren, a hand squeezing mine. Flick, her eyes round with fear. The pain is unimaginable, unbelievable. I must be dreaming. This is a nightmare, and I'm about to wake up.

The ambulance swerves suddenly and I feel nausea rising. Flick grips my hand tighter. 'It's okay,' she whispers, 'everything is going to be okay.' And I wonder who she is trying to convince. I squeeze my eyes shut as pain rips through me. It feels as if I am being torn in half, my body white hot with agony.

It wasn't supposed to be this way, I think, panic flaring between the pain. I am not usually someone who is unprepared, caught off-guard. I am a planner. I have lists for everything – food shopping, the cleaning rota, planning the classes and events at Helygen House – and I am forever pulling scraps of paper from pockets, words scribbled on them, barely legible to anyone but me. I suppose it is a symptom of the OCD, but I feel better with a plan, knowing the direction my life will take. Even when I found out I was pregnant, shocked as I was, I hadn't felt wholly unprepared. I'd slowly moved towards the idea of becoming a parent over the years, so it didn't take long for me to warm to it when the pregnancy test came back positive. I've had the birth planned out in a way I never dreamed up my wedding. I would have a bag packed and ready to go, the nursery finished, every single item on my list ticked off. A hospital bed in Truro, all the pain relief available on the NHS, surrounded by experienced doctors and nurses, Henry by my side. Instead, I'm in an ambulance, rushing towards the hospital with no hospital bag and no husband.

'Alice?' I ask, suddenly remembering my mother-in-law.

'She's following in the car,' Flick says, rubbing the back of my hand. 'She said she's your birthing partner.' The unspoken part of her sentence hangs between us. *In lieu of*

Henry. I'd never considered Henry *not* being here for the birth of his child, so we hadn't planned for this. I couldn't ask Flick, so Alice seems like the natural choice. The only choice.

I nod, gritting my teeth against another wave of pain. The ambulance stops suddenly and the back doors fly open, paramedics in luminescent jackets rushing in. 'This is your stop, maid,' one of them says with a thick West Cornwall accent and a warm smile. 'They'll sort you out here, worry not.'

I am rolled out of the ambulance and through the double doors of A&E, bright lights flashing above me. I let out a moan, my fists clenched by my sides. I remember Lorna's face when she checked between my legs just before I passed out, her hand coming away red as the colour drained from her face. The sheet beneath me is soaked through, crimson splashed against white. So much blood. Is there supposed to be so much blood? Am I dying? Is my baby dying?

NINE

ELIZA

1881

Her first night in Helygen House was strange. The figure of her mother-in-law sitting silently beside her, so still it seemed she was carved from rock, made Eliza clumsy and nervous during dinner, her fork slipping from her fingers, a drop of wine spilling on the tablecloth. She felt out of place, like a figure on a stage, watched by hundreds of pairs of eyes. She tried not to look at the gallery wall at the far end of the dining room, the Foxes of yesteryear sitting in judgement upon her.

She saw a new side to her husband too, and realised again that there was so much about him she did not know. Cassius dominated the conversation, his eyes growing rounder and more sparkling with each glass of red wine he drank. The servant, the young girl with the wild red hair, hovered at the edge of the room, ready to step forward with the pitcher whenever a glass ran dry, watching as Cassius held court. Now he had finished telling his mother about their time in London and had moved on to his latest venture, a scheme he and a friend had dreamed up involving china clay.

'It's all the rage in high society,' he said, lifting his side plate and looking at the mark stamped on the bottom. 'These dainty plates and cups. St Austell has some of the finest clay deposits in the world. Business is booming.'

'Is that so, dear?' Harriet said in a small voice.

'And,' Cassius said, as if his mother hadn't spoken, 'did you know that there's a river that turns white when it rains?' He laughed. 'It's all due to the deposits. They get dumped into the water and change the colour.'

'Wouldn't that harm the environment?' Eliza asked, frowning. 'The animals and plant life that rely on the river?'

'It's much better than the filth that runs into the Thames, my dear,' he said, waving a hand. 'I say, London truly is the most disgusting city in the world. The air is utterly poisonous.'

Eliza looked down at her plate. Though she had lived not in London but in Hertfordshire, she could not argue with him. She knew the cholera outbreak had carried off her brother, who had been beloved by her parents, when he was just five years old, and that there had been uproar about the quality of the water. She also knew that her birth a year later had been a disappointment to her parents, who had hoped to replace their heir.

'This food is exquisite,' she said with a bright smile,

trying to shake off her memories. 'Your cook is an absolute wonder.' Harriet did not reply but gave a small smile, which made Eliza brighten. *Perhaps she is warming to me*, she thought hopefully.

'We had the heartiest meal after the wedding, didn't we, my dear?' Cassius said. 'It was truly divine.'

'Roast goose with apple and herb stuffing,' Eliza said, remembering. 'It was delicious.' She caught Harriet's eye and blushed. 'Though I have always favoured beef,' she added, cutting into her meat and watching the reddish liquid ooze out. In truth, she preferred it well done, but chose not to say so.

'And the cake!' Cassius exclaimed around a mouthful of food. 'Glorious. What was it again, Eliza?'

She smiled at the memory. 'Lemon, I believe. And there was fruitcake too. I confess, I was quite the glutton!'

'And you paid for it the next day,' Cassius added with a grin. Harriet spluttered and Cassius looked alarmed. 'Are you quite well, Mother?'

'Yes, yes,' she said, patting her collarbone with her palm. 'Please excuse me.'

Eliza watched as Harriet left the room, one hand pressed to her mouth, and turned to her husband, confused.

'Delicate constitution,' he said, waving his fork in the air. 'Women, you know. We'll join her in the parlour when we're done.'

After dinner, Cassius drank two glasses of brandy before announcing that he would be in his study, leaving Eliza alone with her new mother-in-law for the first time, but she soon became so fatigued that she felt herself falling asleep in the armchair before the fire. The parlour was warm and almost cosy, and she was lethargic after such a heavy meal. *Wake up. This is the perfect opportunity to get to know her*, she berated herself. But while she was trying to think of something to say, Harriet rang a bell and the maid appeared.

'Tea, please,' she said. 'Eliza appears to need a little pick-me-up.'

Eliza felt her cheeks redden. 'My apologies. I am rather tired.'

'You had a long journey. Did you manage to rest earlier?'

'I was too excited. This house – *your* house – is incredible. And a bathroom with hot, running water!' She smiled. 'I am not used to such luxury.'

'Cassius is rather proud of that,' Harriet said, staring into the crackling flames. 'Though it came at great expense.'

'I'm sure,' Eliza murmured, though in truth she had no idea how much such a thing would cost or even how one might go about obtaining it. 'He is very generous.'

The maid slipped into the room and placed a tray on the table between the two women, pouring tea into china cups. As she put the teapot back on the table, the maid knocked into the sugar bowl and a cube fell to the floor.

'Be careful, Mary,' Harriet snapped. 'I would not have you scald my new daughter-in-law on her very first day here.'

'Sorry, madam,' the maid mumbled, while Harriet picked up the milk herself and added a drop to each cup, clearly not trusting the girl to do it without further spillages.

Eliza bent and picked up the sugar cube, holding it out for Mary to take. She dropped it into her open palm with a smile. 'No harm done,' she said. 'Thank you for the tea.' Mary, her cheeks red, dipped a curtsey and left the room.

'That girl is a liability,' Harriet muttered, cupping her tea between her hands. 'I only took her on as a favour.'

'Oh?' Eliza dropped a sugar cube into her cup.

Harriet seemed to jump, as if she had forgotten Eliza were there. 'Tell me,' she said, sipping her tea. 'What does your father do? Cassius wrote to me, of course, but his letters are often short and to the point. Unlike his soliloquys,' she added, and Eliza fancied she saw the ghost of a smile playing around her lips.

'My father owns a factory,' Eliza said carefully. 'He makes soaps and perfumes.'

Harriet lifted an eyebrow. 'Not one I would have heard of?'

'No.' Eliza shook her head, embarrassed. 'He is not very well known. But successful enough,' she added hurriedly. 'He is very proud of his business.'

'Of course. Men so often are, even if there is very little to be proud of.'

Eliza was silent for a moment, letting the words sink in, wanting to ask what Harriet meant but not daring to. She needed to make a good impression; she didn't want her mother-in-law to think she was a silly schoolgirl, incapable of comprehending the world around her. She took another sip of tea, hoping it would settle her stomach. *Is it nerves, or something I ate?* she wondered. *Perhaps I just ate too much. I do not want Cassius to think me a glutton.*

She felt her eyelids grow heavy again, and placed her teacup on the table in case she spilled it. 'I'm afraid I must retire,' she said, forcing back a yawn. 'I cannot seem to keep my eyes open.' She felt a sudden pain in her stomach and gasped, a hand fluttering over her mouth. She got to her feet quickly, while Harriet watched her with steely grey eyes, her hands folded neatly in her lap. 'Excuse me,' Eliza whispered before hurrying out of the room.

She managed to rush upstairs and reach the bathroom before nausea hit again, causing her to stagger towards the toilet as her stomach growled angrily. Vomit splattered against the toilet bowl, the stench enough to make her want to throw up again. She stood and flushed it away before stumbling over to the sink to rinse her mouth. Her fingers gripped the side of the sink and she tried to breathe deeply, swiping the back of her hand against her forehead. *Too much food*, she thought, looking up and catching her reflection in the mirror. *Too much wine. I just need to rest.*

Eliza looked longingly at the bath. She wished she could sink into the hot, comforting water, but she began to sway on her feet and knew she could not stand for much longer. *Tomorrow*, she told herself as she bent to splash her face with water. When she looked up, a figure was standing in the doorway, the shadow stretching across the tiled floor.

'Cassius?' she called hopefully, patting her face dry on a towel hanging on a rail beside the sink. 'Forgive me, darling, I –' She stopped, one hand on the door frame, her eyes taking in the empty room.

TEN

JOSIE

2019

I wake to a world of white. I blink once, twice, the over-head lights too bright. *Where am I?* I try to sit up but pain ripples across my abdomen. I gasp, pushing down the white sheets and pulling the hospital gown aside to find a large bandage taped across my stomach. The skin around it is sore when I press it, and I picture an angry scar hidden beneath.

'You're awake.'

I turn to see Alice sitting in a chair beside the bed. The breath catches in my throat as my brain registers the bundle in her arms. 'Wh-what happened?'

'You had to have an emergency caesarean,' Alice says. 'She was extended breech, and you'd lost so much blood . . .'

She. My daughter. I take in her features and feel a rush of emotion. 'Is . . . is she okay?'

'She's fine. Small. Five pounds, four ounces, but otherwise

perfectly healthy.' She gives a watery smile. 'She has hair just like Henry's. Look.'

I reach out for my daughter, whose tiny head is covered with light tufts of hair. *Our daughter*, Henry whispers in my ear. For a second, I think Alice is about to refuse to hand her over to me, but then she shuffles forward, carefully placing the bundle into my arms. 'Hello, Willow,' I say quietly, bending to inhale her scent. 'Welcome to the world.'

'Willow?' Alice's voice is sharp and I look up in alarm. 'You can't . . . You haven't . . .'

'Ah, hello, Mum,' a voice says from the doorway. I'm relieved to see Sharon, my midwife, smiling widely at me. 'How are we?'

'Okay,' I say, unsure. My whole body aches, as if I have fallen down a flight of stairs and bruised every part of me. 'Tired. Thirsty.'

Sharon glances at Alice as if in reproach before reaching out and filling a plastic glass with water. She drops a straw into it and holds it to my lips while I drink. 'She's a precious one,' she says, nodding at Willow. 'Keen to make her entrance into the world.' She takes the empty glass away. 'I thought we'd try some breastfeeding before we look at expressing,' she says, sitting on the edge of the bed. 'If you still want to, that is.'

Alice makes a noise in the back of her throat, and I can hear her thoughts as if she has spoken them aloud. I know what she thinks of the decision Henry and I made to express milk for our daughter so he could take some of the night feeds. *Sorry about that*, he says inside my head, and I feel a flicker of anger. If he did . . . what Alice says he did, then he would have known he would be leaving me to bring up our daughter alone. How could he do that to me, to us?

'Yes,' I tell the midwife, pushing the emotions away. 'I'd like to try.'

'Fab. And it looks like the little one is waking up. Are we hungry, sweetie?' She touches a finger to Willow's cheek before glancing up at me. 'Do we have a name yet?'

I swallow, thinking of Alice's reaction and not understanding it. 'Willow,' I say cautiously, but Sharon only smiles.

'Oh, that's beautiful,' she says. 'Right then, Willow, let's get you fed.'

After a few false starts, Willow finally manages to latch on, her mouth closing around my nipple. The sensation is strange, almost painful, and I must grimace because Sharon places a hand on my arm.

'It can take some getting used to,' she says. 'And there's always formula if you need it.'

'Should you really be encouraging that?' Alice snaps. 'Breast is best, it always has been.'

'Yes,' Sharon says, drawing out the word. 'But sometimes we all need a little helping hand, don't we?' She turns back to me. 'Looks like you've got the hang of it anyway, Josie. Well done.'

Willow has placed her fist against my breast, her tiny fingers curling in as she suckles. I smile down at her, taking in her fair hair which already seems to be curling just like

Henry's did. She has a tiny button nose and smooth pink skin, and when her mouth slips from my nipple and she looks up at me, I see that her eyes are a bluey-grey. Then her eyelids begin to droop, her breathing becoming slow and steady. I can feel her heart beating against my own chest. I cannot take my eyes off her, this perfect bundle which Henry and I created. I am not the kind of woman who believes that having a child completes me; I was a complete person before, with a whole, fulfilled life. But there's something about holding Willow that makes everything feel just . . . right. *This is it*, I think. *This is my life now.*

Except everything isn't quite right. Henry should be here with us. He should be sitting beside me, his hand cupping our daughter's head, his eyes shining with tears. *Our daughter*, he says again inside my head, and I feel a pang of grief. He should be a part of this picture. Tears prick my eyes and I bend my head towards my sleeping daughter again, pressing my lips against her soft cheek. I will take my comfort from her, this girl who means everything to me. I can almost feel my world shrinking, my senses sharpening to be in tune with her, to focus only on her. I feel my arms grow heavy and realise I am falling asleep again too.

'Let's put baby in her cot,' Sharon says quietly. She reaches out for Willow and I tense, not wanting to let her go. 'I just need to check you over now, sweetie,' she adds with a sympathetic smile. 'And we don't want to disturb the little one.' Reluctantly I hand her over, watching as Sharon carefully places her in the cot beside the bed before turning back to me. 'How are you feeling?'

'Exhausted,' I say truthfully, blowing out a breath. 'I feel as if I could sleep for a week. Everything hurts.'

'Shall we check your scar?' I nod, letting the midwife move the hospital gown aside. 'I know it probably looks bad, but it's a perfectly normal c-section scar. It looks like it will heal nicely.' Her expression turns serious. 'But I'm afraid you'll have to be on your best behaviour. No lifting for at least six weeks.'

'Six weeks?' I echo. 'Not even—'

'You can carry Willow,' she clarifies with a smile, 'but nothing heavier. And considering she's teeny tiny, that means not much at all.' She holds up a hand and begins ticking things off on her fingers. 'Avoid driving if you can, no intense exercise, try not to do much cooking or cleaning. Just take it slow, don't overexert yourself. Do you have someone to help you with day-to-day activities?'

'I can help,' Alice says. 'Of course. You can stay in the main house, where you're closer to me. We could—'

'No,' I say, sharper than intended. Something flickers across Alice's face and I try to swallow down my guilt. 'Sorry. But no. I'd like to go back to the apartment. Willow's nursery is mostly done, and it's where . . .' I trail off, unable to mention Henry. Not now. Not yet. 'It's where I feel most comfortable,' I finish.

'Marie can help with the cleaning then,' Alice says after a

beat. 'And meals. There'll be no need for you to cook. Halka will make extra and bring it to you.'

I open my mouth to protest – I have never let Marie clean our rooms before, and although we did regularly eat with Alice, I always went into the kitchen to see if I could help Halka. The cook is a large, formidable woman who said very little in the beginning, but now we have a chat while I help her chop vegetables or stir bubbling pots while she is busy doing something else. Sometimes Henry would come with me, as uncomfortable as I was with having live-in help, but it's something Alice seems to take for granted, as if she deserves to have someone at her beck and call every hour of the day. Poor Marie never seems to stop, always rushing around with a feather duster in hand or dragging the hoover up the stairs. It's a good job Alice only uses certain rooms now and not the whole house. One woman couldn't possibly keep it clean alone.

'Fine,' I say with a sigh, resting my head against the pillows. 'Thank you, Alice.'

'I'll leave you to rest,' Sharon says with a pat on my hand. 'I'll see you again before you go home, see if we can get the hang of expressing.'

I nod, but my eyes are closing as she rises, and by the time she has left the room, I am asleep.

I wake with a gasp, my heart beating wildly in my chest. What was that sound? I look around the darkened room, searching for the source of the noise. It sounded like . . . My eyes land on Willow and I shift towards her, gasping again at the stinging pain in my stomach. Is she crying? Is she hungry, or wet? But as I go to lift her up, I see that her eyes are closed, her lips slightly parted. She's still asleep. A dream, then? Or another baby on the ward? I am in a private room, but the walls are thin and I can hear the usual hospital noises from beyond the door. Machines bleeping, shoes squeaking against the linoleum. Babies crying?

I strain my ears, trying to listen, but there is nothing. If a baby had been crying, it has stopped now, probably resting against its mother's chest, being soothed back to sleep.

I lie back down, one hand resting on the side of Willow's cot. I suddenly wonder where Flick is and reach out to pick up my phone. I remember her being with me in the ambulance but everything after is a blank, until I woke up here with Alice holding Willow. Perhaps she wasn't allowed in because she isn't family. I unlock my phone with my thumb and, squinting at the brightness of the screen, open my messages. There's one waiting from her.

> I've gone home. They said you were out of surgery and both doing well. I can't wait to see her. Call me if you need anything, day or night, and I'll be there. Well done, Corbs xxx

The use of Henry's nickname for me sends a flutter of sadness through me. I go to reply to her message, but my fingers are slow and clumsy. Will I ever stop feeling so tired? Or will this exhaustion creep into my bones, entwining itself with the very fibre of my being until I remember nothing else?

I put the phone down, my eyelids heavy. I'm just drifting off when it comes again, an almost furious shriek, but it feels far away this time, and sleep drags me back down.

ELEVEN

HARRIET

26th August 1849

A storm blew in last night, and I knew by the way my limbs suddenly felt heavy that my child would be coming soon. Edgar would have been three years old now, and as they say, time heals all wounds, although I could not say that I have healed from his passing. Rather, I have learned to live with it.

I also knew – in a way that would make Edmund frown and begin a lecture on the perils of spiritualism, if I were to tell him, which I will not – that this child would be a boy. The spare, now the heir. Clara, who is two, seemed to know it too. 'Brother,' she said last night, pointing at my large stomach from her place at my feet. She smiled then, a wide smile that caused such a rush of love. She is a dear child. Angelic in looks, with the same fair hair as my sister and the Fox slate-grey eyes, she will be a beauty, someday.

The pains started after dinner, just as the first roll of thunder rumbled in the distance. I attempted to count the seconds between them, and got to fifteen before the next boom and, barely a second later, another contraction. I was in sync then, with the storm. I only hoped this labour would be swifter than the previous two, and, thank God, it was. Edmund rang for the doctor as soon as the pains started, but of course, the storm was too fierce by that point, and I knew the boy he sent would struggle to make his way to the doctor's house. So I lay abed with only Sara to comfort me, and I was grateful for her presence. She'd learned about midwifery from her grandmother, she told me, who, in her youth, had been a highly regarded midwife in her home village of Polperro. I trust Sara with my life, who has already seen me through two births, and now this one too. Edmund found her for me when we were newly married, and she truly is the most loyal of servants, kind and gentle, and sharp too. She is altogether too intelligent for a woman of her social status, or even a woman of mine. Perhaps I could believe in reincarnation if it meant next time Sara would be reborn as a man.

An hour later, the child was delivered. I could see the relief on Sara's face as she wrapped him in a towel, carefully cutting the cord and cleaning him up before placing him in my arms. The afterbirth was swift in coming too, and just as Sara had covered me over with a clean sheet, lightning flashed across the sky, splitting it open. I turned my face to the window to watch the rain begin to lash down. The glass bottles on my dressing table shook as the thunder rolled overhead, and the child began to cry, his wails piercing the silence between the fury of the storm. I tried to hush him, tried to comfort my dear boy, but the look of alarm on Sara's face gave me pause. Perhaps she was just worried about the horses. They are so easily spooked, but her own nephew is one of the stable boys so they were in good hands. I put my son to my breast and he finally quieted, suckling with one fist pressed against my chest. I tried to relax, to enjoy this time with my son, but the storm continued to rage and I could not calm my fluttering heart.

To my surprise, Dr Everest arrived a few moments later. I hurriedly covered my breast, but knew I could do nothing more to make myself look presentable.

'Ah, Mrs Fox,' he said, removing his hat. 'It would appear that I am not needed at all.'

'Nonsense,' I said automatically, my good breeding winning out over my exhaustion. 'You have arrived at precisely the right time.'

While Dr Everest checked the boy over and weighed him, I found my eyes were drawn to the windows and the storm outside. 'It appears to be abating,' he said, holding the baby out to me before turning to the window. 'The storm, I mean. My carriage seemed to drive straight through it on my way here, as if it were leading me to you.' He jerked, as if coming back to himself, and cleared his throat. 'All seems to be well, Mrs Fox. A fine, hearty boy. Do we have a name?'

I thought back to the conversation with Edmund on this very topic, the name he would choose for his second son. I was grateful he did not suggest Edgar, for while it is a fine name for the Fox heir, I could not have borne the removal of my first boy's memory. 'Cassius,' he said decisively, his eyes not lifting from the papers before him. 'Liberator, philosopher and Shakespearean hero.' I did not list the other possible descriptors: turncoat, assassin. Our boy would be the beloved Fox heir, after all. Such words would not do.

'Cassius,' I told the doctor, and I am certain I saw something flicker across his face, something close to what I had kept carefully concealed when my husband told me the name he had chosen. Uncertainty.

'Very good, madam,' he said respectfully, and left to tell Edmund the good news. Sara stayed with me a while, ensuring I was clean and comfortable before taking the child into the nursery where the nanny, who was still taking care of Clara, would care for him too. A deep exhaustion settled over me then, turning my limbs to lead, and my eyelids grew heavy, pulling me down into a deep, dreamless sleep. But I woke not a few hours later to the sound of a baby crying, loud, furious cries that seemed to echo around my room. Unlike Clara and Edgar, whom I rarely heard crying from my room, Cassius seemed to have a strong pair of lungs on him. I waited, my body tense as I listened for the sound of Nanny going into the nursery, but all I could hear were Cassius's cries. I dithered, unsure if I should go to him myself, but then he quieted, and I was allowed to drift off to sleep again, and when I woke, the sky was clear and bright, with no sign of the storm from the night before except for a few fallen branches down by the lake. And my boy, who had been born in the very eye of it.

TWELVE

JOSIE

2019

A few days later, I am finally allowed to go home. I breathe a sigh of relief as the car turns down the private track that leads to Helygen House. Willow is sleeping in her car seat in the back and I am beside her, watching Alice navigate the tight bend that turns into the wide, gravelled driveway. I will never stop enjoying this view, I think as Alice parks by the front door. The house from the front is exquisite, truly majestic, with its white frontage and tall windows reflecting the greenery that shields the house from the road. There is a true feeling of isolation here, as if the house wraps its arms tight around you, protecting you from the outside world.

I get out of the car and move carefully around to the other side, but Alice shoos me away. 'I'll get her,' she tells me firmly, and I stand back, staring up at the house.

'It's good to be home,' I say, leaning down to touch Willow's cheek when Alice lifts the car seat out of the car. 'Welcome to Helygen House, little one.'

'Let's get you indoors,' Alice says, locking the car and marching towards the front door, gravel crunching underfoot. I follow slowly, one hand on my still round stomach. *I'll need to go to one of Flick's classes*, I think as I go up the steps into the house. *Get my body back into shape.* I have always prided myself on being as fit and healthy as I can be, eating well most of the time and moving as much as I can. I am grateful for what my body can do, after seeing what MS did to my once strapping father. I watched him waste away, the disease eating him from the inside out, and I vowed to always value what my body does for me. And now my movements are slowed by the caesarean, the scar tight and itchy across my stomach, I have to remind myself that it is temporary, that I will get my health back.

I follow Alice into the sitting room, which she insists on calling the parlour, and settle into a comfortable chair by the radiator. It is cold today, November making its presence known with wintry fingers finding their way through the cracks. I realise that Christmas is only around the corner, and suddenly I am remembering the first one after my father died, the complete and utter wrongness of staying in London for the festive season instead of my usual trip home. But there were new tenants in his flat, the only home I'd known until I went to university, and there was nothing waiting for me in Cornwall, so I stayed with Flick and her then-girlfriend, trying to get into the spirit of the season, but instead finding myself in a bar after a dinner I'd only picked at, downing shots and trying to blur my mind enough so the memories weren't quite so sharp.

There will be no vodka-soaked Christmas this year. Although Willow will not remember it, I will make sure her first Christmas is a happy one. Perhaps Flick will come, since she is no longer with Jaz and her mother usually goes to Belfast for the holiday, to visit family Flick doesn't like. Perhaps we can be alone together, and I can stave off the grief that will be waiting for me.

'Josie?' I look up to see Alice staring at me, and her tone suggests this isn't the first time she's said my name.

I shift in my seat. 'Sorry, I was miles away.'

She purses her lips. 'I've been into the nursery and finished setting up. Everything should be ready for you now.'

I push down the flare of irritation at her words. It had been ready enough before the birth. Willow's cot was built and I'd made sure the changing table was well stocked. We'd even painted the walls, a strip of blush pink in the middle with fresh white paint beneath. The top of the wall opposite the cot is covered in metallic rose-gold Dalmatian stickers. It took almost an entire day to do them just right, but it was worth it. The only things left to do were to paint the old rocking chair Alice had given us and set up the baby monitor. Has she moved the cot out of my bedroom? I know she didn't like the idea of co-sleeping, tutting over the cot which was attached to my side of the bed, but she wouldn't have taken it out, would she? I want to go and check, but my swollen ankles are throbbing and I'm too comfortable to move.

'Thank you,' I say instead.

'Are you certain you don't wish to move in here?' she asks. She reaches down to brush a finger against Willow's cheek. 'It would be so much easier if I could help.'

I try to smile warmly at her. 'I'll be fine. Honestly. I'd prefer my own bed, especially after being in hospital.'

She purses her lips. 'Very well. I'll bring you some dinner later.'

I nod. I don't have the energy to argue with her now. I can't keep fighting her every step of the way. Whatever I say, she has a different idea that is always better than mine. We never seem to agree on anything. Henry really was the glue that bound us together. Our shared love of him is the only thing we seem to have in common.

And yet . . . The way she spoke to the police officers on the day I found him still niggles at me. She seemed so ready to accept that her son had taken his own life. But why? I want to ask, but I daren't open that Pandora's box yet. I don't have the strength to fight her on this, not now, but I make a mental note to call the police tomorrow and request an update. I haven't heard anything since that day, and I've assumed that Alice has been dealing with it all, but she hasn't mentioned it to me either. I look down at Willow and can't help but smile at her angelic face. *It's all for you*, I tell her silently. *You deserve to know the truth about what happened to your father.*

I suddenly long for familiar surroundings, for the cosiness of Little Hel and everything it is to me. I bend carefully to pick up Willow, waving Alice away, and move slowly towards the corridor. I use my key to let myself into the apartment through the internal door, and as I lock it behind me, I remember that it had been open on the day of Henry's funeral. Had he unlocked it before he died? I can't remember the last time we'd used it, but perhaps Henry had done so on the day of his death. But why? What does it mean? Could someone have come through the house and killed him? Could they have used an entrance not covered by CCTV, somehow found Henry's shotgun? Is that the only reason the police don't seem to believe it could be anything other than suicide, because it was Henry's gun that had been used? So many unanswered questions that I don't have the energy to face. Not yet, anyway.

I groan as I place Willow's car seat on the floor in the hall and put a hand to my lower back. My whole body still aches, my mind fuzzy with fatigue, and I feel my limbs grow heavier still when my eyes find the place where I found Henry that day, blood pooling on the tiles beneath him. I creep closer, searching for a sign of what happened here, of the event which changed my life forever, but I know there is nothing. No stray blood, no cracks in the floor. The stool on which he sat has been tucked back under the breakfast bar, the wood cool beneath my fingers. I sigh, pressing the heels of my hands against my eyes. I need to rest. I turn, carefully picking the car seat up, and climb the stairs towards the bedroom, my progress painstakingly slow. I breathe a sigh of relief to see the cot still attached to the bed, and marvel at how tiny Willow looks when I place her in it. 'Sleep tight, little one,' I whisper, smiling down at her and trailing a finger over her cheek. I dither for a moment, wondering if I've missed anything. Should I feed her first? Change her? But she's already asleep, so maybe I shouldn't disturb her. I crawl into bed beside her, fully dressed, darkness rushing up to catch me.

I wake to a hand shaking me, fingers tight around my shoulder. 'Josie!' a voice hisses in my ear. 'Josie, wake up!'

My vision is blurry, my head thick with sleep. 'What?' I mumble as I blink several times. Alice's face comes into view and I try to sit up. 'What is it?'

'Can't you hear it?'

'Hear what?' And then it hits me, a high-pitched wail. *Willow.* My breasts feel full and uncomfortable, and I realise she is overdue a feed. I push back the cover and try to slide my legs out of bed, but they're too heavy and I don't have the energy. 'How long has she been crying?'

'A while,' Alice says, her voice cold. 'Why isn't the baby monitor working?'

'What? I haven't set it up yet.' Confused, I look down at the cot and my heart lurches. It's empty. I leap out of bed, my eyes searching the room. 'Where is she?'

Alice tuts. 'What do you mean? Who?'

'Willow. I put her right here.' I lift the blanket, as if she would be hiding beneath it. 'She was right here, Alice.'

'Josie.' Alice puts a hand on my arm. 'She's in the nursery, of course. I'll go and get her.'

'The nursery?' I go to move past her, but Alice pushes me back down onto the bed, none too gently.

'Stay there. You're too weak. You'll drop her.'

Anger fizzes through me. I won't drop her. I won't drop my own child. But my body refuses to move and so I sit back against the headboard, the wood cold against my back, as I wait for Alice to bring my daughter to me. How could Alice move her while I was sleeping? How did she even get in here? I close my eyes, trying to clear my mind. It feels as if I'm drunk, my memory patchy. I remember locking the door behind me. I remember putting Willow in this cot. I definitely did those things. Didn't I?

Alice returns, and Willow's crying stops as soon as she's in my arms, her face nudging against my breast. 'She's wet, too,' Alice says, and I know I'm not imagining the reproach in her voice. I take a deep breath, trying to ignore the pain as Willow latches on.

'I'll change her after.'

'I'll do it. Where are the nappies?'

'Top drawer in the changing table. There should be some small enough for her. Fresh Babygros too.' My eyes are closing as I speak, my arms tingling with the effort of holding Willow. Is this normal? Am I supposed to feel this weak?

'Josie.'

My eyes flutter open and I realise my arms are empty. I inhale sharply. 'Where's . . .' I look up to see Willow in Alice's arms, swaddled in a pink knitted blanket.

'All clean,' she says, pressing her lips against Willow's head.

'Thank you,' I mumble. 'I'm so . . . I'm just so tired.'

'You need to rest. I'll look after Willow for a while.'

I want to say no, want to tell her that she is my child, and I will look after her, but the exhaustion is too much and I feel myself slipping away before I can speak again.

THIRTEEN

ELIZA

1881

Eliza woke in the middle of the night, unsure what had disturbed her. The space beside her was empty, a painful reminder of Cassius's absence. During their honeymoon they had slept together every night, though it was true that he had not reached for her since their wedding night. Yet now she was to sleep alone in Helygen House, her husband in the room next door. She turned over, resting her cheek against the soft pillow, and just as her eyes began to close, it came again. A cry.

She sat bolt upright, heart pounding. Was there a baby in the house? How could there be, when so few people lived here? Perhaps one of the servants had a child? She thought of how tentative Mary had been when she helped her undress for bed, her fingers slippery on the buttons. Far too young to have a child of her own, and Cook was far too old. So who?

The cry came again, and before she realised what she was doing, Eliza had slipped from the bed, the floor cold beneath her feet as she padded towards the door. The hallway outside was pitch black, all the doors tightly closed. She blinked, waiting for her eyes to adjust as she listened carefully. Silence. She tiptoed along the corridor, her hand gripping the banister on her right. If she followed it all the way around, she remembered, she would reach the stairs, but where to from there? She knew Harriet's room was on this floor, but there was a whole other wing she hadn't explored yet, and she assumed the servants' quarters were on the floor above. Could the sound of a baby crying reach that far?

Her foot touched something cold and wet and she jumped back. A leak? She looked up but the ceiling was too high and dark to see if anything was dripping from it. Something skittered to her left, scrabbling against the closed doors, and she felt her heart begin to pound, the blood rushing in her ears as her eyes darted left and right, searching for the source of the noise. She took a step back, then another, and screamed when she came up against something solid.

'Eliza!' She turned, her hands flying out in front of her. Something grasped her wrists and she stifled another cry. 'Eliza! It's me.'

'Cassius?' His name came out as a gasp. His outline was taking shape now, his eyes wide, his fingers digging into her wrists.

'What are you doing out here? It's the middle of the night.'

'I thought I heard something . . .' She trailed off as she looked around again, remembering the sound. Had she really heard a baby crying?

'What? What did you hear?'

Eliza held her breath, listening for a moment. Nothing. She felt her husband's arms go around her, pressing her against his chest. 'It was probably a bad dream,' he said into her hair. 'Let us go back to bed. You must be exhausted.'

She nodded, suddenly feeling tired. She let Cassius guide her back into the bedroom, his hand on the small of her back, and fell asleep curled up beside him, grateful for his warmth against her.

'Good morning,' Eliza said brightly as she entered the dining room the next morning. She wondered why they did not take breakfast in a smaller room as she had done at home. Harriet must have felt lonely when Cassius had been in London, eating here by herself. Harriet looked up, glancing at the empty doorway behind Eliza. 'Cassius will be joining us shortly,' she explained as she took her seat on Harriet's right. 'I left him shaving in the bathroom. He told me to come down when I was ready.'

Harriet nodded. 'Did you sleep well?'

Eliza paused, considering whether she should mention the crying baby. 'Very,' she said, deciding against it. She didn't want her mother-in-law to think her feeble. 'The bed is most comfortable.'

Harriet lifted a small bell and rang it once. A moment

later, a door at the back of the room opened and Mary appeared. 'Tea,' Harriet said, 'three cups. My son will be down in a moment.'

'Yes, madam.'

'Two sausages for me, two slices of toast and an egg.' Harriet looked up questioningly. 'Eliza? What will you have?'

Eliza hesitated. At home, they had served themselves from the sideboard, but it would appear that Mary was expected to serve them breakfast as well as dress Eliza and probably Harriet too. It all seemed too much for one young girl to handle, but she told herself that she just had to learn the ways of Helygen House. Mary may be young and somewhat nervous, but she knew what she was doing. Eliza swallowed, the smell of the food making her queasy as she remembered how unwell she'd felt the night before. 'Just tea for now, please,' she said. 'Perhaps some toast in a little while.'

Harriet looked as if she was going to speak, but then Cassius appeared in the doorway. 'Ah, now, this is a sight for sore eyes!' He made his way around the table to sit on his mother's left, opposite Eliza, and she wondered why he did not sit at the head of the table. 'My beautiful wife and my wonderful mother, together.' He grinned at them both.

'Good morning, dear,' Harriet said. 'I hope you are hungrier than your wife.'

Cassius glanced at the cup Mary placed before Eliza. 'Not hungry, darling?' She shook her head. 'Well, I'm absolutely ravenous. Mary!' He gave the maid a winning smile. 'A bit of everything, please, and don't skimp on the bacon!'

She nodded, keeping her eyes averted. 'Here is your tea, sir,' she mumbled, her cheeks flaming as she brought it over.

'Is that coffee I can smell?' He looked at his mother who nodded. 'Black coffee then, no sugar.'

Mary bobbed a curtsey and scurried back to the sideboard to fill a cup with steaming coffee instead before plating up Cassius's food. Harriet waited until it was placed in front of her son before picking up her own cutlery.

'This is delicious,' Cassius exclaimed around a mouthful of tomato. 'Absolutely divine! My dear, you are missing out.'

Eliza smiled. 'Perhaps a slice of toast then, and maybe a poached egg?' She looked to Mary who was hovering on the edge of the room. 'If it's not too much trouble.'

'The eggs are scrambled,' Harriet said briskly while the maid dithered. 'We have poached eggs on Saturdays.'

'Oh.' Eliza glanced at her husband, who was shovelling food into his mouth as if he hadn't eaten for days. 'Scrambled is fine. Thank you, Mary.' She smiled again as the maid put the plate in front of her. She took a bite of the egg, hoping it would settle her stomach, but her mouth flooded with a metallic, fishy taste which threatened to choke her. 'Lovely,' she managed, forcing the food down. It was the nerves, she told herself. A new house, a new husband, a new way of life. A new mother-in-law who seemed to dislike her from the moment she'd set foot inside Helygen House. It was no wonder her appetite had disappeared.

They ate in silence for a few minutes, Harriet cutting off

tiny pieces and popping them daintily into her mouth, chewing for what seemed like a long time. Though her plate was still half full, she placed her cutlery to the side and picked up her teacup. 'What are your plans for the day, Cassius?'

Cassius leaned back from his empty plate and patted his stomach. 'I thought I'd head over to St Austell, get this show on the road.'

'So soon?' Eliza asked. She had thought they would take a tour of the estate today; there was still so much she had not seen, and she had been looking forward to exploring with her husband.

'No time like the present!' he said with a grin. 'I'm sure you can amuse yourself today, darling. Or perhaps Mother could show you around?'

Harriet looked less than thrilled at the prospect and Eliza suppressed a sigh. 'No, no,' she said, forcing a smile. 'I'm sure I can find my own way around. It'll be an adventure.'

'Marvellous.' Cassius stood, his chair scraping across the wooden floor. He leaned down and pecked Eliza on the cheek, the scent of coffee on his breath enough to make her feel nauseous again. 'I'll take the carriage, Thomas is getting it ready. Have a pleasant day, ladies.' And then he was gone, the front door closing behind him with a bang.

Eliza glanced at her mother-in-law, who was staring up at the gallery wall, her eyes vacant. She cut off another piece of toast and forced herself to eat it, taking a large swallow of tea to wash it down. When she looked up again, she noticed Harriet staring at her. She placed her cutlery to the side of her plate and took another sip of tea, her mouth suddenly dry. Mary came over then to clear the plates away and Eliza gave her a small smile.

'Are there many more servants?' she asked, remembering the small group of people who greeted her when she arrived. 'It must take a lot of hands to keep an estate of this size running smoothly.'

'They have good leadership,' Harriet said in a way that made Eliza think she was speaking about herself rather than Cassius.

'Is Cassius often from home?' she tried again in a light tone. 'Does he travel a lot?'

'He has a great deal of business to take care of.' Harriet sipped her tea. 'Though only one of his father's factories remain.'

Eliza considered this. 'Is that the reason for the new venture? To build up his businesses?'

'His empire,' Harriet said, her eyes straying to a portrait hanging on the wall opposite. Eliza followed her gaze, but she was too far away to read the plaque beneath it. 'My late husband,' Harriet explained, her voice wobbling.

'My condolences. Was it a recent bereavement?'

'Almost twenty years. Though it feels like only yesterday that he was taken from me.'

Eliza tried to hide her surprise. Twenty years? Why then

was she still dressed in full mourning? She had heard that the queen had been in mourning for Prince Albert for almost the same length of time, but was this to be usual now, for women to live and die in their widow's weeds? She shuddered at the thought and stood up, moving closer to the portraits to hide her emotions. Her eyes found a painting of a young girl and boy, similar in height and colouring to one another. 'Benjamin and Maisie Fox, 1857,' she read aloud. 'Your children? Cassius did not mention any siblings.'

'Did he not?' Harriet snapped. Eliza turned back to her mother-in-law, flinching when she saw that her face was a mask of cold fury.

'N-no,' she stammered. 'Should he have?'

Harriet stood then, the sudden movement making Eliza jump. 'You may explore the gardens,' she said, lifting a hand towards the window. 'The weather is fine, if a little cold. Take a shawl.'

'I thought I would go down to the kitchens afterwards,' Eliza said, trying to keep up with the change of subject. 'I should meet the rest of the staff. I suppose I shall have to learn the running of the house now.'

Harriet stared at her for a moment, her lips pressed into a line, before nodding once. 'I shall leave you to your explorations then. You have much to learn.'

'What time is dinner served?' Eliza asked, following her mother-in-law out of the dining room. 'I may not hear the bell, if I am in the gardens or the west wing.'

Harriet turned then, her hand snaking out to wrap around Eliza's upper arm. 'We do not use the west wing,' she said sharply, her fingers digging into Eliza's skin. 'That is the first thing you shall learn here. You will not wander where you are not permitted.'

FOURTEEN

JOSIE

2019

When I wake next, my head feels clearer than it has in days. I check my phone, surprised to see it is almost six o'clock in the morning. I must have slept straight through.

I sit up, swinging my legs over the edge of the bed. The rug is soft beneath my feet. I rub my toes against it for a moment, remembering when Flick gave it to me as a Christmas present all those years ago. I'd been eyeing it up for weeks, pausing at the charity shop window every time we passed on our way to work, but it was too expensive for me then. I was so disappointed when it disappeared, only to discover it waiting for me beneath the tree, wrapped in sparkly silver paper.

I reach out and disconnect the charging cable from my phone, feeling a pang of guilt when I see another message from Flick is waiting for me, her previous one having gone unanswered.

I close my eyes, trying to push down the guilt at how she must have felt the day Willow was born. Three years have passed since she buried her own daughter, born too early and having never drawn breath, and time has not dulled the agony of it. I should go and see her. Her mum only lives in Devon, just over an hour's drive away from here, but the idea of it seems insurmountable right now. Maybe she could come here? But what if seeing Willow is too much for her? I know she's been struggling lately, but she's my best friend, I remind myself. Above anything, she'll want to meet Willow.

I begin to tap out a reply, but I'm interrupted by the sound of Willow grizzling. I stand, grateful that my back no longer aches quite so much, and go into the nursery. I'd let Alice put her down in the nursery last night, since she'd been taking care of her while I slept, but she will be back in my bedroom tonight. 'Good morning, little one,' I whisper as I bend down and lift her into my arms. 'Did you sleep well?'

She reaches out to touch my face, her eyes wide, her lips parted as if she would reply. I kiss her on the cheek before placing her on the changing table. When she's clean and changed, I pick her back up and sit in the rocking chair, rocking slowly back and forth while I feed her. It's still a bit painful, but I relish the warmth of her tiny body against mine, the way her fingers curl into a fist that rests against my chest. She is so precious, so unbelievably beautiful. The rush of love hits me again and I almost gasp at the intensity of it.

I hear a clatter of claws and look up to see Ivy entering the room. I realise suddenly that Halka must have been taking care of her while I was in hospital. I can't believe I hadn't thought of it until now. 'Hello, girl,' I say quietly, reaching out a hand towards her. 'I'm sorry for neglecting you. Are you ready to meet your sister?' As if in response, her ears go back against her head and she slowly shuffles forward, sniffing Willow's leg first, then her back. Ivy is the gentlest of dogs and she has always been fond of children, so we never had any concerns about how she would be with the baby.

'You're going to be the best big sister ever, aren't you?' I say as she gently nudges Willow's cheek with her nose. Willow's eyes fly open in surprise, her lips detaching from my nipple. I cover myself then turn her so she can see the dog. 'Willow, meet Ivy,' I whisper in her ear. I laugh as Ivy's tongue flicks out and catches the tip of Willow's nose. Willow reaches out then, her tiny fingers stretching towards Ivy, and I'm about to bring her closer when Alice appears in the doorway.

'What on earth are you doing?' she demands, striding into the room and taking Ivy by the collar.

'They're getting to know each other.' I struggle to my feet, pain flaring in my stomach. 'Let go of her, Alice.'

She does in an almost flinching way, and Ivy moves to sit down beside me, her head tilted up to sniff at Willow's foot. 'I'm not . . . I just don't know if she's . . .'

'Alice,' I say calmly. 'Ivy wouldn't hurt her. She loves children, you know that.'

'Children, yes,' Alice says. 'But a newborn? What if she—'

'She won't,' I say, firmer now. 'I know you're not a fan of dogs, but she would never hurt Willow. And it will be so special to see them grow up together.' I smile. 'There's nothing quite like that bond. Henry told me that.'

Alice relaxes a fraction. 'Yes, I suppose he did. He loved that great lumbering beast.' She smiles too. 'Henry was five when we got him. Basil. Such an odd name for a German shepherd, but it was Henry's choice.'

I nod, smiling. 'I've seen pictures. They were so close.'

Something flickers across Alice's face and her eyes take on a faraway look. 'Yes. They were.' She shakes herself. 'Anyway, I meant to tell you that it's the will reading today. The solicitor is coming here.' My stomach drops. Today? I'm losing track of time. 'But if you're not feeling up to it, I can do it alone,' she continues. 'You still need to rest.'

I shake my head. 'I'm feeling better today. I'll be there.'

She looks at me for a moment as if considering whether to argue. 'Very well,' she says after a beat. 'The solicitor will be here in an hour.' She reaches out to touch Willow's hand. 'Would you like me to watch her while you get ready? I can take her back to the house with me. I'm sure you're desperate for a shower.'

I laugh. 'Hint taken.' I *do* feel a bit grubby. My hair hasn't been washed in a week, and although I've been keeping the scar clean, I'd love nothing more than to step into a hot shower. 'That would be great, thanks.' I hand Willow over, bending to kiss her cheek. 'See you in a little while.'

The shower is glorious. I turn the temperature up as I shampoo my hair, luxuriating in the coconut scent. This bathroom is one of my favourite rooms in the apartment, with its white metro tiles and huge clawfoot bathtub. I'd always wanted a rainfall shower, having grown up with only a bath and then a useless handheld thing in my student house that took an age to rinse my hair clean, but what I love most about this room are the original features, especially the beautiful ceiling rose. We fitted spotlights around it but kept as much intact as possible. I love lying in the bath, gazing up at that ceiling and wondering how many other pairs of eyes have looked up at it over the years.

I rinse the conditioner from my hair then apply a leave-in cream, deciding it could do with some TLC after the week it's had. Besides, I'm not sure I have the strength to straighten out my natural loose waves right now. I shave my underarms then wash my body, being careful around the scar. The skin is already starting to look better, less puckered and angry.

I step out of the shower, grabbing a towel from the rail and wrapping myself in it, enjoying the softness against my skin. At the sink, I brush my teeth and pluck a few stray hairs from my eyebrows before padding into the bedroom to get dressed. What do you wear to a will reading? Will it be just like the Hollywood films, a group of us gathered together to hear the last will and testament of

Henry Fox? I shake my head. I'm the sole executor, and Henry and I had mirrored wills, so there shouldn't be any surprises. I take down a comfortable pair of navy trousers and a loose black top, then sit at the dressing table to do my make-up. My skin looks paler than usual, though the rings beneath my eyes are slightly less obvious than before. I struggled to sleep after Henry died, unable to rid myself of the image of him lying on the kitchen floor, but since Willow was born I've been too exhausted to dream up my dead husband.

I smudge some concealer under my eyes and apply a lick of mascara, then switch on the hairdryer, hovering the large diffuser bowl over my hair. It's still slightly damp when I switch it off, but I'm running out of time. I'm moving much slower these days. Ivy gets up from her bed in the living room and follows me as I slip my feet into my comfortable trainers and grab my jacket. I decide to go the long way out of the front door and through the grounds, desperate for some fresh air. It's slightly warmer today, though the sky is still overcast. I should bring Willow out here, show her around the place she'll call home. There's so much for her to explore here.

Ivy trots along beside me as we follow the path around the side and up the steps to the door which leads into the formal dining room. I glance up and see the CCTV camera, and remind myself to bring it up with Alice again. I need an update on the case. Surely there will be an inquest at some point? I realise how little I know of these matters and wonder if I should ask the solicitor for some advice. I'm so out of my depth.

I find Alice in the sitting room pouring tea into two dainty cups, while Willow sleeps in her Moses basket. I sit in the chair beside her and Ivy moves to the other side, lying down and resting her head on her paws, her eyes trained on my daughter. I scratch behind her ears, realising that I almost feel happy, and immediately feel guilty about it. My husband hasn't even been dead a month. But don't I deserve to be happy? Doesn't Willow? She deserves more than a mum who is constantly grieving. She deserves a full life, and my complete, unwavering love. I straighten up as Alice passes me a cup of tea, smiling my thanks, and resolve to give Willow the best life she could ever have, here, in Henry's house, where she is surrounded by his presence.

The doorbell rings and Alice hurries to answer it. I frown. She usually lets Marie answer the door, even when she's expecting someone, but perhaps she doesn't want anyone else to be present for this. I feel a pang of sorrow for her. She has lost her son, and yet here she is holding the rest of the family up, taking care of Willow for me so I can rest and shower. She's so energetic and full of life that I sometimes forget she's over sixty. She can walk for miles without resting and has been known to do things like mow the huge lawns and fix leaky taps by herself. I know money was tight when she moved in here all those years ago, as it's been running low again in recent years, so Alice had to learn how to do certain things by herself. That's why Henry and I came up with our grand schemes to run workshops and retreats and even weddings one day, to make the estate pay for itself. I've been trying not to think about those plans we had, and what will come of them now, but at least today I should get some answers about that side of things.

A thin man I don't recognise follows Alice into the room. He has a long nose and, to my surprise, a strong Bristol accent. 'Jeremy Wilcox,' he says, holding out a hand for me to shake. I smile and stay seated while Alice hovers behind him.

'Tea, Jeremy?' she offers. 'Or perhaps coffee?'

'Tea would be lovely, thank you. No sugar.' He sits down in the seat Alice indicates for him and lays his briefcase across his lap. 'Oh, hello,' he says, noticing Willow beside my chair. 'Congratulations.' His smile dims when he remembers the purpose of his visit. 'And, uh, my condolences too, of course.' He clears his throat, nodding as Alice places a cup of tea by his elbow. She sits in the chair beside mine, her hands folded in her lap, and we wait for Jeremy to begin.

'Right.' Jeremy opens his briefcase and pulls out a sheaf of papers. 'This really is a formality, Mrs Fox, and, uh, Mrs Fox,' he adds, glancing awkwardly at Alice.

'My surname is Corbyn,' I remind him with a smile. 'But Josie is fine.'

Jeremy gives a funny kind of jerk, as if he, in any other circumstances, might make a joke about our names, but instead he clears his throat again. 'Josie, right. Of course.

Since you and Mr Fox had mirrored wills, there is very little to go over. You see—'

'What does that mean?' Alice cuts in. 'Mirrored wills?'

'We had them drawn up together,' I tell her. 'If I die, he gets everything. If he dies . . .' I trail off, since that is no longer an *if*.

'And what of Helygen House?' she demands, sitting forward. 'Surely that was not in your power to bequeath?'

I glance at Jeremy. 'Perhaps you could go over that? I'm not entirely certain either.'

He nods, looking down at his papers. 'Yes, of course. The house and estate belonged to Henry Fox, of course, and so they have been left to his wife, Josephine Corbyn, along with everything else.' He looks up and gives a small, wary smile. 'This is not unexpected, I hope?'

Not to me, I think, watching Alice's fingers tighten on the arms of the chair out of the corner of my eye.

'Rather,' Jeremy continues, 'Josie has inherited the house and estate until his eldest living child comes of age.' He glances down at Willow. 'Until your, uh, daughter, is twenty-five.'

'But *girls* cannot inherit,' Alice splutters, and I turn to look at her properly now, bewildered by her outrage. 'It has always been this way. The eldest male heir must inherit Helygen House. That is why *I* did not inherit.'

I am certain I'm not imagining the bitterness in her voice. 'But Alice, there is no male heir,' I begin, but she cuts me off.

'Or nearest living relative. *Male* relative.'

I sit back, stunned into silence. As one of the women who had been passed over, I would never have expected Alice to uphold such an outdated practice.

Jeremy is shaking his head. 'I'm not sure what went before, Mrs Fox, but this is Henry's last will and testament, and Helygen House was indeed his to bequeath.'

'I will contest it!' Alice slams a fist against the arm of the chair and I jump.

'You will contest it?' I repeat slowly. 'You will contest your granddaughter's inheritance? Where she will *live*?' My voice rises until it is almost shrill and Alice looks at me then, as if seeing me for the first time. 'This is Willow's home, Alice. Do you really want to take that away from her?'

She shakes her head, dropping her gaze to the carpet, her hair falling into her face. What has got into her? I have never seen her like this. It's almost as if she is possessed.

'To be clear,' Jeremy says, shifting in his seat, 'you are not contesting the will, Mrs Fox?' Alice says nothing, only shakes her head again. He clears his throat. 'Very good. Shall we proceed?'

FIFTEEN

I see the solicitor out, Willow held in the crook of my arm. Alice hasn't said a word since her outburst, and while I want to see if she is okay, I am also silently fuming. How dare she say she would contest the will. How dare she almost threaten to throw her newborn granddaughter out onto the streets. Henry would have been furious. *I* am furious. But a part of me knows she is still grieving, and perhaps that is the reason for her uncharacteristic behaviour. At least, I hope so.

I'm about to turn back towards the sitting room when Halka bustles into the hall. Her lips spread into a wide smile, her hands coming together beneath her chin as if in prayer.

'Oh, there she is,' she says, coming closer. 'May I hold her?' Despite having lived in the UK for most of her life, Halka still has a slight eastern European accent. I've heard her speaking in Polish on the phone before and marvelled at the quickfire language. She coos at Willow, who stares back with her wide, intelligent eyes. She is such a quiet baby, I am learning, content to watch the world go by. I pass her over and smile as Halka rocks her in her arms. 'She is so beautiful,' she says, making the kind of faces people only tend to make at babies and small animals. 'And how are you?' she asks, looking up at me and frowning. 'Alice said you had a difficult birth.'

I swallow, trying not to remember the pain and fear. 'I'm fine,' I tell her. 'Still a bit sore, but fine.'

'You had a caesarean, no?' She nods towards my stomach. 'You be careful with lifting. If you need anything, you call me. Okay?' She fixes me with her gaze and I nod, touched by her concern. 'I'd better get back to work,' she says with a wink, passing Willow back to me. 'I'll bring you dinner tonight?'

I'm about to nod again when I pause. 'Actually, I think I'll eat with Alice tonight. What are you making?'

'Tonight we have soup, followed by lamb chops and cheesecake for dessert. I also have apple crumble if you like, but Marie has had her eye on it all day.'

'Cheesecake is great,' I say with a smile. 'Six o'clock?'

'As always.' She gives me a pat on the shoulder as she passes before disappearing down the hall.

I take a deep breath, holding Willow close. Tonight, I am going to eat with Alice and demand some answers. Tonight, I am going to get to the truth.

I go back to the apartment, Ivy on my heels, and put Willow down for a nap in her Moses basket. While she's sleeping, I make myself some toast and eat it on the sofa, feeding Ivy the crusts. My phone buzzes and I pull it out, which reminds me that I haven't finished the text to Flick. I want to ask her to come over, now I have seen the solicitor and everything has been put to bed. Henry has left everything to me, though Alice can continue to live in Helygen House until her death if we both wish. I hate the idea of throwing my mother-in-law out of her ancestral home, but I need to remind her that Willow is my first priority. If she threatens my daughter's future, I will not hesitate to act. Surely she knows me well enough to know that. Surely it is the least one expects from a mother.

This also means that the plans Henry and I made can continue. It's a good thing, since my phone vibrated with a calendar reminder that says BUILDERS. Tomorrow at eight a.m., workmen will be coming to start on the stables. It'll be the beginning of the wedding venue plans, creating three six-bedroom apartments and a one-bedroom luxury guest suite. I unlock my phone and type out a message to Flick.

So sorry I haven't replied, I'm exhausted! Come and see us next week? We have the retreat to discuss, and the renovations are due to start tomorrow. I'm looking forward to having something to focus on again. I hope you're okay xx

I sit back and listen to Ivy snoring on the sofa beside me, her nose almost touching the Moses basket. My gaze drifts until it finds the lake, glittering in the weak afternoon sun. I'd forgotten all about the building work, though I suppose it's no surprise in the circumstances. I open my mouth to speak, forgetting for a second that Henry is no longer here beside me, and groan instead, putting a hand over my eyes. Will this ever get any easier? Or will I always look for him in this house, expecting him to be on the sofa next to me, or in the kitchen making poached eggs on a Saturday morning, or coming in through the back door in muddy wellies? A part of me doesn't want to forget him, doesn't want to erase him from these spaces, but I know I'll never find peace if I keep seeing his ghost everywhere I turn.

I must fall asleep, because when I open my eyes the sky outside is darkening. Ivy has moved to her bed, face pressed against the raised side, and the heating has kicked in, the radiator behind me growing warm. I sit up, groggy, and reach out for my cup of tea to find it's gone cold. A glance at the clock tells me it's four o'clock. Willow is still sleeping peacefully and I have a couple of hours until dinner, so I decide to put a load of washing on and tidy up the kitchen. I haven't cooked properly in days, maybe weeks, and I realise the kitchen sink is still full of washing-up from the day Henry died. I try not to think about the fact that some of these mugs and cutlery will be among the last things Henry touched. Instead, I tap DS Fergus's number into my phone from the business card pinned on the fridge and listen to it ring while I load the dishwasher. I leave a message when his voicemail kicks in.

'Hi, DS Fergus, it's Josie Corbyn here. I'm just calling for an update on the . . .' The word *case* sticks in my throat. Henry wasn't just a *case*. 'On what happened to my husband.

Can you please give me a call back?' I reel off my number and hang up, my palms sweaty with nerves. Have I been avoiding making this call because I'm afraid of what the police will tell me? Because I'm afraid that they'll tell me my husband took his own life, when his wife was only weeks away from giving birth, when we had so many plans for the future? I'm afraid that my husband knew something he didn't want to tell me, *couldn't* tell me, and he saw no other way out. Is that the man I knew? I shake my head, reaching out for a dirty glass. It slips through my fingers and smashes against the tiles, and I jump back, my heart thudding. A cry starts up and my head jerks towards the Moses basket as if on a string.

'I'm sorry, sweetie,' I call as I grab the dustpan and start to sweep up the shards. The last thing I need is for Ivy to cut her paws, or for me to step on an errant piece in the middle of the night with Willow in my arms. No more hospitals. No more grief. I need to look forward, to focus on what is to come.

Willow is screaming by the time I reach her, her face bright red with fury. 'All right, little one,' I hush her, picking her up and cradling her hot little body against my chest. She is rigid, still screaming her piercing scream despite my murmuring. I move over to the sofa and sit down, rocking her in my arms in the hope that the motion will calm her, but she balls up her fists as if to pummel me, as if she is so utterly furious that I would wake her so violently and then leave her to cry for even a few moments.

Unexpected tears prick my eyes. 'I'm sorry, little one,' I whisper, pressing my lips against her cheek. 'I'm sorry, I'm sorry.' Eventually she begins to calm down, her face relaxing. She opens her eyes and stares up at me, almost reproachfully, as if I have disappointed her by crying. I swipe the tears away from my eyes. 'Sorry, darling,' I say quietly. 'I'm probably going to do that a lot.'

After I have fed and changed Willow, I strap her into her car seat and carry her through to the kitchen, where I slip on my shoes and jacket. Ivy comes up beside Willow and nudges her foot with her nose. 'Sorry, girl,' I tell her. 'You've got to stay here this time.' I fill a bowl with food and refresh her water bowl, then leave a Bonio out for her.

'You spoil that dog,' Henry used to say with a grin, knowing that he did the same.

'She's my baby,' I said, unabashedly, unapologetically, as if daring him to ridicule me. But he never did. He loved her as much as I do, and had in fact been pestering me to get a dog ever since we met. Our first London flat had been too small, but when we moved to another place a bit further out with a tiny private garden, we finally agreed that it was the right time. We drove to Kent to collect Ivy one sunny day in April, to a quaint little town in the middle of the countryside. Though I had grown up in Cornwall, I'd spent most of my time in the towns of Liskeard and Bodmin, rarely able to properly explore the beautiful countryside and coast that surrounded me. My dad didn't have a car and

I didn't learn to drive until I was a student, and so I'd never truly appreciated the county I called home. Until now. Now I am in love with it. When we moved back here, Henry took Ivy and me on weekly trips to Wheal Coates and Tintagel and St Nectan's Glen. We went to farmers' markets in Lostwithiel and food fairs in Truro and on river cruises along the Tamar from Saltash, gazing up at Plymouth standing proudly above the Sound. Willow will have all of this too. She is privileged, I realise that. She will grow up with everything I never had – this large, beautiful home, extensive grounds to get lost in, an education to be proud of. But she will also grow up without the only thing I ever had – a loving father. I have to be that for her. I have to be everything, mother and father. Guardian, protector, friend.

We leave Ivy tucking into her dinner and go out through the front door, but instead of turning towards the house, I begin to make my way across the grass and down to the lake. We installed high-power security lights throughout the grounds last year, as well as pretty solar-powered ones dotted along the winding path leading from our patio down to the willow tree. I pause there, one hand on the trunk, Willow's car seat in the other, breathing in the clean air. There is something calming about still water, as if you can drop your worries into it and let them sink to the bottom, where they will be held until you are strong enough to unearth them again.

After a few moments, I turn back towards the house, following another, darker path up to the back door of the main house. Lights flick on as I get near, allowing me to climb the stone steps without risk of injury. As I'm wiping my feet on the mat, I notice drops of water on the wooden floor leading up the corridor. It hasn't rained today, not that I'm aware of, and Alice certainly wouldn't go swimming in the lake on a November evening. Bemused, I follow the water down the hall and pause in the kitchen to say hello to Halka.

'Are you prepared for battle?' she asks with a wry smile.

I feel my stomach drop. 'What do you mean?'

'She's . . . well, let me say that she's not in a good mood. I'm sure you noticed the water out there? We think it's coming from Marie's bathroom, those old lead pipes.' I make a face and Halka sighs. 'Do you want some wine, to fortify yourself?' She indicates a bottle on the counter.

I shake my head. 'I'm breastfeeding.'

'Girls still do that? I thought it was all about the bottle now, so the men can't get out of the night feeds.'

I laugh. 'Actually, I was planning on expressing milk for that exact reason.'

The smile falls from Halka's face. 'Oh, I am sorry. It was insensitive of me to joke.'

'No, Halka.' I reach out to touch her arm. 'We have to talk about him. We can't let him fall away into the past. He would be laughing now, if he could hear us.'

'I think he can,' she says, nodding. 'I am Catholic, you know? Well, I was *raised* Catholic, but I was also raised to become a dancer, and look what happened there.' She rubs her admittedly large stomach and chuckles. 'But I do believe in angels. Spirits, yes? They live on around us. I know it.'

I've heard Halka speak of ghosts and angels before, and always nodded and smiled and pretended I didn't think she was talking a load of nonsense, but this time a shiver runs through me. She nods again as if I have spoken. 'You feel him too. It's this house. It remembers people. It's like you give a piece of yourself to it, a piece that stays trapped here forever.'

SIXTEEN

HARRIET

21ˢᵗ June 1859

It might seem as if I only ever write to you, dear diary, about death or tragedy, and here I am again. Forgive me for neglecting you, and for only turning to you in my hours of need. I do not know who else to turn to. My beloved Sara has been unwell, with dark purple beneath her eyes and an even paler complexion than usual, and I have noticed small bruises along her arms. She has no brute of a husband or father who could be hurting her, and she very rarely visits friends or even her ailing grandmother. Whenever I ask her about the marks on her body she says they are nothing, that she must have banged herself while cleaning or carrying water about the house, but I do not believe it. She has become almost distant towards me of late, going about her duties without her usual warmth, and so I find myself utterly alone in my grief.

Has it truly been a decade since I last wrote to you? It

feels as if hardly any time has passed at all. Cassius is now a strapping boy of ten, and Clara is the most beautiful girl, with long, fair curls and sparkling eyes. I can already picture her in a fine dress when she makes her debut, all heads turning in her direction. Though she has a fiery disposition, inclined to bursts of frustration and stubbornness, I am certain she will grow out of her wilfulness.

After Cassius was born, I'd thought perhaps my days of childbearing were over, but then along came Maisie and Benjamin a few years later, one after the other. I can hardly bear to write her name; my hand is shaking so. Maisie, my dear, sweet cherub. Only six years old and yet so bright and eager to learn, even Edmund was impressed with her — though he still refused to engage a governess for the girls. Oh, how he must regret that now. Maisie would sit on his knee after breakfast and read the newspaper to him, pausing to ask questions which Edmund delighted in answering. He does love to show off his worldly knowledge. He would even tell her about the quarries and factories which have been in his family for generations, the running of which he mostly leaves to his very capable foremen, and he would show her the slate and granite used to build parts of this very house. She was fascinated, and though I myself do not find the practical side of my husband's business very interesting, it was truly heart-warming to see how proud he was that one of his children was taking a keen interest.

'A shame Cassius does not show the same passion,' he said one day over luncheon, thankfully when the children were out of earshot. 'It is he who will inherit, after all. Perhaps Maisie should have been born a boy.'

I wrestled with my emotions, knowing I could not speak my thoughts aloud. Lately, I have been wondering why it is always the boys who have such bright futures ahead of them, and yet all my daughters have to look forward to is a good marriage and fine, healthy children. If they are lucky.

And yet, Maisie now has nothing to look forward to. My heart aches as I recall her small, limp body and her pale, almost translucent skin. She looked as if she was sleeping, her eyes closed, her lips slightly parted, but no breath fluttered from between them.

He found her in the lake. The children had been shooed from the house while the servants began the spring clean, as they are of an age when they like to get under one's feet, and the new housekeeper Mrs Lane is not the most tolerant of women, though she gets the job done, I suppose. Edmund was out at a business meeting and I was in the library, staying out of the way and enjoying the peace and quiet. Cassius was going to teach Benjamin to swim, and Clara was supposed to be watching them from her place under the willow tree, a book of French verbs in her lap. Though only a year older than Benjamin, Maisie was already a strong swimmer – she had taken to it like a fish, as if she was never supposed to walk on land – and she often swam alone in the lake, the willow tree her only companion. Which is why I cannot seem to make sense of what happened. Clara had disappeared at some point, and Benjamin had grown bored of swimming and gone to climb a tree on the edge of the lake. And then, chaos. Mrs Lane heard a shout from where she was stringing sheets up on the line outside the kitchen door and hurried down towards the lake. She found Cassius pulling Maisie out of the water, her body slack and unresponsive. She sent Cassius to fetch me, his feet leaving wet footprints on the floorboards, making them slippery underfoot, while Sara knelt down in the mud beside my youngest daughter.

'Madam,' she cried. 'She's not breathing. I've tried everything, I . . .' She trailed off, her eyes full of tears, while Mrs Lane looked on, her lips pursed in either disapproval or grief, I could not tell.

I confess I knew not what to do. I told Mrs Lane to fetch the doctor, though who knew where he would be and whether he could come to us in time, and besides, Sara knows as much as he does about medicine, as far as I am concerned. But by the time he arrived, Edmund had returned and moved Maisie's body into the house, wrapped up in a blanket. How small she looked, how young. Such a waste of life.

'It was an accident, Papa,' Cassius told Edmund. 'A terrible accident.' He looked so young too, so terrified. How awful for him to watch his sister drown. I gathered him in my arms after, smoothed down his still-wet curls and held him close. So much tragedy in one house. I must remember to be thankful for the happy times, however short, and for the children still living. They must be my priority, despite the pain in my heart.

SEVENTEEN

JOSIE

2019

'It's nice of you to join me for dinner, Josie,' Alice says with what seems to be a genuine smile. I try to return it as I take my seat on her left, placing Willow's car seat on the table beside me. She is sleeping peacefully, wrapped up in her pink knitted blanket. 'It's been a long time since I had company,' Alice adds, and I wonder if I am imagining the bitterness in her voice. Surely she did not expect me to dine with her after Henry died and I was drowning in grief? Halka had sent trays of food up to my room when I was staying here, which remained mostly untouched when Marie collected them again. Surely she does not hold that against me?

Or maybe she is just lonely, I chastise myself. *Maybe she's grieving, just like you are.*

'Yes,' I reply, holding my smile in place. 'I thought it was time we settled into a new routine.'

Marie enters the dining room carrying two large bowls and a bread basket with the skill of an experienced waitress. I suppose she has had to get used to it, waiting on Alice as her personal servant. I feel a prickle of distaste as I often do when I am here in the main house, uncomfortable, as I am served food or drinks and asked, 'Is there anything else?' This has been the hardest part of living at Helygen House for me. I was a waitress myself when I was at university and suffered with aching feet and a sore back and a constant headache from the noise and forced smiling at often rowdy, sometimes rude customers. *How the other half live*, I muse, not for the first time, as Marie puts my bowl in front of me.

'Thank you,' I say, giving her a warm smile, and she flashes me a quick one in return. I notice, as I always do, that Alice does not thank her. She has been used to this her whole life, I suppose, people scurrying around, waiting on her hand and foot, wanting to please her. It feels so antiquated, as if such a wide gap between the classes should have been left behind in the 1800s. But what about when Henry and India were young, and they first moved into Helygen House? Alice has hinted that they had very little money back then, while they'd waited for her late husband's estate to sell, so she must have had to cook and clean like a normal person. Yet somehow, I can't quite imagine it.

Marie comes back with a bottle of wine and offers it to Alice, who nods. 'Very good,' she says. 'Halka has fine taste in wine.'

'None for me, thanks,' I tell Marie as she moves over to

my glass. 'Breastfeeding.' I see Alice wrinkle her nose and try to ignore the ripple of frustration which passes over me. 'Is there any lemonade? Juice? Anything really.'

'I'm sure there's some lemonade in the pantry,' Marie says, 'but it won't be cold.' She glances at Alice as if waiting for a reproach.

'That's fine,' I say quickly. 'I don't mind. Thank you.' She hurries off to fetch me a drink while Alice sips her wine. I nod towards my bowl of soup. 'This looks excellent. I've missed Halka's cooking. I know she's sent food over, but I've often been asleep or feeding Willow and had to heat it up later, so it's not quite the same.' I realise I'm babbling and shut up as Alice studies me over her wine glass.

'You know you are more than welcome to join me for dinner any day of the week,' she says evenly. 'I did so look forward to our Sunday lunches together.'

I feel a rush of sadness. Despite everything, I too enjoyed having Sunday lunch here with Henry and his mother. It wasn't so much that I liked having a break from cooking – I've always enjoyed it, as it was something Henry and I often did together – but it felt like such a treat to come here. Halka's roasts are to die for, her potatoes absolutely perfect in a way I have never mastered, and Alice was always on her best behaviour when Henry was around. She truly did worship him, and he adored her, despite their differences. I realise that she must have felt abandoned, left alone in this house with only her grief for company. I should make more of an effort with her. But then I remember that I'm here to get some answers, and I need to choose my words carefully.

'What was it like,' I ask, once Marie has deposited a glass of lemonade before me, 'when Henry was a child? You moved in here when they were quite young, didn't you?'

Alice looks surprised by my question. 'Yes. Henry was four, and India seven. We lived in the east wing then, where your apartment is now. The rest of the house was an utter mess.' She picks up her spoon and I do the same, tucking into the potato and leek soup. I break apart a piece of crusty bread and dip it in, and we eat in silence for a few moments.

'I wish I could've seen it,' I say when I've eaten my second slice of bread. 'The house back then, before you started the work.' I look around the vast dining room, with its dark wood panelling and green wallpaper. 'Did you change much in here?'

Alice shakes her head. 'No, I kept as many of the original features as possible. This is the same wallpaper that was hung when this room was first built, back in the nineteenth century.' She smiles proudly. 'It's lasted so well.'

'How did you manage it all, with two young children? Was there a lot to be done?'

'Oh, the kitchen was fine, though quite outdated, and of course there was no central heating. It took a lot of time, and a lot of money, but we got there in the end.' She places her spoon on the side of her empty bowl. 'Your apartment was quite different back then. The staircase was rotten so we could only use the rooms downstairs at first.'

I smile. 'Henry said it was a death trap,' I say without thinking. The word hangs in the air between us and a chill runs through me, as if I have summoned Henry's ghost. I shake myself. 'So you lived in the downstairs rooms? How did that work?'

'Yes. There was no kitchen in that part of the house, as you'll remember, and the plumbing was a bit haywire. But once the stairs were fixed we could use the bathroom – *your* bathroom now – and it's easy enough to get to the kitchen through the old servants' corridors. It was fine, for the most part. We managed.'

I nod, remembering Henry telling me about it. 'Henry had such fond memories of his childhood here. Do you have any old photos of the place? I'd love to see them.'

Alice smiles vaguely. 'Oh, I'm sure there are some around somewhere. I'll have a look.'

Marie comes in then with plates of lamb chops and new potatoes. She whisks the soup bowls away and comes back with a little dish of mint sauce.

'Thanks, Marie,' I say before she disappears again. I look down at my plate and feel my stomach rumble, despite the soup starter. Alice reaches out for the mint sauce and adds a dollop to her chops before handing it to me. I feel nerves bubble up as I start to eat. While I am interested in the history of Helygen House and the Fox family, I've really been gearing myself up to talk about the important thing: what happened to Henry. I decide to wait until after we've finished eating, in case Alice chokes on a chop bone and I have to perform the Heimlich manoeuvre.

Willow fidgets and I place a hand on her stomach. The now-familiar worry that I'm doing the best I can for my daughter niggles away at me. Is she comfortable in that car seat? *Not for much longer,* I tell her silently. *Then I'll tuck you into your nice warm bed.*

Despite its deliciousness, the food sits heavily in my stomach, and I suddenly want to be back in Little Hel, curled up on the sofa with Willow and Ivy, watching some rubbish on the TV. That was one of Henry's favourite Sunday evening pastimes, snoozing in front of a soap rerun or documentary, comfortably full from lunch. I wonder what our new routine will be without him.

Marie clears our plates away and I sit up, bracing myself for this conversation that needs to be had. But as I take a deep breath, Alice speaks first. 'I heard from the police today.'

My mouth falls open. 'Really? What did they say?'

'That you had left the DS a message.' She smiles, but there is little warmth in it. 'The Chief Inspector is an old friend. He went to university with my brother.'

'Your brother?' My mouth suddenly feels dry; I take a sip of lemonade, feel it fizz along my tongue. 'I thought you grew up in Australia?' I remember Henry telling me about his mother moving to England when she was eighteen and marrying an Englishman, Henry's father, who died in a car accident when Henry was young. I realise now that she has never had any trace of an Australian accent, only the rounded vowels of received pronunciation.

'We did. The Chief Inspector spent his gap year with us and then decided to study in Sydney.' She is still smiling. 'Cornwall is a small place. Everyone knows everyone, as they say. And so I trust the Chief Inspector to do the right thing with regard to Henry's death.' Her expression turns serious then, and she pauses to sip her wine before continuing. 'There's nothing on the CCTV to suggest it was anything other than suicide, Josie. It's a hard truth, but we just have to accept it.' I am shaking my head, my skin growing hot. 'Henry must have been so very troubled,' she continues, 'and he did not wish to burden us.'

'No.'

'We must strive to put it behind us,' she says, as if I have not spoken. 'We must move on, for Willow's sake, if nothing—'

'No!' The word bursts from my lips, echoing around the room.

Alice falls silent, her lips pursed into a thin line. 'He was my son, Josie.'

'And he was my husband,' I hiss. 'He would never have killed himself. Never. Especially not with Willow on the way.' I place a hand on my daughter's stomach again and take a deep breath, trying to centre myself. 'You said there's nothing on the CCTV? How can there be nothing?'

Alice sighs. 'Well, there are some gaps . . . Something to do with the app, I don't quite understand it.' Her eyes are sad now. She reaches a hand across the table but I flinch away. 'I know how hard this is for you, Josie. It is so very hard for me too. To believe that my son . . .' She drops her gaze, fiddles with her napkin. 'I can hardly believe that he would do such a thing. But the estate was – *is* – in a lot of debt, perhaps even more than Henry led us to believe.'

'We were fixing things,' I tell her, my jaw clenched. 'We had plans to start making money, make the estate pay for itself. It would have worked.'

'You know very little of the workings of an estate like this,' she says softly. 'Considering your . . . background.'

'You mean the council flat I grew up in?' I snap. 'I may not have grown up in a fine house with a name and grounds and *fucking servants*.' I see her recoil at the swearword and feel a buzz of triumph. 'But Henry taught me all about how it needs to be run. We were partners in this venture. We knew what needed to be done, and we were doing it. I am still doing it.'

'What do you mean?' Alice sounds alarmed. 'What do you mean, you are still doing it?'

'Flick and I will continue with our plans. Yoga classes, the retreats. And the builders are starting work tomorrow on the stables for the wedding venue.'

'They cannot. I won't allow it.'

I glare at her. 'You don't get a say, Alice.' Somewhere deep inside, I am surprised at how vicious this conversation has turned so quickly. I try to calm myself down. 'Look. It makes sense for us to proceed as planned. I know this place has been haemorrhaging money for some time. It's the only way, unless you want to sell it to the National Trust.'

Alice gives a bark of laughter. 'You mean give it away.' I say nothing, only watch her as she processes my words. Her jaw is set, her eyes full of steel as she meets my gaze. 'What are these plans then? You cannot mean to keep them from me. This is my home too, even if it is not my house.'

I feel something release inside me. 'I'm sorry, I shouldn't have . . . I'm just . . . Alice, you can't seriously believe Henry would have killed himself?' My eyes search her face for a flicker of doubt, but she gives nothing away. I feel my eyes fill with tears and I brush them away. 'I can't believe it. I just can't believe he would leave me like that. Leave us.' I run a finger down Willow's cheek and try to suppress a sob.

Alice sighs. 'I don't want to believe it either. But there is little evidence that it was anything else. And the note—'

My head snaps up at the word. 'Note? What note?'

She stares at me with undisguised pity. 'Don't you remember, Josie? He left a note.'

I shake my head in disbelief. Nobody has ever mentioned a note before, I'm sure of it. 'What did it say? Can I see it?'

'The police have it, of course. I told you what it said, don't you remember?' I shake my head again and Alice takes a breath. 'It said: *the night is dark and I am far from home.*'

I stare at her. '*The night is dark and I am far from home?*' I echo. 'What does that even mean?'

'The money, I suppose. The debts. He must have felt so lost and alone.'

'Do you really think he was hiding things from us?' *From me?* I want to add. *He hid plenty of things from you, but from me?*

'He must have done. And we can find out, now you have access to his bank accounts.' She reaches out and squeezes my hand. 'We can go into town tomorrow if you like, speak to the bank manager.'

I suddenly realise that I have always had access to Henry's accounts. How had I not considered it before? I could tell her, whip out my phone and show her now, but instead I nod. If Henry was hiding anything from me, I want to find out first, away from Alice's judgement.

Back in the apartment, I feed Willow and sit with her in the rocking chair until she falls asleep. She sleeps well for a baby, or at least, I think she does. Does she sleep too much? She rarely wakes more than twice during the night and goes down for her naps easily enough. Perhaps I should ask the midwife when I see her next. Whenever that is. My brain has gone to mush since the birth. It's a cliché, but 'baby brain' has only seemed to hit me since Willow was born. Before, even while I was pregnant, I kept everything under control: reminders set on my phone, appointments logged neatly in the calendar. Now everything is a mess. I've lost control of my life, and with Henry gone, there's no one else to pick up the slack.

I put Willow down upstairs and pad into the kitchen to make a cup of tea. Ivy lifts her head when I sit down on the sofa but doesn't get up from her bed. 'You miss him too, huh?' I whisper as I scratch behind her ears. I glance up at the stool Henry had been sitting on, picture it as it had been that day, imagine the clatter as it fell to the floor when Henry pulled the trigger. Is that what happened? I close my eyes, trying to force the image away. *The night is dark and I am far from home.* What on earth does that mean? Why would Henry write such a thing?

Taking a deep breath, I pull out my phone and open the banking app. Henry gave me access to the business account for Helygen House when he appointed me as a director. Another thing for me to sort out, I realise with a groan. Despite my outrage at Alice's words, I do know very little about running a business. I suppose I have inherited his shares, but do I have to inform anyone of his death? Perhaps Jeremy Wilcox could help me with that.

One thing at a time, Corbs, Henry says in my head as I scroll through the accounts. While the figures are a bit concerning, there is nothing untoward here, nothing I did not already know about. Could Henry have taken out another loan elsewhere? Surely there would have been some correspondence? I suddenly realise that I haven't received any post in a while. It all usually goes to the box outside the gates of Helygen House, and Marie brings our letters to us if we don't collect them first, but I can't remember receiving anything since Willow was born. I glance at the clock: almost ten. Too late to go and bother Marie about it now. I make a mental note to ask her in the morning and settle down in front of the TV, staring at the blank screen, wondering when I will get used to the silence.

EIGHTEEN

ELIZA

1881

Eliza watched as the carriage travelled out of the gates and down the road, disappearing around the hedges at the end. She felt something heavy sitting in her stomach at the sight of her husband leaving, as if she had swallowed a stone. She turned back towards the house with a sigh, but instead of going inside she followed a side path, shoes crunching on the gravel as she walked. She hoped Cassius would find some success in his new venture. Although she knew little of his father's business, she knew that the quarry had been lost some time before, though Cassius had not told her how and she was hesitant to pry. She knew all about the pride of men, and how fiercely they could guard their affairs.

The path opened up to a large lawn, and in the near distance she spotted the willow tree standing guard over the lake. Her step quickened as she headed for it, smiling as the sun broke through the clouds and cast a glow upon the water. It looked as if it was full of diamonds, sparkling in the sunlight. The bank was slightly muddy, but Eliza placed a hand on the willow tree's solid trunk to steady herself as she gazed across the water. *It is so peaceful here*, she thought, smiling to herself. The lake was vast and no doubt deeper than it looked, and although Eliza loved to be near water, she could not stand to be in it, not since she had almost drowned during a family holiday in Margate when she was ten and a strange man had dragged her onto the shore where she flopped like a fish, gasping for breath. She shuddered, trying to push the memory away. She was no longer a helpless child. She was a woman now, a married woman, with a fine husband and a beautiful new home. She had, despite the odds, done well for herself, and she did not intend to spoil things now.

A bird flew overhead, landing on a branch amongst the trees on the opposite side of the lake, where it watched her, head tilted as if listening to something. She could hear nothing but the sound of the leaves rustling. The lake was still, the breeze barely touching the long grass along the banks. Leaves the colour of fire fell to the ground, but the willow tree remained untouched by the change of the season. *And soon it will be Christmas*, Eliza thought happily. *How glorious Helygen House will look when it is decorated.* She found she was looking forward to spending the holiday here, with her new family. Of late, the day had become overshadowed at her parents' house, no longer a celebration but a chore, with strained smiles and barely concealed disappointment. 'Things will be different here,' she whispered to the willow. 'I will be happy.'

She turned to make her way back across the lawn, skirting the carefully pruned bushes and passing the rear entrance. This must be where the servants came and went, and where deliveries were made. She noted that the door could do with a fresh lick of paint. Perhaps she could make some changes here, and the thought made her smile. Though she adored the dark wood panelling and intricate wallpapers, she wondered if she could do something to make the house more fashionable. It did not appear to have been changed at all in recent years, though she was not surprised, since Harriet had been living there alone for such a long time.

The path wound around the back of the house, and, with the ancient woodland on her left, Eliza made her way down a slope towards the west side of the estate. She passed through the formal gardens, admiring the neat stone paths and beautiful flowers, some hardy enough to withstand the autumn air. A fountain burbled as she passed, her step light on the path, and birds hopped from one branch to another, twittering away. She knew there was a bath house out here somewhere, a stone structure sunk into the earth by Cassius's grandfather, but she feared she might get lost in the gardens by herself. Perhaps Cassius would take her to see it tomorrow.

As she turned to go back to the house, something caught

her eye. A shape lying beneath one of the shrubs, its orange fur barely distinguishable from the fallen leaves. A fox. She recoiled when she noticed the blood trail on the path behind it. It looked as if it had been dragged into the bushes and left there, but by what? Were there predators here in Cornwall, in the grounds of Helygen House? She shivered and wrapped her arms around herself, before turning away and hurrying back up the path. She was surprised to find Harriet waiting at the back door, wrapped in a heavy shawl, thick gardening gloves held in one hand. She had a smear of mud on her dress and a strand of hair had come loose from its bun.

'Have you been gardening?' Eliza asked with a smile, unable to quite picture it.

'Where have you been?' Harriet demanded, ignoring her question.

'Exploring. The gardens are so beautiful.'

Harriet pursed her lips. 'It is almost time for luncheon.'

'Already? Forgive me, I had no idea so much time had passed. Allow me to get changed and then I will join you.' Eliza made to step around her, and, for a second, she thought the older woman was not going to move, but after a beat Harriet stepped aside and let her into the house. 'There was a dead fox,' Eliza said as they walked through the corridor. 'Under a bush. Poor thing looks as if it's been mauled to death.' Harriet made a noise in the back of her throat but said nothing. The corridor led them past the back stairs and the kitchen, and the scent of luncheon cooking made Eliza's stomach rumble, pushing all thoughts of the fox aside. They parted ways at the door to the dining room, Eliza hurrying up the stairs towards her bedroom, where she stripped off her gloves and washed her hands and face in the sink, patting her skin dry with a towel, before smoothing down her hair and spraying perfume on her wrists. Within a few minutes she was ready, and she rushed back down the stairs, her hand trailing along the banister, but when she arrived at the dining room, she was surprised to find the table not yet set, Harriet's chair empty. Frowning, she moved along the corridor towards the drawing room, but that room too was empty. As she turned back, she saw Mary scurrying along with a tray held carefully in front of her.

'Mary?' Eliza called, and the servant stopped as if she had run into a wall. 'Do you know where the mistress is?'

'Having luncheon, madam,' Mary said, avoiding her gaze.

'But the dining room is empty.'

'The mistress always takes her luncheon in the sitting room, madam, when the master is from home.'

'The sitting room?' Eliza frowned again. 'I do not believe I have seen it. Would you take me there, Mary?' She nodded towards the tray. 'I assume that is where you are going?'

'Yes, madam,' Mary said with a nod. 'Follow me, madam.'

Eliza followed the maid down another corridor poorly lit with lamps. She had to hurry to keep up with the girl's pace and quickly found herself out of breath. They passed through an arch and into some kind of antechamber, with a fine leather seat in the large window and a row of bookshelves lining one wall. Harriet's library, perhaps, Eliza thought, where she might relax with a book in peace and quiet. Again, Eliza struggled to picture her mother-in-law engaged in such an activity. What did she do when she was alone?

'Where are we, Mary?' she asked as they approached a set of double doors, struggling to get her bearings. 'Which part of the house is this?'

'This is the east wing, madam,' Mary replied. 'Below your chamber, if I'm not mistaken.'

A staircase spiralled up to their left, and Eliza wondered where it led. She must search for it upstairs, she thought, if Mary was right and they were directly beneath her bedroom. She suppressed a shudder at the idea of Harriet creeping up those stairs and watching Eliza sleep.

'The mistress's sitting room, madam,' Mary announced as she pushed open the door. Eliza saw Harriet sitting by the fire, a cup of tea at her elbow.

'Ah, there you are,' Harriet said with a raised eyebrow as Eliza entered murmuring apologies. She nodded at the maid, who deposited the tray on the table between the two chairs and removed the lid, revealing a platter of sandwiches and cakes. She laid out cups and placed the teapot beside Harriet before hurrying away. 'A strange child,' Harriet muttered, watching the maid leave the room. 'Always so nervous.'

I wonder why, Eliza thought, then chided herself for her unkind thoughts. 'She is very nice,' she said instead. She watched as Harriet poured her a cup of tea. 'This is a lovely spread, but I confess I am still full from breakfast.'

Harriet raised an eyebrow. 'But you hardly ate a thing this morning, dear. And you need to keep your strength up, if you're going to be galivanting around the estate.'

Eliza prickled at the word. 'I was exploring,' she said evenly. 'There is so much to see here, so much beauty. And history! I would love to know more about this house and your family.'

'Drink up,' Harriet said, nodding towards the cup in Eliza's hands. 'And have a sandwich, won't you? These sponge cakes are glorious too.'

Eliza obediently took a sip of tea and selected a sandwich and a small sliver of cake, which she dropped onto her plate. She licked her lips. 'Is this mint tea?' she asked.

'Yes. It is good for digestion,' Harriet said with a knowing look, and Eliza reddened, remembering how unwell she had been since arriving here.

'Will you tell me more about Helygen House?' she asked, taking another sip. 'Where did the name come from?'

'From the willow. Helygen means "willow tree" in Cornish.'

Eliza was surprised. 'I had no idea they had their own language. Do you speak Cornish yourself?'

Harriet smirked. 'Oh, no. Only a few words. Why, do you wish to learn?' Her tone told Eliza what she thought of that idea.

'Do many speak it? I wonder if it might be useful to communicate with more people here.'

'Only the lowly sorts. I doubt you will have cause to communicate with any of *them*, dear.' She nodded towards Eliza's plate. 'Eat up.'

She nibbled dutifully at the sandwich. 'How long has Helygen House been in your family?'

'The Foxes have always lived at Helygen House,' Harriet said, her voice so low Eliza struggled to hear her. Harriet blinked as if coming back to herself and reached out for a slice of cake. 'You are comfortable here, I trust?' she asked. 'You have everything you need?'

'Oh, yes,' Eliza replied, trying not to think of the large bed she occupied alone. 'Everything is just perfect.'

Harriet nodded before taking a bite of cake. Eliza sipped her tea, trying to wash down the bread which she feared had become stuck in her throat. Her stomach roiled and she felt a sharp stab of pain, and Harriet looked up in alarm. 'Are you quite well?' she asked.

'Yes, yes,' Eliza said, waving a hand. 'I'm fine, thank you.' She wondered if it was her time of the month. She had never been regular, though this was not a topic she had ever discussed, nor would she ever discuss it, especially not with her new mother-in-law, so perhaps her courses were in fact quite normal. Perhaps it was the food. She had grown used to eating simpler food in recent years, so perhaps the richness of the meals at Helygen House did not agree with her. She put down her cup and folded her hands in her lap, trying to swallow down the nausea. 'Will Cassius be joining us for dinner?'

Harriet finished her cake and returned her small plate to the tray. 'He did not say.'

'I do hope this new venture is a success,' Eliza said. 'Who is the friend he has gone to meet?'

'Mr Dixon.' Harriet's expression turned sour. 'Or Dickie, as he calls himself. An ill-mannered brute. He and Cassius have always got up to mischief together.'

Eliza looked at her in surprise. 'Mischief? I cannot imagine Cassius getting up to mischief.' And yet, somehow she could. With his twinkling eyes and ready grin, Eliza could imagine her husband as a younger man, brazen and bold with the knowledge that the entire world was at his feet. Mischief was the least such men could get up to, she knew.

'It would appear,' Harriet said, staring into the fire, 'that you do not know your new husband very well at all.'

NINETEEN

JOSIE

2019

I am up and ready by seven thirty the next morning, crunching my way towards the front gate, Ivy trotting at my side. I feel stronger today, so I am carrying Willow in a sling on my front, her head resting beneath my chin. Her face is turned to one side, her eyes wide and staring as she takes everything in. It is cold this morning, my breath misting the air before me, and I'm glad of my daughter's warmth against me.

I hear the low rumble of an engine as I near the gate and turn to see a van coming up the track towards the house. 'They're on time,' I whisper to Willow. 'That's a turn-up for the books.' Ivy is sniffing around the grass at the side, so I swing open the gate and stand back to allow the van to park up on the driveway. Three men exit the vehicle, their clothes spattered with what looks like paint or cement, their boots caked in mud, but otherwise they look fresh and ready to begin this new project.

'Darren?' I ask, heading for the oldest man. He nods and holds out a hand for me to shake. 'Josie. Nice to meet you.'

'Sorry for your loss,' the builder says in his thick Cornish accent, and from the way he looks at me, I half expect him to doff an imaginary cap. 'Henry were a good sort. We'd worked with him a few times in the past, ain't that right, lads?' The other two nod.

I feel my cheeks begin to heat up. I will not cry, not here, not in front of these men. 'Thank you,' I say, aware that my accent is weaker than Darren's, my voice posher. When did that happen? 'Shall we get on?'

'Lead on, maid,' Darren says. 'Let's have a look at what we're dealing with.'

The men follow me to the stables, their boots crunching over the gravel. I go over the plans again, though Darren knows them already and better than I do, before offering cups of tea and bacon sandwiches.

Darren grins. 'The royal treatment, eh?' He glances at one of the other men. 'Todd here is a veggie, though, awkward sod.'

I consider for a moment. 'I think we have some Quorn sausages in the freezer, if that's any good?' I'll have to buy some more before Flick comes back to visit. If she does.

Todd nods. 'Ideal, thanks very much.'

I whistle to Ivy and we make our way back to the apartment. I know Alice will disapprove, but I refuse to ask

Halka to cater for the builders. I'm here, and I'm perfectly capable of making a bacon sandwich. Or a Quorn sausage one, for that matter.

I place Willow in her Moses basket and set it on the floor well away from the hob. Ivy lies down in front of it, sniffing at Willow's feet before resting her head on her paws. They both watch me as I dig out the bacon and Quorn sausages from the freezer. I butter thick slices of bread while the frying pan fizzles and spits, and find sachets of tomato ketchup and brown sauce in one of the drawers, probably pinched from a restaurant or service station. The kettle clicks and I pour hot water into three mugs, one with two sugars, two without, all with just a splash of milk. I wrap the sandwiches in tin foil to keep them warm and load up the tray before pausing. Can I carry Willow as well? I have a sudden vision of me stumbling and the mugs tipping over, scalding my daughter. Surely it would be easier if I just run the food over to the builders, leaving Ivy in charge? It will only take a minute, two tops. They'll be perfectly safe.

With another glance at my baby, who seems to be fascinated with Ivy's tail, which is draped over her legs, I open the front door and hurry across the gravel, trying to hold the tray still. A drop of tea splashes onto my hand and I wince, but I'm glad it's me and not Willow. I enter the stables and place the tray on a windowsill. I can already hear banging coming from what will be the small kitchen area and the news blasts from a radio, a muffled voice reporting on a serious crash on the A390. I lift a hand to one of the men who is sitting on a bright yellow digger and point towards the tray before hurrying back towards the apartment.

I am out of breath when I open the front door, and I feel a surge of guilt when I hear the crying. 'Oh, darling,' I say, rushing into the kitchen. 'I was just —' I stop, the breath leaving my body. The Moses basket is empty. I look around the large room, moving past the breakfast bar and into the lounge area. Empty, and Ivy is nowhere to be seen either. Where are they? Willow is a newborn for Christ's sake, she can't have gone far, and Ivy can hardly have carried her anywhere.

The cry comes again and I follow it, my heart racing. It sounds as if it is coming from the ground floor, so I bypass the stairs and instead check the toilet and utility room before opening the door to Henry's office. The breath catches in my throat. I haven't been in here since he died, and it looks utterly untouched, as if he left only a moment before. His chair is pulled out, and there are papers scattered across the desk, a pen without a lid sitting atop a leather-bound diary, and I notice a space where his laptop should sit, taken away by the police in an evidence bag. But I can almost feel his presence in here, can almost believe that he isn't gone for good.

My head snaps up when I hear Willow cry again. I hear something else then, a *shushing* sound, and race out of the room towards the hallway. I wrench open the internal door separating the apartment from the main house and have to stop myself from swaying with relief. Alice has Willow in her arms, jiggling her up and down as my daughter screams. I reach for her, almost snatching her from my mother-in-law.

'What are you doing?' I demand, holding Willow close. Her cries quieten as I rock her from side to side. 'Why did you take her?'

Alice glares at me. 'She was distraught. I heard her crying from the drawing room. Where were you?'

I feel my cheeks flush with indignation, with guilt at being caught out. 'I was only gone a moment.'

'A moment too long,' she snaps.

Before I can retort, Ivy lets out a low growl and I look down at her in surprise. She has never growled at anyone before. 'It's all right, girl,' I tell her, placing a hand on her head and she sits, leaning against my legs. I turn back to Alice. 'How did you get in? That door was locked.'

'I needed to speak to you,' she says, ignoring my question. The door had been locked, hadn't it? 'She lunged at me when I picked Willow up, you know. Your wretched dog.'

'Lunged at you? Ivy doesn't lunge at people. She wouldn't harm a fly.'

'Hmm,' Alice says, crossing her arms over her chest. I glance down at Ivy and see that her body still looks tense, as if ready to strike. 'I wouldn't trust her around Willow if I were you. She's too unpredictable.'

'She was probably just protecting her.'

'From me?' Alice tuts. 'As if I would ever hurt her, my own grandchild.'

'You did snatch her from my kitchen, Alice,' I snap.

Ivy barks then, a sound I have never heard from her before. It is low and almost a snarl, nothing like her usual barks for attention or when it's time for a fish chew. Alice takes a step back, her eyes widening. 'You need to control that animal,' she says, pointing at Ivy as she backs away. 'Before something terrible happens.'

I am hanging up a load of washing when the knock comes. Willow is sleeping in her basket beside me – I haven't dared let her out of my sight since this morning – and she doesn't stir when I lift and carry her through to the front door. Darren is standing on the doorstep, his face creased with worry.

'I'm afraid we've got a problem,' he says, wringing his hands in front of him.

'What's happened?' I feel my skin prickle, Alice's words echoing inside my head. *Before something terrible happens.*

'You'd better come with me, maid,' Darren says. 'See for yourself.'

I quickly slip on my shoes and follow him across the gravel, the basket heavy in my arms. I feel a twinge in my stomach as my ankle turns and I stumble. I hope I haven't torn a stitch. But I right myself and keep going, trying to ignore the feeling of dread as I wonder what is waiting for me in the stables.

TWENTY

'A child?' Alice's voice is high-pitched, almost strangled. We're in the drawing room, and she is pacing the floor while I sit in a highbacked chair, Willow in her basket beside me. 'What do you mean, they've found a child?'

'Bones,' I tell her with a sigh. I fidget, trying to find a more comfortable position. My back is aching, and I can feel the beginnings of a migraine pulsing behind my left eyebrow. 'Small bones that look like they came from a child.'

'How on earth would they know? They're builders, not archaeologists.'

'Regardless, they've had to stop the work. The police are on their way.'

She stops suddenly, turning towards me. 'The police?' she echoes, her voice even higher now. 'The police are coming here again?' She throws up her hands. 'Goodness me, what a year this has been.' She pauses before speaking again. 'Are they certain they are human remains? It could be an animal for all we know.'

'I saw it myself, Alice. It looks like the skeleton of a small child.' I glance down at Willow and feel my heart lurch. 'When were the stables first built?'

'Oh, they've been there for years, though I know they were rebuilt at some point in the 1800s. It used to be a wooden structure and not a very strong one, so they replaced it with proper walls. And I had the roof redone about twenty years ago, but we never did any excavating.' She exhales loudly. 'A small child? Are you sure?'

I shake my head. 'I'm not certain, no, but I'm sure that it's not an animal.'

'Might they be ancient? Saxon or Roman? I'm sure there are medieval burial grounds all over.'

'I have no idea.' I sigh again, leaning back in the chair. The bones had certainly looked old, and they were buried beneath several feet of concrete, according to the builders, but I'm no archaeologist either. Could they be more recent? I suppress a shiver at the prospect.

Alice glances at me. 'I suppose the work will be delayed now?'

I nod, trying to ignore the note of triumph in her voice. I sent Darren and his men home, though luckily they'd seemed rather unfazed. Perhaps they've seen this kind of thing a few times. There are probably bones buried all over the place in this country, homes built upon battlegrounds. 'The police will be here soon,' I tell her. 'They've told us not to touch anything in the meantime.'

'Goodness,' Alice says, sitting down on the settee opposite. 'What a day. And it's not even noon!'

I follow her gaze to the clock on the wall. 11.37. I feel as if I've been awake for days. My limbs feel heavy, weighed down by this discovery and Alice finding Willow unattended. I shake my head, pushing away the guilt. I was only gone for a few minutes. Alice overreacted, that's all. Willow was fine. Willow *is* fine. But what if she wasn't? What if something had happened to her? I fight the urge to touch my hands together, my fingers tingling as I shove them between my knees.

The doorbell rings and I jump out of my seat to answer it.

'Marie will get it,' Alice says, but I ignore her. Marie is probably busy in the bowels of the house, and besides, the drawing room is right next to the front door. I wrench it open to find DS Fergus and a woman standing on the doorstep and stand aside to let them in.

'Hello again, Mrs Fox,' DS Fergus says with a nod at Alice, who is now hovering by the window. 'This is DC Wallis.'

'Take a seat,' I say, indicating the settee. 'Thank you for coming so quickly.'

'Thank you for calling us,' DC Wallis says. She is young, in her early twenties perhaps, with black hair smoothed back into a neat bun. She smiles sympathetically. 'We understand this discovery must have been . . . distressing.'

'Quite,' Alice says with a sniff.

DS Fergus clears his throat. 'Yes, well. We're just waiting for forensics to arrive. We need to ascertain the age of the bones before we can take any action.' He looks at me when he says the word *action*, and for a second I wonder if he suspects me of some kind of wrongdoing. Or does he think it might be linked to Henry's death? I open my mouth to speak but Alice cuts in.

'Of course, Detective. Whatever you need.' She smiles warmly, her earlier prickliness gone. 'How about a cup of tea? Coffee?' She lifts the bell she uses to summon Marie, and I feel a wave of frustration wash over me. Who uses a bell to ring for tea in this day and age? It's a wonder Marie hasn't shoved that thing up Alice's—

'Tea would be lovely,' DC Wallis says, interrupting my thoughts. 'One sugar, please.'

'I'll make it,' I say quickly, moving to the door. 'DS Fergus?'

He nods. 'Same again, thanks.'

I slip out of the room and through a side door which creates a shortcut to the kitchen. This is the servants' corridor Alice told me she'd used to get to and from the kitchen when work was going on in the house. *She must have left Henry and India alone sometimes*, I think, immediately irritated by my own pettiness. Alice just cares about her granddaughter, is that really so wrong? I emerge into what was once the scullery but now houses the washing machine and tumble dryer, both of which are spinning loudly, and walk through to the kitchen where I find Halka stirring something on the hob.

'Kettle has just boiled,' she says with a knowing smile. 'You know where everything is.' I nod my thanks and go to the cupboard to pull out four mugs. 'Nasty business,' she says while I spoon out sugar. I turn to see her frowning at me. 'It's bad luck to disturb the dead.'

I fill the mugs with hot water. 'I'm sure they will be reburied with dignity once the police have worked out who they are. Were.'

She tuts. 'This is an omen, Josie. I can feel it. First Henry, now—'

'Halka.' My voice is sharper than intended and she looks up in alarm. I take a deep breath. 'I'm sure it's nothing to worry about. England is such an old country, there must be bones everywhere.' I place the mugs of tea on a tray and attempt to smile at the older woman. 'There's no such thing as omens. Nothing bad is going to happen.'

She says nothing, but as I pass back through the scullery, I think I hear her mutter something that sounds like 'something bad has already happened', and the words send a shiver up my spine.

TWENTY-ONE

HARRIET

1st January 1862

A new year. A new decade. Another loss, and I live in fear of the next.

Edmund says that fear is in the mind, but if that is the case, then my mind lives *in* fear. Constant, crippling fear that another one of my children will be taken from me. Again. And there's nothing I can do to stop it.

My eldest daughter, my one remaining girl, is gone. Killed by a jealous suitor, Cassius said. My darling boy. He is only eleven years old and, though he will be off to school in September, I still see him as that small, fair-haired boy of four who never failed to make me laugh. But I must admit that he and Clara were never close. I fear Clara took her role as the eldest rather too seriously and was prone to bossing her younger siblings around. It was as if she saw herself as apart from them, older and wiser and with better things to do than babysit them. Perhaps she was right. Perhaps I should have given her more freedom and less responsibility. The children have enough minders, from dear Sara who so often tends to them, to the new governess, Mathilde, a rather strict French woman Edmund employed to teach all of the children, Clara included, despite his earlier reservations about educating girls. Still, I know Clara resented the governess and not being able to go away to school like her brother will do this year. She was remarkably bright, my daughter, but she did not seem to understand the limitations of her sex. Just as Maisie would have had to grow out of her tomboyish ways, Clara too would have had to settle down into the boundaries of womanhood – if she had lived.

Oh, Lord, why must you punish me so? How many children can one mother lose? How much pain and hardship can one woman take? Sara told me that she was one of nine children, though seven of them were lost in infancy. Seven. Her poor mother. She died in childbirth with the last one, and, God help me, I suspect it may have been a blessing.

Edmund tells me that the boy who pushed Clara has been found. I can hardly bear to recall the details, but I must. There must be a record of what happened to her, a true record. It is the least I can do for her now. The only thing I can do for her.

Though it feels like years have passed, it was only last night that tragedy struck. It was Cassius who alerted us to the fact that Clara was missing. We were entertaining, as we often do at this time of year, with a group of close friends and some of Edmund's business associates. Though still only fourteen, Clara was allowed to eat dinner with us, and she was pretty as a picture in her beautiful green gown. She behaved impeccably throughout the meal, truly. I could see Edmund was so proud of her, and watched him eyeing up some of the men as potential suitors. But it would appear that Clara had other plans for her future.

We sent her up to bed after dinner and she went with a demure smile, apparently quite pleased with herself. But it was not until later, when Cassius burst into the ballroom, breathless and red-cheeked, that I realised why she'd looked the way she had. I can only tell this to you, diary, for I could not bear the shame if anyone else found out. It would seem that Clara had arranged a secret liaison with a boy, a farmer's son of all people, out on the edge of the estate above the river. It is a dangerous place, with a sheer drop down to the water and unsteady ground, and the children are forbidden from going there, yet that is where she was found, on a rock halfway down the cliff face, her body broken from the fall.

When I asked how Cassius had known where she would be, he said he had watched her sneaking out on several occasions and this time his curiosity got the better of him, so he followed her. He had looked ashamed when confessing, for he had not told us of his sister's illicit activities, but he had only been protecting her from punishment. He is a good boy, thoughtful in a way which is unexpected in a child so young, and it is not his fault.

The party was spilling out onto the patio when Cassius

came to get us, and the sky was dark, the moon half hidden by heavy clouds. I remember worrying that we would have to dash inside if the heavens opened. What strange, insignificant things we concern ourselves with, when real tragedy is only around the corner.

I know not what they will do to the farmer's boy. I know not why he wished to harm my dear Clara. Perhaps he had an infatuation which was not reciprocated, but surely he knew that nothing could ever happen between them? Perhaps that is why he killed her, because she refused him. My poor, beautiful Clara. However will I go on after this? How can I live with this grief?

TWENTY-TWO

JOSIE

2019

The police have gone, leaving us with strict instructions not to continue any work until they come back to us. I return to the apartment and lie down on the bed, Willow sleeping beside me. My stomach hurts; I lift my shirt to find blood blooming between the stitches. I overdid it, making bacon sandwiches and carrying Willow around the estate, and I can almost hear Henry's gentle chiding. *You need to take care of yourself, Corbs.* I reach for my phone to check when the nurse is supposed to be visiting and am surprised to see a message from Flick.

How are you and little Willow? I can visit tomorrow if you like. I'm sorry I've been a rubbish friend lately, but I'm back on the wagon and have no intention of falling off again. Love you xxx

I feel a rush of guilt as I read her message. I've neglected her in her hour of need. Flick has always been there for me. She came back to Cornwall with me for my father's funeral; she helped me pack when I moved into that first flat with Henry. I remember that day vividly. She had just discovered she was pregnant, her joy so clear and bright it almost hurt to look at. We were twenty-five, that weird age when you still don't feel old enough or mature enough to do adult things like buy a house or get married or have children, and yet you do them anyway and hope for the best. Flick and her then-boyfriend Alex had been living together for over a year when they discovered they had a baby on the way. We all felt so settled, our futures mapped out in front of us, and yet I remember a keen sense of anxiety too, of feeling as if I was standing outside of my own body, watching myself make decisions and do things a part of me didn't quite feel ready to do.

Flick's pregnancy flew by. Her bump was small, her body hardly changing to accommodate the tiny human she was growing, and she was positively glowing throughout. She continued to teach yoga until two weeks before the birth – something she later blamed for what happened. Or rather, something Alex blamed her for. He said some unforgiveable things in those dark days after Flick gave birth to their daughter who never drew breath. Perhaps he was so distraught, so utterly devastated at losing his child, at almost losing his partner during the traumatic birth, that he was simply lashing out, but his fury was too much for Flick to take on top of her grief, and so she found herself on Water-loo Bridge, wanting to end it all.

And now here I am, with a baby Flick has been desperate to meet, and yet it is all too much for her to bear, too hard. I understand why she left the hospital when Willow was born. I hadn't been with her when she gave birth – it had all happened in the middle of the night, with a desperate ambu-lance ride not dissimilar to my own – and by the time I saw her missed calls in the morning, it was too late. My own experience was so close to hers, except my baby survived. No wonder it seems to have sent her on a downward spiral.

I stroke Willow's cheek, feeling my eyes well up. I could imagine and empathise with the depths of Flick's grief before, but now the idea of something happening to my own child creates an almost visceral response inside me. I feel the urge to protect my daughter, to curl my body around her to keep her safe, like I did when she was still in my womb. I will never let anything happen to her. After losing Henry, I couldn't bear to lose her too.

I reply to Flick, telling her that she is welcome to come tomorrow. I won't tell her the details about what the build-ers found beneath the stables, and besides, The Hut is on the opposite side of the house, far away from any hidden bones. I hope.

The sound of the alarm shocks me from sleep, tearing me from a dream which lingers as I sit up in bed, rubbing my eyes. I take a deep breath, trying to calm my racing heart.

The dream had felt so real, and yet it is slipping away from me even as I try to cling on to it.

I hear a cry and swing my legs off the edge of the bed, pausing when I feel a tugging pain in my stomach. I cleaned the stitches up yesterday and they didn't look too bad afterwards. The bleeding had only been minimal, but I need to take it easy today. I look down into the cot to find Willow staring up at the ceiling, her arms held up in front of her as if she is reaching for something.

'Good morning, little one,' I whisper as I lift her out of the cot and move into the nursery to sit in the rocking chair with her in my arms. While she feeds, I lean back and look up at the ceiling. The detail is so intricate, the plaster smooth around the large rose in the middle. I suddenly picture Henry and India lying together as children, staring up at the ceiling. Did they miss their old home, their friends? At least they'd had each other, I suppose. Growing up as an only child could be lonely, and I feel a pang as I realise that is probably the fate of my own daughter.

You're still young, Corbs, Henry whispers in my ear, but I shake my head. I cannot imagine ever remarrying or having more children. Not now, not without Henry.

My dad had been an older father. He was thirty-nine when he had me, my mother thirty-eight. Women are having children older now, but was it her age that put her at greater risk of dying after childbirth? I was four weeks old when a blood clot travelled to her lung and killed her. Sometimes I've wondered if my dad ever thought about remarrying. By the time I was old enough to consider him having another relationship, the MS was so advanced that Dad could no longer get out of bed. I knew little about my parents' relationship, though I know they were together for fifteen years before they had me, and I never thought to ask why they waited so long to have children. There are so many unasked questions I can now never find the answers to.

My eye is drawn to the corner of the room. To the left of the large window, still covered by the light grey curtains, is a dark patch on the ceiling. I squint, cursing my vanity for not wearing the glasses I am supposed to. Is it a damp patch? Spider eggs? I shudder. I'll have to ask Marie to take a look for me; she doesn't seem to mind creepy crawlies.

I burp and change Willow, moving slowly, bending with my knees to reach a sock dropped on the floor. I only gave birth two weeks ago, I really should be taking it easy. I try not to think about how it might have been, or how it was supposed to be, with Henry here to help with the feeding and changing and managing the estate. I should be on bed rest, letting my body heal, but instead I find myself a single mother, desperately trying to keep everything together, and suddenly I feel very alone. Alice is here to help, but since Henry's death I've felt an even bigger void opening up between us. I still refuse to believe that he took his own life, and there's something niggling at me about Alice. But can my mind be trusted? The old tendencies are starting to creep back, the obsessiveness, the anxiety. Am I reading too much into things? Or is there something Alice hasn't told me?

TWENTY-THREE

ELIZA

1881

When her monthly courses did not come for the second time since the wedding, Eliza knew that something was happening. Cassius had not touched her since their wedding night, but she knew well that once could be enough. She recalled her mother's failed pregnancies and felt trepidation prickling at her skin, but she pushed it away as she hurried down the stairs towards the dining room, where her husband would be breakfasting. She hoped he would be pleased. From the hallway, she could hear him speaking to his mother and she stopped, breathless, and listened. She rested a hand against the dark wood panelling, her eyes drawn to the deep blue paper above, picking out the intricate yellow flowers and tiny birds. *How clever,* she thought as she admired it, *for the artist to create this masterpiece on such a small scale.* She adored the décor in this house, though she longed to do some decorating herself. She hoped to turn her attention to the nursery now, which was in serious need of some updating. *Now I have a use for it*, she thought with a smile.

'Do stop pestering me, Mother,' Cassius said sharply, and Eliza's attention snapped back to the present. 'I am well aware of the situation.'

'Are you, indeed?' Eliza was surprised to hear Harriet speaking so harshly to her son. She usually reserved her contempt for her daughter-in-law. The two women had remained at a distance, despite Eliza's attempts to get closer to her mother-in-law, and these days she often felt unwell, retiring early with nausea and stomach cramps, and a pounding headache which had kept her in bed on more than one occasion. *I will have to start taking better care of myself*, she thought, *now I have another to consider.*

'Two months have passed, and there is still no sign,' Harriet said, as Eliza began to move towards the dining room door. No sign? Could she mean . . .? A loud crash made her jump, the sound of a fist against wood making the crockery clash together.

'I do not need to be hen-pecked,' Cassius said, his anger pulsating through the open doorway. A chair scraped against the floor. 'I shall be in my study,' he announced, and before Eliza could move, he was right in front of her, his chest almost connecting with her forehead.

'Darling,' she said, smiling warmly at him. The anger was still on his face, but his expression began to soften as she spoke, like clouds clearing away to reveal a blue sky. 'Good morning. I thought we could explore the gardens together today; the weather looks set to be fair.'

'I am afraid I'm on my way to my study.' He lifted her hand and kissed the back of it. 'I have a lot of work to do. But feel free to go alone.'

Eliza tried to hide her disappointment. 'Of course. Will I see you at dinner?'

'Certainly,' Cassius replied, smiling back at her. 'Seeing your pretty face will be just the ticket after a hard day's work.' He moved past her then, striding towards the study and closing the door behind him. She sighed, hands pressed over her corseted stomach. *Later*, she told herself. *Good things come to those who wait.*

Harriet was drinking tea when Eliza entered the dining room, while Mary hovered by the sideboard. She wondered if her mother-in-law had been speaking about the absence of a child, and hoped she would be happy once Eliza could share her good news.

'Good morning,' she said brightly. 'Tea, please, Mary.'

'No food again?' Harriet asked with a raised eyebrow.

'Oh, I was going to ask for some fruit,' Eliza said, directing her words at Mary as the maid poured her tea. 'A pear, perhaps?'

'Pear? For breakfast?'

'And an apple, please. I'm sure I saw you picking them from the orchard this morning, Mary?'

The maid blushed. 'Yes, madam. They're lovely this time of year.'

'Stop babbling and get on with it then,' Harriet snapped, and Mary curtseyed awkwardly before hurrying out of the room.

'I peeked inside the ballroom yesterday. Do you use it much?' Eliza asked when her breakfast had been delivered. She speared a chunk of pear with her fork and popped it into her mouth, savouring the rich flavour.

Harriet chewed her mouthful for a long time before answering. 'The ballroom has not been used in some time. We have not had the need for it.'

'Oh, but it would be perfect for entertaining,' Eliza said, smiling at the thought of the swish of pretty dresses and the tinkling of crystal. 'I was hoping to invite my parents to stay. Perhaps we could throw a ball around Christmas, or to welcome in the new year?'

'We do not celebrate the new year,' Harriet snapped, setting her cutlery down with a clatter. Eliza opened her mouth to speak, then closed it again at the look on her mother-in-law's face. Why was she so snappish, so secretive? She could feel a thousand questions bubbling up inside her but she pushed them away, knowing they would not be welcomed. Had Harriet always been this way? Haunting the house like a ghoul, mourning her long-dead husband? So many of the rooms in Helygen House stood empty, filled only with dust and faint memories. Was there never laughter here? The joy of small children, the excited barking of a puppy, the sound of cutlery against china as friends dined together?

The two women sat in silence, Eliza nibbling her fruit

and Harriet sipping tea, her eyes fixed on a point on the gallery wall. Eliza followed her gaze and shuddered. This room was her least favourite, she decided. It was too dark, the walls too crowded with portraits. Too many eyes watching her. 'Who is that?' she asked, indicating a large portrait that must be as tall as her and almost double her width hanging above the fireplace.

'Lord Edward Fox,' Harriet replied without interest. 'My husband's grandfather.'

Eliza studied the two children standing beside Lord Fox's chair. They had matching blonde curls and light blue dresses. 'And the girls beside him?'

'His twin daughters, Elizabeth – or Bess, as she was known – and Tabitha.'

The one on the left is Bess, Eliza thought to herself, *and on the right is Tabitha. Did he ever call her Tabby, I wonder?* 'Do twins run in the family then?' she asked, turning back to her mother-in-law, whose face had lost its colour. 'Are you quite well?'

'Yes,' she said quietly. 'Twins do run in the family.'

Eliza wanted to ask more, wanted to prod the older woman, turn her upside down until all her secrets spilled out, but then Harriet was on her feet, her napkin fluttering to the rug beneath the table.

'Excuse me,' she said before striding out of the room.

'Oh dear,' Eliza said to herself, pushing her empty bowl away.

'She doesn't like talking about them.' Mary's voice made

Eliza jump. She turned to find her tidying up the sideboard, carefully stacking plates atop one another.

'Who doesn't she like talking about?'

'The twins.'

Eliza frowned. 'Bess and Tabitha?'

Mary shook her head. 'No, madam. *Her* twins. The mistress had twins, once. A boy and a girl.' She lowered her voice to almost a whisper. 'She had lots of children, did the mistress. But only the master survived.'

Eliza shivered at the word *survived*. The poor woman, to have lost so many children. 'How old were the twins when they died?' she asked.

'Only babies, madam,' Mary said, then hesitated. 'Well . . .'

'Go on.'

'Well, my ma, Annie – she was a maid here back then, before she had us children – my ma said that the poor lad died in his sleep. Suffocated, she said. He were barely a few days old. Archie, he were called, madam.'

Eliza suppressed a shiver. 'And the girl? The other twin?'

'That's the thing, madam.' Mary's eyes were wide with fear. 'There are two headstones in the family graveyard, one for each of the babes, but they only brought one little body down from the nursery that night. Nobody ever saw Flora again.'

TWENTY-FOUR

JOSIE

2019

'What do you mean, there's damp?' Alice's tone is snippy as she peers up at the corner of the room. I had let her in and led her straight up to the nursery, today's meals from Halka left on the kitchen side. Willow is crying, her bottom soggy beneath my hand as I hold her against me. Alice glances at her. 'Is she hungry? Does she need changing?'

'There's damp on the ceiling,' I say, ignoring her. 'Can't you see it?'

'I think it's just a cobweb,' Alice says, raising her voice over Willow's screams. She's staring at me with an unreadable expression. 'Shall I change her for you?'

'I'll do it,' I snap, turning to lay Willow down on the changing table. 'It's not a cobweb. Do we have a stepladder I can use?'

'You're not going up a stepladder,' Alice scolds. 'You've just had a baby.'

'I'm aware of that,' I mutter. 'Maybe Marie could check? What if it starts to spread?' I look up in time to see Alice make a face. 'I saw water in the corridor by the kitchen in the main house. Halka said there was a leak. Damp can cause all kinds of problems in babies,' I add crossly. 'Asthma, for one. It's not healthy for her.'

'Well, it's not like she's sleeping in the corridor,' Alice mutters, before sighing. 'I'll ask Marie to take a look. But really, Josie, Willow is fine.' Her expression changes to the one most people wear when looking at babies. 'Aren't you, darling?' Willow, quiet now, stares up at her as Alice caresses her cheek. 'Do you think . . .' Alice glances at me and hesitates before continuing. 'Do you think you could do with some help?'

I frown. 'Help with what?'

'With everything. Willow, the estate. You're juggling so much, Josie. You need to rest.'

I clamp my lips together to stop myself from snapping at her again. This isn't the first time she's hinted at hiring a nanny, but I thought Henry and I had made ourselves clear. *But things have changed*, Henry says inside my head. *Because of you*, I snap at him before inhaling sharply. I close my eyes, trying to calm down, telling myself that Alice means well.

'I don't need any help,' I tell her, trying to keep my voice even. I open my eyes and meet her gaze. 'I have you, and Marie and Halka do plenty for me. And Flick is coming over to today to discuss the—'

'But the police said we're not to do any work,' she cuts in.

'Only on the stables. Flick is going to be doing up The Hut.'

She tuts. 'I really don't think you should be working, Josie. Not in your condition.'

'I'm *fine*, Alice. Really.' The doorbell rings and I hand Willow to her grandmother. 'That'll be her now.' I hurry down the stairs and through the kitchen to the front door where Ivy is waiting, tail wagging. Flick stands on the doorstep with a huge bunch of flowers in her arms and a shopping bag hanging off one wrist.

'Jose!' she cries, engulfing me in a hug. Emotion clogs my throat as I sink into her arms.

'I'm so glad you're here.'

She steps back as if seeing me for the first time. 'Are you okay?' she asks and I nod, forcing a smile. 'Well, where is she then? The star of the show?'

I laugh. 'In the nursery with Alice. Come in, I'll go and get her.' I lead Flick into the kitchen and indicate the breakfast bar where she sits down and starts to fuss over Ivy.

'You still haven't got a dining table?' she chides playfully.

'She has no need of one,' Alice says from the foot of the stairs, surprising me. 'The dining room seats up to eighteen people, after all.'

'Eighteen,' Flick repeats. 'Really? I've never seen it.'

'Haven't you?' I take Willow from Alice's arms. 'We'll have to give Auntie Felicity the tour, won't we, Willow?' I approach Flick cautiously, but she is holding out her arms, a wide smile on her face before her expression changes.

'No, wait.' She gets up and moves to the sofa. 'This is better.' I place Willow into her waiting arms and sit down beside them. 'Oh, Jose,' she whispers, staring down into my daughter's face. 'She's beautiful. She looks like you, you know.'

'Poor sod,' I joke and Flick laughs.

'She has Henry's eyes,' Alice says, coming into the living area. 'The Fox eyes.'

'She does,' Flick agrees. 'And his intense stare.'

'Henry? Intense?' I laugh. 'I think you've mixed him up with someone else.'

'Oh, he could be,' Flick says. 'Especially when he looked at you, Josie. It was as if everything else in the world ceased to exist.' I feel my cheeks heat up. *Oh, Henry.* Flick carefully reaches out and squeezes my hand. I give her a watery smile. 'Still,' she continues, 'she'll be a beauty.'

'And a brain,' I add.

'All of the above,' she whispers. 'All of the above and more.'

After some hesitation, I leave Willow with Alice and take Flick on a tour of the house, Ivy padding along behind us. She took some persuading to leave Willow too, and I can't help remembering the way she growled at Alice before. She's always been protective, especially of me and even more so when I was pregnant, so perhaps that has simply extended to her new sister. She's a lovely dog, I remind myself, there's nothing to worry about. Anxiety prickled up my spine as I settled Willow and left her with Alice, but it will do them both good to spend some time together. And it will do me good to spend some time away from her, to remind myself of who I am aside from being Willow's mum.

'I can't believe I've never shown you around before,' I say to Flick as we stand in the hallway, fingers twitching as I try to fight the urge to touch them together. 'I suppose it does feel a little bit . . .'

'Showy?' Flick teases. 'It's like a National Trust property. Should I have paid to get in?'

'Don't say that too loudly.' I flick a glance towards the drawing room where Alice is with Willow. 'Alice has a fit whenever the National Trust comes up.' Flick claps a hand over her mouth in mock embarrassment and I laugh. 'I'd like to redecorate down here,' I tell her as I lead her along the corridor towards the dining room. 'It's all a bit too dark. But Alice won't hear of it.'

Flick gazes around the dining room in wonder. 'She still uses all of these rooms?'

'Not all of them. Henry tried to encourage her to portion off a section of the house to use as her private apartment, like we have, but she insisted on staying in the main house and just using certain rooms.' I watch as Flick wanders around the room, fingers trailing along the dark wooden sideboard. 'Which is why we're transforming the stables into accommodation instead, at least until the west wing is sorted out.'

'What have you got planned for that?' Flick turns back to face me, but her eyes land on something to my right. 'God, Josie, doesn't that girl look like Willow?'

I turn around, startled. 'What girl?'

'Up there.' She points at a portrait above my head. 'The one standing next to the dog. Is that a golden retriever as well?'

I take a few steps back and stare up at the painting. The girl is about three or four, with long fair curls and striking grey-blue eyes. The dog sitting beside her is taller than her, its head cocked slightly to one side. 'I think it's a Labrador,' I say after a moment, skin prickling. Although Willow is still so young, the similarity is uncanny.

'Maisie Fox, 1856,' Flick reads out from the plaque beneath the painting. 'Who was she?'

'I'm not sure. I don't know much about the family history.' I frown, my eyes searching the faces of the people hung above us. I've dined in this room so many times since moving in, why have I never taken more of an interest before?

'They're all so fair,' Flick says. 'And their eyes are all the same. Oh, who's this?' She steps closer, craning up to read the tiny writing. 'Eliza Fox.'

'That one I know. She was Alice's great-grandmother.'

Flick is frowning at the portrait. I follow her gaze and feel Eliza's eyes settle upon me, and I suddenly have the mental image of her climbing out of the frame, like the woman in *The Yellow Wallpaper*. I feel a shiver run through me. 'Let's move on. There's so much more to explore; you could get lost in this house for days, you know.'

I take Flick through the old ballroom, now used as a

storage room. 'So much of this room is glass,' I tell her, my voice echoing in the large space as I point towards the ceiling. 'It's more like a conservatory. But the frames are all rotten and some of the glass is damaged, and there was definitely a rat problem last year.' Flick makes a sound of disgust. 'I'd probably tear it down and start again, if money and time were no object, but for now it's easier to keep it shut away. There's no need to go through here at all really, but I do love this room. It makes me think of grand balls and formal dancing.' I smile as I picture it, women in large gowns gliding across the room on the arms of handsome men, music and laughter filling the air.

'You know,' Flick says, peering through one of the floor-to-ceiling windows, 'from the outside, this house looks so huge and imposing, but even though the rooms are large, they almost feel tiny once you get used to them. Like the walls are pressing in on you.' She turns to me, a strange look in her eyes. 'Do you ever feel like that?' I tilt my head, considering her words, but she speaks again before I can reply. 'It's like when you're on the Tube at night. It's supposed to be full of people, you know? But it's empty at that time, there's just you and maybe a few others dotted around. It's like you can still feel the energy of all those people who were there earlier in the day, as if there's still a part of them in there with you. Like they've left a part of themselves behind.' She snaps her fingers, and the sound bounces off the walls. 'That's it. This house feels full, but there's nobody here.' I stare at her, trying to fight the strange feeling creeping over me at her words. She shrugs, and her face clears as if she had been daydreaming. 'What's next?'

'The kitchen,' I say, clearing my throat. 'Maybe Halka can rustle us up a cup of tea.' Flick gives me a sideways glance and I smile. 'Yes, I know.'

'It's like going back in time. Does her maid, like, *bathe* her?'

I laugh. 'I don't think so. Marie mostly does general cleaning and helps serve food at mealtimes. That kind of thing. I hate it,' I confess, lowering my voice. 'I suppose this is why I've never shown you around properly. It's all a bit . . .'

'Antisocialist?' Flick offers. 'What would Corbyn say? The important one, I mean.'

I elbow her. 'It's funny, I always assumed people who live in these grand houses were absolutely loaded, but often the estates themselves haemorrhage money.' I lock the ballroom door behind me and lead Flick through the narrow passageway towards the scullery. Ivy trots ahead, tail wagging. 'They cost so much to run. Hence the plans Henry and I came up with.'

'To avoid selling to the National Trust,' Flick says with a nod. 'Having known Henry outside of this house, I would never have guessed he'd grown up here. He was so down-to-earth, and he really cared about people.'

I nod. Henry used to spend his weekends working at food banks and soup kitchens, or running errands for the elderly and disabled members of our community. He spent one summer helping at an activity club for disadvantaged kids, giving them something to do other than roam the streets, and it had been more popular than we'd expected it to be. He often paid for things out of his own pocket too: pizzas for the teenagers on a Friday night, tickets to a football match for a young carer, a haircut for a homeless man going for a job interview. The first time I realised how much I loved him was when we were doing the food shopping for an elderly couple who lived in our block of flats. It used to be council-owned, but it had been sold off to a private developer in the late nineties and the rent was extortionate. The couple had lived there since the fifties, having married not long after the war, and had brought their three children up there. They didn't want to leave the only home they had ever known. The man had carefully counted out the money for the shopping from an old tin in the kitchen, and Henry and I had seen how little was left afterwards. When we got back from the supermarket, arms laden with bags, Henry had called through that he would put their change away while I started to unpack the shopping, and I turned to see him slip all of the money the man had given us back into the pot. *I love this man,* I thought, my heart filling with pride as he smiled sheepishly at me. *He is good, and I am utterly in love with him.*

'Yes,' I say, smiling at the memory as I push open the door. 'He really did.'

Halka is sitting at the table in the middle of the room, a cup at her elbow, a pencil clenched between her teeth as she stares down at the crossword in front of her. She looks up as we enter and goes to rise.

'Stay there,' I tell her firmly. 'We're just going to make ourselves a cup of tea.' I nod towards her mug. 'Do you need a fresh one?'

She smiles. 'I wouldn't say no.'

I take the mug from her and go to fill the kettle. 'Flick, this is Halka. Halka, this is Felicity, my best friend and soon-to-be business partner.'

'Ah, the yoga teacher?' Halka says. 'I might have to come down for one of your lessons when you're all set up. My back often gives me trouble.'

Flick sits down opposite. 'Where does it hurt?'

I turn away, leaving them to it. Like Henry, Flick just can't help herself. She's forever talking to people about their aches and pains, asking questions and recommending stretches. Her lessons and retreats are going to be so popular, I wonder if she'll need to move closer than her mum's house in Taunton. Maybe she could move in with me. The apartment is certainly big enough, and we've lived together before, so unless she's developed new, distasteful habits, I'm sure we could make it work again.

If she can cope with living with a baby, I think as I add sugar to the mugs. Perhaps living with a newborn would be too much for her. Or perhaps she would enjoy it, playing as big a part in Willow's upbringing as she wants to. Who better to help guide my daughter through life than my best friend?

Certainly better than me, Henry says. *I was a bad influence.*

You were, I tell him, smiling. *The worst.*

My heart aches whenever Henry speaks to me. I know it

isn't real, and that's what makes it hurt so much. My mind is filling in the gaps where he should be, refusing to let go of him. But all I have left are my memories. I need to keep them for a little while longer.

I place the mugs on the table and sit down beside Flick. 'Has she cured you yet?' I ask Halka with a wry smile. 'She's magic, this one.'

'Is it true you are running free sessions?' she asks. 'How will you make any money?'

I glance at Flick, registering the guilty look on her face. 'Some sessions will be free or cheaper for some people,' I say carefully. 'We don't want to price anyone out.'

'Everyone deserves to be as healthy as they can be,' Flick adds.

'I can afford to pay,' Halka says, sitting up straight and frowning.

'I know you can,' I say quickly, 'but you live and work here, so getting freebies is part of the deal.' I smile at her. 'Consider it an employee benefit.'

Halka chuckles, her face clearing. 'Well, we don't get many of those, do we?'

We sit and drink our tea for a while, Flick and Halka surprising me by swapping recipes. Flick is all about healthy food, whereas Halka is often quite heavy-handed with things like butter and cheese, but they seem to have found a common ground in how difficult it is to make tasty vegan desserts. Although we rarely have company these days, Halka does love a challenge.

'Eggs are so hard to replace,' Flick says, sipping her tea, 'but I think I've just about managed it with flaxseeds.'

'Flaxseeds?' Halka scribbles something down on the edge of her newspaper. 'I'll have to try that.'

At Halka's insistence, we leave our mugs in the sink – and Ivy lying by the fire, waiting for scraps – and go up the steps towards the corridor which runs parallel to the dining room to continue our tour.

'This was the servants' corridor,' I tell Flick. We are walking single file, the dark passageway just wide enough to accommodate one person at a time. 'Their rooms were up there.' I point towards a staircase leading off to the left. 'Halka and Marie live there now. It's quite spacious actually. A few walls were knocked through at some point and everything was updated by Alice, so it's almost like they have their own apartments.'

'They don't pay rent or anything, do they?'

I glance back at her. 'Of course not. Bed and board is included, plus their salary. And holidays and sick pay. This isn't the bloody Victorian era.'

Flick laughs. 'All right, point taken.' We emerge in the corridor by the dining room and she looks around. 'We went full circle. Though I doubt I could find my way back.'

'I told you, you could get lost in here for days.' I lead her towards the main set of stairs. 'There's another staircase leading from the servants' quarters up to the first floor. I think it was so the nanny could hear the children from the nursery.'

She follows me up the stairs, our footsteps echoing on the wooden boards. 'Where does Alice sleep?'

'On this floor.' I turn as we step onto the landing and point towards the far wall. 'This used to stretch all the way across the house. We put this wall in when we created the apartment.'

'Little Hel,' Flick says with a grin. 'Such a great name.' I smile. 'So what did your bit used to be?'

I laugh. 'A wreck. Mostly bedrooms and reception rooms, according to the old floorplan I found. I'll have to dig it out for you.' I push open the door at the top of the stairs to reveal a short hallway.

'Christ, the Victorians loved their corridors,' Flick says. 'It's like those fun houses at the fair.'

'This used to be the nursery,' I say, opening a door to our left to reveal an empty room with peeling wallpaper. 'That staircase leading from the servants' quarters comes up at the end there.' We step inside the room. The air is cold in here, and dust tickles my nose. 'These rooms aren't used very often, other than Alice's. I've only been in here once myself.'

'It's creepy, isn't it?' Flick rubs her hands up and down her arms.

I frown at her. 'It's just an empty room.'

'Yeah, but . . . Can't you feel it, Jose?' Her voice trembles slightly, and she moves back towards the door. 'It feels like someone was just here, doesn't it? Like they literally just left before we arrived.'

I shake my head, trying to dispel the fear creeping over

me. 'Nobody has been here, Flick. Unless Marie was cleaning, but I doubt she comes in here very often.'

Flick takes another step back. 'I don't know, Josie. It just feels weird in here. Like something isn't quite right. Like the air has been disturbed, and we're trespassing. Like we shouldn't be in here at all.'

TWENTY-FIVE

HARRIET

1st September 1864

A sickness has descended upon Helygen House. Cassius was the first to go down with it, his forehead hot and beaded with sweat, his hands gripping his stomach as he moaned in pain. It began during dinner last night, and he later vomited up the small portion he managed to eat. If only he had spent the summer at school, he might have avoided the sickness. He is fifteen now, strong and healthy, but he looked so terribly ill that I spent the night with him, mopping his brow and praying. *Oh, Lord*, I begged silently as he writhed in his sleep, *I cannot lose another child. Please, take me instead. Deliver the child from my womb and take me instead.*

He slept fitfully, gripped by a ferocious fever. At first I suspected it was something he ate, perhaps the rich food from last night did not agree with him, but then Edmund woke this morning complaining of a headache and stomach pains. His forehead was hot to the touch, his eyes bloodshot and heavy with tiredness, but he still had the wherewithal to tell me to segregate myself.

'You are with child, Harriet,' he said, his eyes half closed, his voice weak. 'You must protect him, and yourself.'

'But Edmund—'

'Sara can tend to us. I will have Cassius brought in here, and you must sleep in your own chamber until this has passed.'

Edmund and I have rarely slept apart in our marriage. I know it is common, and sometimes useful, for husband and wife to take separate bedrooms, but we have been fortunate that our match born of business and necessity transformed into one of love. I love my husband, and we love our children, and I knew that he was right. I had to protect the unborn child inside me. But what if that meant sacrificing a living child? Such a terrible, impossible choice for a mother to make.

I hurried downstairs and asked Mrs Lane to arrange for Cassius's bed to be moved in with Edmund. Sara was in the kitchen, wringing her hands as she watched a pot on the stove. She turned at my entrance, her face creased with worry.

'I am making soup, madam,' she said. 'Chicken broth. It'll help the poor lad keep his strength up.'

'Edmund has fallen ill as well.' I sat down heavily at the long table in the middle of the room and Sara rushed over to me. The bench was hard beneath me, the surface dusty with powder. Flour? I reached a finger out to touch it.

'Don't!' Sara's voice was like a whip and I froze, too

surprised to scold her. 'Apologies, madam,' she said quickly. 'Forgive me, but please, do not touch it. It is arsenic.' She soaked a cloth at the sink and began rubbing at the table. 'We were making rat traps, for the ballroom.'

I was surprised. 'At the kitchen table?'

Sara paused before replying. 'Where else, madam?'

A cry rang out then and I got quickly to my feet, Sara behind me as we hurried towards the sound. One of the maids was stood by the window in the passageway, one hand pressed against her mouth, the other against the glass, her fingers splayed.

'What is it?' Sara asked, putting an arm around the girl. 'Annie?' Annie kept staring out of the window, her eyes wide and fixed on the willow tree in the distance. Sara shook her gently. 'Annie?'

She jumped then, as if only just noticing our presence. Her eyes found mine and I felt something pass over me, a coldness that took hold of my limbs and made me feel light-headed. I stumbled back, my hands finding the wood of the panelling behind me before I fell.

'She's beneath the willow,' Annie said, eyes still fixed on mine. 'They all are.'

'Who?' I demanded. I suddenly wanted to shake the girl, but then Mrs Lane appeared and Annie scuttled away. I turned to Sara. 'What on earth was that about?'

Sara wet her lips, her eyes avoiding mine. 'You mustn't pay any attention, madam,' Mrs Lane said, giving Sara a look. 'Annie is a troubled girl.'

'But who did she mean?' I asked, directing my question at Sara. 'Who is beneath the willow?'

'Maisie, madam,' Sara whispered. 'Annie saw him pull her down.'

I stared at her. 'Down? Don't you mean out, Sara?' I glanced at Mrs Lane, whose mouth was in a thin line. Sara would still not meet my gaze and I felt my frustration growing. 'Cassius pulled her *out* of the lake. He tried to save her.'

'As you say, madam,' she said, bobbing her head and going back into the kitchen.

TWENTY-SIX

JOSIE

2019

After the tour, we find Alice still in the drawing room, a novel on her lap, Willow sleeping peacefully beside her.

'How has she been?' I ask, quietly moving across the room and picking my daughter up.

Alice smiles. 'An angel. How was the *tour*?' I know I'm not imagining the bitterness in her voice when she says the word. She raises an eyebrow. 'I trust you haven't made any other plans for my home?'

I suppress a sigh and force myself to smile at her. 'Of course not, Alice. Flick had never seen the house in its entirety, that's all. We're sticking to our plans for The Hut.'

'Ah, yes,' Alice says, folding her hands in her lap. 'The Hut. Retreats, yoga. Relaxation.' There's something in the way she says the words that make them sound as if they are dirty and undesirable. Perhaps she has never truly relaxed in her life.

'That's right,' Flick says brightly, as if to cover Alice's scorn. 'I'm looking forward to getting started.'

Alice turns her gaze to Flick, her lips pursed. 'And have you recovered now, Felicity?'

Flick's smile falters. 'Recovered? Well, yes, I—'

'Because I won't have my granddaughter in any danger. You understand.'

I stare at her, shocked. 'Alice, Flick is not a danger to Willow. She's my best friend.' I can see what she thinks of my endorsement by the way her eyebrows rise by a fraction.

'Well. I must get on.' She stands and strides out of the room without another word. Flick and I stare at each other in surprise.

'She really doesn't like me, does she?' Flick whispers.

'Don't worry,' I whisper back, trying to hide my shock at Alice's words, 'she doesn't like me much either.'

We go back to the apartment through the internal door, which I lock firmly behind us, slamming the bolts home. I feed and change Willow and put her down in the nursery while Flick makes tea in the kitchen. When I come downstairs, I see that she's rustled up some chocolate digestives from somewhere.

'I brought supplies,' she says, holding up a few takeaway menus. 'Chinese, Indian, or good old-fashioned pizza?'

I laugh and sit down on the sofa beside her, clasping the mug of tea between my hands. 'I think it's got to be Chinese, hasn't it?'

Flick grins wickedly, no doubt remembering the late-night

takeaways we lived off as students, chow mein and chicken balls and egg fried rice eaten while drunk, reheated the next morning to soothe a hangover. I wonder suddenly if these memories trigger negative emotions in my friend, if they make her long for a drink. She places her hand over mine and squeezes gently.

'If I didn't have an image to preserve, I'd eat egg fried rice all day, every day,' she says as if reading my thoughts. 'No cheap wine or watery beer required.'

While she orders online, I study her profile. Her eyes are no longer ringed in purple; her cheeks are back to their usual pink; her lips smooth and without flakes of dry skin. She *is* better, I tell myself. She is. Three years is no time at all when it comes to losing a loved one, and I imagine it'll always be something she has to bear, but she's doing well. I think of my dad, and how delighted he would have been with Willow. Although the MS slowly ate him alive, he was forever the optimist, always looking on the bright side. When he became bedbound, he liked having his bedroom window open all year round to listen to the birds in the morning and the children playing on the green below and the tinkle of the ice cream van in the summer months. He liked two digestive biscuits with his tea before his breakfast, and every Christmas he asked the woman from next door to pick up a gift for me, which he chose himself from the Argos catalogue.

I wasn't always kind to my father. Sometimes I resented having to go home straight from school to cook dinner or bathe him. Sometimes I got bored of our poky flat, watching the same TV shows over and over again, the same well-thumbed novels staring at me from the shelves. Sometimes I just wanted to go to the beach or the cinema with friends, to do normal things and be a normal teenager. To tell the truth, I often felt trapped in that tower block, like Rapunzel staring out of the window at the world below, watching life happen. But, though I didn't know it at the time, my dad was just as desperate for me to get out of there as I was. When I was fifteen and studying for my GCSEs, he swallowed his pride and asked for help. A carer came twice a day to wash and feed him, and they even did the tidying up when they had time, hoovering around me as I sat at the kitchen table revising. And he encouraged me to go further away, to apply to universities across the country. I ended up in London, where I lost myself in the buzzing energy of the capital, feeding off it, and slowly the image of my father alone in his room in the sixth-floor flat, watching clouds and birds and planes pass by the window, began to fade.

Flick puts her phone down and turns to me, bringing me out of my reverie. 'Done. I've gone all out. We're going to have a feast!'

I laugh. 'To us,' I say, raising my cup of tea. 'To our joint venture.'

'To the future of Helygen House,' she says, clinking her mug against mine.

'Speaking of,' I say cautiously, 'I wanted to ask you

something.' She makes a face and I nudge her with my elbow. 'It's nothing bad. In fact, it might be quite good. I was wondering if you wanted to move in here. With me.'

Flick tilts her head to one side. 'Into the apartment?'

I nod. 'There's plenty of space. It feels so empty here now, and besides, your mum's is too far away for you to commute here every day.'

'Commute.' She laughs lightly. 'This is hardly Hammersmith.'

I roll my eyes. 'That's not what I mean. Although the roads can get quite busy during peak season. All those emmets coming down from up country.' I laugh, faltering when I take in Flick's serious expression. 'I just thought it made sense, you being closer.'

'I agree,' she says slowly. 'But Josie – and don't take this the wrong way – I don't think I could live here.'

'Oh.' I try to push down my disappointment. I'd built up the idea in my head, of Flick and me living together again, of late-night movies and weekend takeaways and Sunday strolls with Willow and Ivy. I remember feeling nervous about moving out of our shared flat and into one with Henry. What if I didn't get on with him like I did with Flick? What if he dropped dirty socks on the floor or left the toilet seat up or never picked up a duster? Flick and I had got into a routine with one another. We understood each other, and as far as housemates go, we were perfectly matched.

'It's not what you think,' she says, reaching out for my hand again. 'I just . . . Josie, how can you stand to live here?'

I stare at her in surprise. 'What do you mean? After . . . after Henry?' I try to swallow the lump in my throat.

She shakes her head. 'No, though of course, it was an awful thing to happen. I just . . . I could never feel comfortable here. It feels as if there's always someone standing behind me, like a face pressed against the glass. It's creepy.' My eyes flick up involuntarily to the patio doors behind her, where the sky is darkening, the long winter night drawing in. I can see the willow tree in the distance, leaves dancing in the breeze. 'I'm sorry,' Flick says, and I turn my attention back to her.

'Don't be,' I say hurriedly. 'It's fine, really.' But it isn't. Because at the same moment I hear Willow begin to cry, I think I see something move beyond the window, the figure of a girl turning away.

After we've eaten our body weight in Chinese food, Flick decides to stay the night, as if in protest against her own fears. My imagination is getting the best of me as I turn off the lights, avoiding the patio doors and the blackness beyond them. *I must get some curtains*, I think as I brush my teeth in the en-suite. I've put Flick in the room next to the nursery, the guest room which has never been used, the bedding fresh out of the packaging. Maybe after tonight, she'll change her mind about Helygen House.

In the bedroom, I check on Willow before sliding between the sheets, picking up my Kindle from the bedside table. I feel like I haven't read in weeks, and realise that I probably haven't. Between Henry's death and Willow's birth, I've been too emotional or exhausted to do anything other than fall into a deep sleep each night. I press my fingers into my eyes, breathing through the wave of grief that often comes when I am alone and everything is quiet. When I'm busy, I can almost forget about Henry, or at least put it to the back of my mind. I feel better when I can focus on other things, when I have something other than my loss to occupy my mind. I try to read for a while, but my attention keeps drifting, and I find myself staring at the blinds covering the window instead. I sigh, putting the Kindle back on the bedside table and turning off the lamp. I stare up at the ceiling, the darkness almost impenetrable, and close my eyes.

'Josie!' I wake, heart pounding, to find a hand on my shoulder. 'Josie, wake up!' My shoulder shakes beneath its grip, fingers digging into my skin. 'Josie!'

I sit up, eyes darting around the room. The hand has fallen away and I can't see anyone, but I can feel them. 'Who's there?' I hear the tremble in my voice and hope I sound stronger than I feel.

'It's me, Flick.' I feel my body deflate with relief as the lamp turns on.

'What are you doing?' I demand, anger flaring as the fear drains from my body. I peer into the cot, relieved to find Willow still sleeping, before looking back at Flick. 'You scared me half to death!'

Her brows are knitted together, her fingers twisting

before her. 'You were screaming,' she says. 'It sounded like someone was hurting you.'

I blink at her. Screaming? Surely I would have woken myself up, and disturbed Willow? I shake my head. 'I must have been dreaming,' I whisper. 'Did I say anything?'

Flick's eyes are wide, an expression of anxiety and fear that sends prickles up my spine. 'You said, *not another child. Don't take another child.*'

TWENTY-SEVEN

ELIZA

1881

Eliza lay in the darkness, eyes wide, watching the branches from the trees outside make shapes on the ceiling. The bed felt too big, too empty, for just her alone. The moon was brighter than usual tonight, stars twinkling in the inky sky, and though she did not know the time, she knew that it was late. Too late for Cassius to be out. He had gone to see Dickie that morning, leaving Eliza to suffer through the day with Harriet alone, but he should have been back by now. What if something had happened to him?

Frustrated, Eliza turned on her side, her back to the window, one hand cupping her stomach. She was not yet showing, though there was a little firmness there, a tiny hint at what she was carrying inside her. What she was concealing. Her wedding night baby, whose presence had sparked such excitement inside her. But her joy had turned to ashes in her mouth at Mary's words the day before. *Nobody ever saw Flora again.* Where did she go, that twin girl? The question writhed around inside her like a snake, curling around her heart and squeezing. For some reason, the story of the lost girl had got under her skin, and she could not shake it off. *They only brought one little body down from the nursery that night.*

She shuddered, closed her eyes. *There is a perfectly reasonable explanation*, she told herself. Perhaps the child went to the hospital, or to stay with another relative. There was no reason for the family to explain everything to the servants. But what had happened to Archie, exactly? She knew that babies died all the time, sometimes for unfathomable reasons, but something was prickling at her. She remembered a conversation she'd had with her uncle once, a conversation her mother had deemed inappropriate for a young lady. 'Children die more often when mothers and babies must share a bed,' Uncle Frank had explained, ignoring his sister's icy glare. 'And yet what other choice do they have, when they are ten or twelve to a room and without any proper facilities?'

Fifteen-year-old Eliza had been shocked. Ten or twelve to a room? Despite the fall in her own family's fortunes, she could not comprehend such poverty. Her uncle was a doctor and routinely volunteered his time in the poorer areas of Hertfordshire, ministering to those unfortunate souls who had no funds to seek medical attention, and she went with him one day to a cramped building only a stone's throw away from the bustling market town of Hertford. The family was known to him, the man of the house a farmhand who had been severely injured a few years previous, and he had been called to visit the youngest child that day, a girl of three or four who had, Uncle Frank announced in his grave voice, contracted consumption. Eliza stood behind her uncle as he knelt to check the patient. There were two rooms, with only one door and a small, filthy window at the back, beyond which was a scrap of grass and uneven paving stones, amongst which chickens pecked for seeds. She counted five children huddled on a mattress in the corner of the room, their faces dirty and their eyes wide. She caught the eye of the mother and saw her straighten her back as she held her sick child, her face like stone, as if she was daring Eliza to judge her. Eliza looked away first.

'But why does she have so many children?' she asked her uncle when they left the house. She was grateful to be out in the fresh air and breathed deeply.

Uncle Frank glanced at her with an expression she could not read. 'Do you believe she has a choice?'

He was right, she thought now. That poor woman had had no choice in how many children she had, or how many children she lost, and neither did her mother-in-law. *And neither do I.* She felt a flash of fear and squeezed her hands into fists, nails digging into her palms as a distraction from the sudden realisation that she, too, could lose her child. Her children. What if she was having twins? *Dear God, however will I cope, alone as I am in Helygen House?* She suddenly missed her mother with a ferocity she had never felt before. Though they had never been close, the ghost of her brother forever standing between them, she wished she were there now to guide her through her pregnancy. She suddenly could not imagine having to go through the birth of her child with just Harriet and perhaps a local midwife to support her.

Her eyes flew open at a noise. A door opening, or was it closing? Relief flooded through her as she pictured Cassius stumbling in through the front door, worse for wear after a late night with his friend, but home, safe, with her. And then . . . could it be? Yes, she was certain this time. Somewhere inside the house, a baby was crying. She was up and out of bed in an instant, opening the bedroom door and stepping out onto the landing. A candle disappeared into a room at the far end of the hall and, before she realised what she was doing, she was moving towards it, her steps quick and light, her husband's name on her lips. It must just be Cassius, trying to sneak in unheard. But as she went through the doorway and turned left, she heard the cry again, louder now, closer, and felt a shiver run through her. She was standing at the doorway to the nursery, a room which had clearly been neglected over the years. Two cribs were pushed up against the far wall, a toy box standing beneath the open window, but otherwise the room was empty. Eliza shivered as she crossed the threshold, her shift too thin for the chill, the floorboards cold beneath her bare feet. The net curtain moved in the breeze, billowing towards her as she grasped it and moved it aside to close the window. The catchment was stiff, complaining as she tried to pull it down, then suddenly slammed shut. She jumped back, her heart beating wildly in her chest. *You're being silly, Eliza,* she told herself, forcing herself to breathe deeply. *There's no baby here. It must have been the wind.*

She moved her attention to the two cribs. The room was too dark to see properly, the moon hidden now behind a cloud, and her fingers moved across the wood, nails catching on the flaking paint. This must have been where Cassius had slept as a child, where all of his had siblings slept. Where the twins had died. A chill crept over her skin and she shuddered again.

She heard something behind her. A scuffle, like feet on floorboards. She turned at the noise to find a child with white-blonde hair standing in the doorway, a candle flickering in her hand. She smiled, her eyes glistening in the light before she blew it out, plunging the room into darkness.

'Eliza? Eliza!'

She was curled into a ball, her hands covering her head. She could not open her eyes. She *would* not open them.

Another voice, sharper. 'She is hysterical. Shall I call for the doctor?'

'Eliza?'

'No,' she moaned. She began to fight the hands grasping her, but the grip only tightened, fingers digging into her flesh. 'No!'

'Eliza!'

A sharp blow to her cheek. Her eyes flew open to find Harriet glaring at her, her hand raised as if to strike her again. 'Mother, enough.' Eliza turned to see Cassius behind her, his arms around her as if he was restraining her.

'Cassius?' She blinked as she looked around the room. It was illuminated now by two candles, but the shadows still lurked in the corners. What if the little girl was waiting in one of them? She moaned again, closing her eyes and resting her head against her husband's chest. 'No, no.'

'What is it?' Cassius asked, his breath sour with whisky and tobacco, and yet it was comforting, his arms around her reassuringly strong. 'What's happened?'

'I saw her,' she whispered, her eyes still closed, her heart pounding in her chest so loud it almost drowned out her words. 'I saw the lost girl.'

TWENTY-EIGHT

JOSIE

2019

Flick leaves the next morning, a final worried glance over her shoulder as she drives out of the gate. I wave, my lips stretched into a smile, but both my smile and my arm drop as soon as she is out of sight. I can't stop thinking about what she said last night. It must have been her who was dreaming, sleep-walking into my bedroom and scaring me witless. There's no way I could have been screaming without waking Willow up. I've always been a deep sleeper – 'like the dead', Henry used to say – though since having Willow I seem to wake more easily, thankfully. I remember a conversation Henry and I had when I was a few months pregnant. We were lying in bed, the credits from the movie we'd just watched rolling across the screen. I got up to pee for the seventeenth time that evening, and from the toilet I could see him getting comfy in bed, pulling back the duvet on my side for me to get back in.

'What if I don't wake up?' I called through.

Henry paused, his gaze flicking up and catching mine, amusement in his eyes. 'As in, never again?'

I rolled my eyes at him. 'In the night. When the baby comes.'

'Aren't mothers fine-tuned to respond to their baby's cries?'

I flushed and washed my hands, carefully rubbing between my fingers as I counted twenty seconds under my breath. It was happening again, the obsessive need to do things in a particular way. I knew I had to nip it in the bud, before it took over again.

'Sexist,' I told him as I switched off the light and slid into bed. 'For that, you can do all of the night feeds.'

'I thought I was doing them anyway,' he said with a smile, slipping his arms around me and holding me close. 'You will be a fantastic mother,' he whispered in my ear. 'The best mother our child could ever hope for.'

I look down at Willow now, strapped to my chest, and feel a wave of panic wash over me. I have tried to keep the OCD at bay since Henry died, my caesarean scar stopping me from doing anything more than light cleaning, but I can feel the itch starting up inside me, the thoughts swirling around in my head. Could I have done anything differently? Could I have stopped Henry from dying? What if something happens to Willow now? Am I losing my mind?

I close my eyes, pressing my lips to my daughter's forehead, trying to centre myself. Whatever happened to Henry, whether his death was by his own hand or someone else's, there is nothing I could have done. I know that.

But that isn't true, a voice inside my head persists. *If he was depressed, why didn't you see it? If he was anxious or stressed or desperate enough to kill himself, why didn't you know about it? Alice knew.*

I look up at the house and jump a little to see Alice staring down at me from one of the first-floor windows. She turns away quickly, but for a second, our eyes meet and I feel a chill run through me.

Alice knew.

I need to get out. I shove my feet into some shoes, pull on a coat and leave the apartment. I try not to look at the stables as I pass them, but my thoughts are drawn to the bones the builders found. When will we discover who they belonged to? They had certainly looked old, but I wouldn't know the difference between ten or a hundred years when it comes to the degradation of bones. Someone, at some point, had lost a child at Helygen House and buried them beneath the stables. But who? And why?

I find myself moving around the side of the house, down the narrow pathway that leads towards the gardens. The lost gardens, I call them, for they are hidden behind the lake and the beautiful, sculpted hedges which I can see from the apartment. There used to be a paddock here full of horses which is now a field left to go wild, back to the bees and creatures of the Cornish landscape, until you reach the cliffs and the river beyond which mark the edge of the estate. But if you go down further this side, skirting the house and following the track past the sculpted gardens, you will find the family graveyard.

I am out of breath when I arrive, my chest constricting with anxiety. I feel as if I'm being drawn here, as if Henry is calling to me, chastising me for not visiting him before now.

The gravestones are glistening in the weak sunlight, moist with dew, the names of the Foxes almost worn away by the passage of time. Henry's ashes still aren't ready to be collected, and so there is nothing to mark where his grave will be apart from a plank of wood. Brushing away tears, my eyes settle on another headstone a few feet away. The name sends a flicker of recognition through me – Eliza Fox – and I remember the portrait in the dining room I'd looked at with Flick. Alice's great-grandmother. Moving closer, I feel my stomach lurch as I read the words written beneath her name.

LEAD THOU ME ON, THE NIGHT IS DARK AND I AM FAR FROM HOME

I stumble back, stunned. Those words . . . Where have I seen them before? And then it hits me. The note Alice said Henry had left. Has she got it back from the police? But then, why wouldn't she have shown it to me? Surely the void between us isn't so great that she would purposely hide such a thing from me?

Dizzy, I stop to catch my breath and calm my racing thoughts before making my way back through the gardens.

I need to fix things with Alice. The gap between us is widening by the day, but Willow needs her grandmother, and I know it's what Henry would want. I see a flash of orange dart through the undergrowth and pause, waiting for the fox to reappear, but it has vanished. We get a few visitors here, and once a vixen gave birth in the old swimming pool, empty for decades now and full of vines and weeds and leaves shed from the surrounding forest. Nature is slowly reclaiming Helygen House.

I slip into the house by the kitchen door, hoping Halka has some food ready for me to take back to the apartment, and maybe a cup of tea to warm my cold fingers. Christmas is fast approaching, the air growing colder, the days shorter and the nights darker. I suddenly realise I haven't done any shopping. I haven't even bought Willow a gift.

'We'll have to sort something out, won't we?' I whisper to her as I glance around the empty kitchen. 'For your first . . .' I trail off as my eyes catch sight of something on the wall opposite the door. The winter air is trickling through the open window, the short net curtain blowing towards me like an arm reaching out. And beside it, on the wall, is a bloody handprint.

TWENTY-NINE

HARRIET

7th January 1865

I write by candlelight, my pen scratching against the paper, so loud I fear it will wake the babies. I know not how long it has been since I last left this room. I had to ask Sara what the date was, so confused has my mind become. All I know is that I have to keep them safe.

Edmund is gone. I can scarcely bring myself to write these words, but I must. I must record what has been happening here. And Benjamin, oh, poor Benjamin, whom we had shut in the nursery with the nanny, far from his father and the sickness, or so we hoped. But he too grew ill. He deteriorated so quickly that, despite being summoned immediately, the doctor was too late to save him. He went from a healthy, happy little boy to someone – *something* – I no longer recognised. A ghost, lying there in his bed, his breathing low and ragged, his skin pale, his fingers like ice clasped between mine. How can this happen? How can life be so cruel to one family, to one woman? How many more children must I lose before the Almighty is sated? But it is not God who punishes me so. I know this now. And it terrifies me. I saw him, you see. Cassius had recovered quickly, and despite our instructions, he had gone into the nursery. He said he had been delivering Benjamin and the nanny's meals, but there had been no need. Sara was leaving the tray at the top of the stairs, and Nanny would come out to collect them once Sara had gone. It should have been safe. *He* should have been safe.

'I was trying to help, Mama,' Cassius said when I caught him exiting the nursery. 'I am no longer unwell.' But now I know why he had recovered so quickly, though I can scarcely bring myself to believe it.

I've rarely left this room since he arrived back from school for Christmas. I watched Archie and Flora lying together in the middle of the large bed, the door locked, pretending I was unwell. Twins. It is a blessing, to one who has lost so many to be given two in one go, but I still cannot shake the feeling that they too will be taken from me. That our time is finite and all the more precious. That, sooner or later, they will die, and I will have to let them go.

Even now Cassius has gone back to school, I stay in my room. Sara brings me meals and tends to the babies while I lie in the bath in front of the fire, the water she has dragged up the stairs for me growing cold as I lose myself in my memories, in my grief. She is the only one I trust now, the only person I allow into this room. My devoted servant, my only friend. She is exhausted, I can tell by the deep rings around her eyes and the paleness to her skin, the way she moves slower than before, but the bruises are disappearing and she no longer appears unwell. I suspect I know the reason behind it all, though I cannot speak it. I dare not, lest everything fall down around me. I fear I am losing my mind, but I must protect the twins. They are all I have left.

'You still have me, Mama,' Cassius said when I told him his father and brother were dead, and perhaps in other circumstances, perhaps spoken by somebody else, this would have brought me comfort, but his words sent a chill through me. No, it was not his words, but the look in his eyes. It was the same look he had when Maisie drowned, and when he told us of Clara's demise. Though the sickness took his father and brother, Cassius was spared. If I close my eyes, I can see again the white grains scattered across the kitchen table that day. Arsenic.

THIRTY

JOSIE

2019

'Marie!' The word comes out as a gasp as the woman staggers through the utility room, one hand clutched around her stomach. She looks up, her eyes full of tears, her face twisting into a mask of agony before she stumbles, falling to her knees. I rush towards her, noticing as I do the trail of blood following her into the room. 'Marie, are you hurt?' I drop down beside her, one hand holding Willow's head against my body, and try to check her over, but the woman is curled into a ball now, her eyes squeezed tight, her mouth open in a silent scream. Fear floods through me, the taste of metal on my tongue.

I hear a noise behind me and turn to see Alice coming into the kitchen. 'It's Marie. She's bleeding, I think she's hurt.' Alice hurries over, one hand going to Marie's shoulder while the other traces down her stomach, then reaches behind the woman to touch her trousers. Her hand comes away red. I stare at it in horror.

'Come on,' Alice says, reaching beneath Marie and lifting her up. 'We need to get you to the hospital.'

'No,' Marie moans, her eyes still closed. 'No hospital.'

'Why not?' I ask, panic making my voice shrill.

'Illegal,' she whimpers.

'Illegal?' I glance at Alice, uncomprehending. Then it dawns on me. Marie had been pregnant, and it isn't the healthcare she needs now which is illegal, but rather what she has already done. What she has been forced to do. 'Marie,' I say quietly, cupping her chin in my hand. Her eyes open but she avoids my gaze. 'What have you taken?' She bursts into tears, slumping against Alice, who staggers beneath her weight. 'You need medical attention, Marie. You could become seriously ill.'

She shakes her head, still sobbing. I catch Alice's gaze and silent communication passes between us. 'Come on,' I say gently. 'Let's get you settled upstairs.'

Halka comes bustling into the kitchen then, her eyes widening at the sight of us holding Marie up. 'Oh, my dear child,' she says, rushing over and taking Marie's weight from Alice. I see something in her eyes when she looks at her employer – frustration? Blame? – but then she is gone, half carrying Marie out of the room and along the narrow corridor. Alice and I follow, mute, as Halka shoulders open a door and leads Marie to a small sofa.

'This used to be a room for the cook's children,' Alice says quietly. 'It's mostly used for storage now.' She gestures towards the stacks of boxes lining the walls, the vacuum and mops leaning in the corner.

'Sometimes we rest in here,' Halka says, finding a blanket for Marie. 'Sometimes the sofa is nicer than the kitchen table for taking tea breaks.' When she looks up, her eyes are blazing with defiance, as if daring Alice to scold her. They are staring at one another, tension rippling between them, unspoken words crackling in the air.

Marie moans and I move towards her, bending down to clasp her hand in mine. 'How are you feeling?' Her fingers are clammy, and when I press the back of my hand against her forehead, her skin is so hot I almost jerk away. 'We need to call a doctor,' I tell her, and this time she doesn't argue. I turn back to my mother-in-law, who pulls her gaze away from Halka when I call her name.

'I'll call Dr Thomas,' she says, and at that moment, Marie leans forward and vomits all over my legs.

'I've given her some antibiotics,' the doctor says when he joins us in the sitting room. I've changed my jeans and Willow is in her Moses basket beside me. Thankfully Marie managed to avoid puking all over my daughter.

'Does she have an infection?' I ask carefully. I don't want to say anything Marie wouldn't want me to. She hasn't told us exactly what she did, but I think I know *why* she did it. The guilt on Alice's face told me everything. Marie may have discovered her pregnancy too late, but I suspect Alice had not allowed her to take time off to seek medical care in time. I fight the urge to shout at her while the doctor speaks. There will be plenty of time for that later.

'A mild one, yes, but she'll be fine after a course of antibiotics. Miscarriages at this stage can be dangerous, though, so do keep an eye on her,' he warns. I avert my gaze at the term *miscarriage*. If he is aware that this is self-induced, he isn't showing it. 'If she shows any signs of deterioration in the next forty-eight hours, or if the bleeding starts again, call an ambulance.'

I nod, swallowing. Infections aren't often something you should have to worry about these days. With modern medicine, it's easy to forget how dangerous they can be. 'Of course.'

'You have my number, Mrs Fox,' he says, getting to his feet.

'Thank you, Dr Thomas,' Alice says formally, rising and leading him out of the room. She comes back wringing her hands, her brow knitted with worry.

'What happened?' I demand, my voice too loud in the silent house. 'Why did Marie do what she did?'

Alice looks stricken. 'I have no idea, Josie. I didn't know . . . She didn't tell me . . .'

'But you refused her time off.' It isn't a question, and from the look on her face I can tell I'm right. 'She is entitled to twenty days plus bank holidays, and she is also entitled to seek medical attention if needed. Statutory sick pay is—'

'I know what she is entitled to,' she snaps. 'I've been an employer longer than you've been alive. She's taken all of her holiday for this year.'

I make a face, but Alice continues before I can speak.

'I don't have to justify myself to you, Josie.'

'She still should have been given time off to see a doctor,' I say, glaring at her.

Alice returns it. 'Are you saying it's my fault she got herself pregnant with an unwanted child?'

'Of course not, but you should have supported her in—'

'Murdering her unborn baby?' She laughs nastily. 'I do not hold with such things. No, she brought it on herself.'

I stare at her, not trying to conceal my disbelief and disgust. Who is this woman, the only family member I have left in the world besides Willow? What have I married into?

THIRTY-ONE

Back in Little Hel, I wrap Willow up in warm clothes and tuck a blanket around her in the pram before leaving the apartment. Leaves crunch beneath my boots as we walk, Ivy bounding ahead, her tail lifted as she investigates the garden. I need to blow off some steam. What I'd really like to do is get in the car and drive to Flick's, but I shouldn't be driving yet, and besides, I'm not sure I'd be good company right now. Since Henry died, I've started to see a side to Alice that makes me uneasy. She's always been a bit difficult, even prickly at times, and clearly very used to a certain way of living, but I hadn't thought her cruel or unfeeling. Until now. Now I have seen a side to her which I can barely stand to look at.

I wonder what it was like for Henry and his sister growing up. Was Alice always like this? She is obsessed with appearances, which is why she fights so hard against opening the estate up to make money. She doesn't want to look as if she is in need of funds or help of any kind. But all of Alice's wealth is tied up in this house, and for a while now, it has been too expensive to run without another source of income. Perhaps there was more money when Henry was a child, once his father's estate had been settled. He still went to private school, after all, and then to university, as did his sister. Perhaps there was a trust fund for them both, though I imagine it ran dry long before I met him, as I never heard him speak of one. I wonder what it was like for Henry to come back to this house during the school holidays. Did he look forward to it, or did he dread it? And what about India? She was about seven when they moved into Helygen House, and as far as I know, she didn't move back here after university. I've never even met her; she didn't attend our wedding, and she didn't even come to her brother's funeral. Perhaps this house holds too many ghosts for her.

I fish my phone out of my pocket and find India's Instagram profile. She has been in Australia since September, according to the beautiful photos on her grid. Sparkling seas and sandy toes and bright, clear skies. Cocktails on a veranda and children splashing in a pool. The wind gusts and I shiver in the cold, wrapping my scarf tighter around my neck. Before I can stop myself, I tap the button to send her a message.

Hi India, it's Josie. Henry's wife. I hope you don't mind me messaging you on here, but I don't have a phone number for you. I was wondering

I pause, my fingers hovering over the keypad. What, exactly, am I wondering? What do I want to ask her? Why she didn't come to the funeral? I imagine flights from Australia are expensive at short notice, but surely she could have afforded it? Why hasn't she sent a card or flowers or got in touch at all since her brother's death? Henry had said they weren't particularly close, though they had been as children – 'involuntary allies,' he said with a wry grin – but he always wished her and the girls a happy birthday and merry Christmas, sending them cards and gifts, and he usually got a similar response from them. Was it because she didn't have any contact details for me? We don't have a landline in the apartment, but I'd have thought she's got the number for Helygen House at least.

I sigh, delete the message and shove my phone back into my pocket. India is another puzzle I don't have the energy to solve right now. I have more pressing things to be getting on with, starting with the renovations. I had hoped that we would be ready to open for weddings by the summer, but with the delays caused by the discovery beneath the stables, I'm worried we'll be put off for another year. I need to speak to the police again, see if they have any information for me. I need some good news.

I call for Ivy and look down at the pram. Willow is awake, her eyes fixed on my face. 'Hello, sleepyhead,' I whisper. 'Did you sleep well?' She really does sleep a lot for a newborn. Is she sleeping too much? Am I waking up when she does during the night? I feel a prickle of anxiety, my fingers tightening around the handle of the pram. I really do need to speak to the midwife. Maybe I should have asked Dr

Thomas earlier, but my mind had been too full of Marie. Poor woman. I don't know how she tried to end her own pregnancy and I don't want to know, but my heart aches for her. I just wish she'd felt she could come to me for help. How desperate does one have to be to take such extreme measures? It feels so archaic, bringing images of filthy instruments and herbal concoctions, procedures performed in the back of a dark room. I shudder, remembering my own thoughts when I first discovered I was pregnant. Terrified at the idea of becoming a mother, anxious that I would get it wrong. I still feel that way sometimes, when I allow the doubts to creep in. As they are now. Is Willow sleeping too much? Is she unwell? What kind of mother allows something like this to go on for so long? Tired of berating myself, I pull out my phone again and find the number for the midwife. It rings out so I leave a message, aware as I'm speaking that my voice is too high, too breathless, that I might sound deranged, but I'm too worried to care. Now I have built it up into something that needs addressing immediately, I cannot seem to shake my anxiety. I grip the handle of the pram too tightly, trying to touch the bar in just the right way, but I can't seem to get it. *Stop it*, I tell myself, releasing the pram for a moment and shaking my hands out. *Don't let it take hold of you again.*

Ivy trots ahead to the front door, sitting on the step and waiting for me to catch up. The sky is darkening already, though it is barely three o'clock. How short these winter days are. How long and cold and empty are the nights. I unlock the door and as I'm reaching down to lift the pram up the step, I notice a brown box sitting in the corner, next to the front door. Probably something I ordered from Amazon a while ago and forgot about. I pick it up and tuck it under my arm as I clumsily manoeuvre the pram into the apartment. As always, I'm struck by the silence of the house whenever I return. It was hardly a loud home before Henry died, but I could always feel his presence, even when he wasn't physically there. Now I can't feel him at all.

I change and feed Willow before filling Ivy's food bowl and putting down fresh water, then I lay my daughter on her play mat in the living room and lie down next to her. Ivy pads over, sniffing Willow from head to toe before settling down beside us, her head resting on her front paws. I smile, scratching behind her ears. She really is the gentlest dog. Then I remember the way she growled at Alice and frown. She has never behaved that way before, not even as a puppy when she would nip and growl in play. That was different. Had Alice hurt her? Or perhaps she was just feeding off our anxiety? She opens one eye and watches me in her calm, steady way, before lifting her head and licking my hand. No, she would never hurt anyone, especially not Willow.

We spend the afternoon together, just the three of us, the absence of Henry stronger than ever. I can picture him sitting between us, Willow in his arms as he reads to her, Ivy lying by his side. It is almost perfect, until his image shimmers and dances like a flame in the wind, before disappearing entirely.

It isn't until Willow is in bed and I'm making a cup of tea that I remember the parcel. I grab it from the kitchen side and sit down on the sofa, carefully opening a packet of biscuits so the rustling doesn't wake the dog. She doesn't understand that she isn't allowed chocolate, and is highly skilled at making you feel guilty for not giving her something that would poison her. I read the label on the side of the box as I dip a biscuit into my tea.

HENRY FOX

LITTLE HEL

I frown. Where's the rest of the address? How did it get here without it? Maybe someone dropped it off. I rip off the tape and fold back the top of the box. Lying at the bottom is a book, the front cover worn and unrecognisable. I lift it out, feeling the weight in my hands, and flip open the front cover.

FAMILY BIBLE
To Mr & Mrs Edmund Fox
A gift from our family to yours, on your wedding day
6th October 1845

THIRTY-TWO

ELIZA

1881

Eliza watched the shadow in the corner of the room, listening to something scrape against the window, like fingers clawing to get in. *It's just the branches*, she told herself, moving closer to her husband. Cassius did not stir. He slept the sleep of someone who had never been haunted.

Night dragged on, the light and safety of morning still hours away, but despite the comfort of her husband beside her, Eliza could not rest. Every time she closed her eyes she saw the child again, her features illuminated by the flickering candle, and heard the baby crying, its wails turning to screams in her ears. Was it real? Her husband and mother-in-law seemed to think not, and yet she could not forget that image, could not force it from her mind. She knew what she had seen, but ghosts do not exist, do they?

As soon as the sun rose, Eliza dragged herself from the bed, pausing on the edge of the mattress for a moment before standing. Her legs felt weak, her limbs heavy with fatigue. She made her slow, painful way into the bathroom, where she used the lavatory and waited, shivering in her nightdress, for the bath to fill. *I have been ill*, she told herself as she slid into the water. She had had food poisoning, eaten something which did not agree with her, and it had made her see things. There were no children in this house, other than the one growing inside her, and only she knew of its existence. *Ghosts do not exist. Ghosts do not exist.* But her mother-in-law was hiding something, of that she was certain, and she was not sure if she wanted to find out what it was.

She stayed in the bath until the water was cold, when Cassius finally stirred and came into the bathroom.

'How are you this morning, my dear?' he asked. 'Better, I trust?'

'Yes,' she said, unsure who she was trying to convince. She forced herself to smile. 'Much better. Thank you for staying with me, darling.'

Cassius nodded, holding out a hand to help her from the bath. Wrapped in her dressing gown, Eliza sat at the dressing table, staring into her own eyes in the mirror as if searching for something, while her husband washed. She could tell by the way he had avoided her gaze as he wrapped her in a towel that he had not been convinced by her recovery. Perhaps she had shamed him last night, with her outburst in the nursery. She must not slip from his good graces. She should tell him today of her pregnancy, and then write to her mother. Though it was still early, she desperately wanted to share her good news. She would write about the baby and invite her parents to stay at Helygen House. She would not mention the child she saw in the nursery. She would not give life to her imaginings. She straightened in the chair, reaching out for the brush and beginning to smooth out her hair while Cassius went into his bedroom to get dressed. *I am Eliza Fox, a woman grown, wife and soon-to-be mother*, she told herself firmly as Mary came in to dress her. *I am not afraid of the dark.*

Downstairs, Cassius was drinking coffee when Eliza entered the room. The scent hit her like a blow and she tried to fight against the nausea rising inside her. She sat down opposite her husband, offering him a smile, but his eyes went straight to the newspaper folded up beside him. He was due in St Austell again today for a meeting with some potential investors. He was stressed, she could see it in his jerky movements as he cut up his breakfast, his brow furrowed as he read the news. He did not need his sleep disturbed by her wild visions.

A cup of tea was placed before her, and she was surprised to find Harriet there with a small plate containing some eggs and a sausage. 'Thank you,' she said politely, though the food did not look appealing. She sipped her tea, the sugar sweet on her tongue, then cut a small piece of sausage and popped it into her mouth, feeling her mother-in-law's gaze upon her. 'Very good,' she murmured when she had forced the mouthful down. The nausea was passing, she realised gratefully, as she slowly made her way through the food.

'I must get on,' Cassius said, startling her. She had not had a chance to tell him her news, and he did not even look at her as he rose and left the room. What had upset him so? He had been kind to her last night, even spending the night and comforting her, but was he furious with her after all? She looked down at her empty plate, her stomach cramping with anxiety.

'He is a very busy man,' Harriet said as if reading her mind. 'He has no time for the troubles of women.' She looked pointedly at Eliza's stomach. 'He was under the impression that you were . . . unable.'

Eliza stared at the older woman. 'Unable?' Then her meaning dawned and she felt herself flush. So they knew. Cassius must have seen her stomach as she got out of the bath. Was that the reason for his change in attitude towards her? 'I see. I had . . . I had not dared to hope, but I thank God that it has happened.' She saw a flicker of something pass over Harriet's face, a brief glimpse at her true feelings before she slipped the mask back on. Fear.

'Excuse me,' Eliza said, rising from her chair. 'I must write to my mother of my news.' Without waiting for a response, she hurried from the room, feeling, as she often did, as if she was entangled in some kind of game with her mother-in-law. A game she was destined to lose.

Dearest Mama,

I hope this letter finds you and Papa in the best of health. I am writing with the most wonderful news – I am with child! Cassius and I are overjoyed, of course. We hope you will come to visit when the child is born. I am told Helygen House is at its best during the summer, or perhaps you would wish to visit sooner, for Christmas? It would be our pleasure to receive you here any time.

Cassius is working hard on his new business venture. A friend of his has recently come on board, and my husband is most confident. I know very little about it but he says the china clay industry is booming, and he has high hopes for the mine. I am very proud of him, as I know you will be too.

What news from home? Is Uncle Frank still on the continent? I do hope he is well, and that we will see you all again soon.

Your loving daughter,

Eliza

She sighed, thinking of all the things she could not say, and began to search the writing desk for an envelope. She pulled open drawers to find spare pens and more sheets of paper, a rubber stamp and a spare bottle of ink. Pushing the chair back, she opened the cupboard beneath the desk and found a stack of envelopes sitting neatly at the bottom, but when she reached in for one, her hand knocked against the shelf above and the contents spilled out onto the floor. She cursed under her breath as she dropped to her knees to retrieve the papers. They were folded, some a few sheets thick. Curious, she opened one of them and began to read the words inside. Her throat tightened as she read, picking up another and another, finding them all covered in the same words.

Help me. They are trying to kill me. I am Ada Fox. Help me.

THIRTY-THREE

JOSIE

2019

I have never seen a book like this before. I've never even heard of a family bible. It appears to be a King James Bible but with additional pages at the front detailing the Fox family tree, with the first entry dating back to October 1845, when Mrs Fox, whoever she was, received it as a wedding present. I scan down the entries, not recognising most of the names.

6th October 1845: Edmund Fox m. Harriet Hale
26th August 1846: Edgar Fox b.
4th September 1847: Edgar Fox d. (1 year). Fever
17th November 1847: Clara Fox b.
26th August 1849: Cassius Fox b.
12th March 1853: Maisie Fox b.
9th September 1854: Benjamin Fox b.

15th April 1859: Maisie Fox d. (6 years). Drowning
1st January 1862 Clara Fox d. (14 years). Murder
21st September 1864: Edmund Fox (43 years) & Benjamin
*   Fox (8 years), d. Fever*
13th October 1864: Archie Fox & Flora Fox b., twins
7th May 1865: Archie Fox, d. (6 months). Suffocation
UNREADABLE
3rd September 1881: Cassius Fox m. Eliza Atkins
21st December 1881: Fire at Helygen House

I sit back, the book heavy on my lap. So that's when the west wing of Helygen House burned down, in 1881, and nobody has managed to restore it in all the years since? No names are listed beside the entry, so did it kill anyone? Or did the family manage to escape? I had been wanting to know more about Henry's family, of Willow's heritage, but this list does not go beyond the fire. What happened to Eliza? Did she and Cassius have children? They must have done, but it looks as if they had only been married for a few months before the fire, so what happened to them afterwards? I know the house passed to Alice's father after the Second World War, so someone must have inherited before then, after Cassius. I wonder if Alice has seen this bible and whether she would like to add to it. It seems like something she would be proud to own. But who would have sent it to Henry?

I read the entries again, sympathy washing over me. Poor Harriet, to have given birth seven times and for only one of her children to make it into adulthood. No – two. I cannot find a mention of Flora's death, so she must have survived beyond the fire at least. I think of Willow's birth and shudder. If something like that had happened in the 1800s, both Willow and I may well have died. Death in childbirth was so common back then, it's a wonder the human race continued at all. And SIDS, which I assume is what caused Archie's death, though they didn't know it then, is still a concern today. So much tragedy to befall one family, in such a short space of time.

My eyes find Clara's entry. Murder. There is no mention of her killer or any details at all, but it must have been reported at the time. Perhaps I can find some old newspapers online. A glance at the clock tells me it is too late to go further down this rabbit hole; somehow it is almost ten o'clock. I have lost hours to this mystery, and I am left with more questions than answers.

My eyes are drawn to the line between Archie's death and Cassius's marriage to Eliza. It is scratched out, the pen lines so deep I can feel them beneath my fingers. What happened here, between 1865 and 1881? What has someone tried to erase?

I am woken the next morning by my phone ringing. I snatch it up without checking the caller ID.

'Hello?'

'Hello, may I speak to Josie?'

'Speaking.'

'It's DS Fergus here. Is this a good time?'

I rub grit from my eyes, trying to wake myself up properly. 'Yes, of course. Hi. What can I do for you? Is this about the CCTV?'

A pause. 'Uh, no. It's about the discovery, on your property. Forensics have come back, and it would appear that the bones are over a hundred years old.'

I blink, absorbing the information. The family tree in the bible comes back to me, the list of children who died. Could it have been one of them? 'Oh,' I say quietly. 'I see.'

'Which means you can go back to what you were doing,' DS Fergus says as if I haven't spoken.

'The renovations? They can restart?' A flicker of excitement as he agrees. As interested as I am in the past, in the story behind the skeleton buried beneath the stables and the Fox family tree, I am even more interested in the future. Helygen House depends on it. 'Thank you for letting me know.'

Willow starts to cry, so I hang up and dress quickly before picking her up and taking her into the nursery. It's almost half past eight and she only woke once in the night, so she must be hungry. I change her then feed her as I make myself a slice of toast in the kitchen to stop my own stomach grumbling. It is only as I'm stepping into my shoes that I realise Ivy hasn't appeared. She sometimes likes to stay in bed if we get up too early, but she would usually have come down for breakfast by now.

'Ivy!' I call, strapping Willow into the freshly washed

baby carrier. I stand at the bottom of the stairs and whistle, straining my ears for the tell-tale whomp of her wagging tail against the door frame. Nothing. I'm about to go upstairs when I hear a scrabbling at the patio doors and turn to see the dog standing on her hind legs, front paws battering against the glass. 'What on earth?' I hurry over to unlock the doors, grimacing as she tracks mud across the living room floor. She is soaked through, her usually light fur dark and flattened against her, her legs and belly coated in mud. 'Where have you been?' I ask, as if she can answer, as I snatch some paper towels from the kitchen side and try to rub the worst of the mud off. I try to think back to last night, to when I let her out for the last time. She did come back in, didn't she? Of course she did, she must have done. I wouldn't have left her out overnight. What kind of dog owner would that make me?

'I'm sorry, girl,' I murmur as I dry off her paws. She needs a proper bath, something Henry always did because Ivy is too heavy for me to lift, even without a caesarean scar to worry about, so she'll have to make do with a shower now. 'Come on then.' She follows me upstairs, tilting her head when I open the cubicle door and gesture for her to go inside. 'I haven't got all day,' I say with a smile, and she walks in, far too big for the space. Willow wriggles against me and I go to fetch her Moses basket, placing it on the floor and unclipping the carrier. 'We can't have you getting wet too, can we?'

I turn on the shower, holding the spray against the glass

while I find the right temperature, then begin hosing off the dog. She never fails to get into any river or pond you pass by, and she's forever swimming in the lake here, leaping through the water like a salmon, which is why she isn't left alone outside for any length of time. But how did she get out today? I'm certain she came to bed with me last night, but perhaps she didn't. Perhaps I'm losing my mind.

THIRTY-FOUR

HARRIET

12th July 1873

I have not written for some time. I have hardly dared put my thoughts to paper, lest he find them and discover what I have suspected for a long time but have never been able to prove. Even though he has been away these last years, first to boarding school and then to university, I know that he has his spies. That he keeps track of me. He has spent the past three years abroad in Germany, learning whatever young men learn in foreign countries, and he has not visited since last Christmas. But next month he will return, and he has written to tell me that he will not be coming alone.

I should have expected this. He is a young man of twenty-four, almost at his majority. He stands to inherit this estate and must begin to turn his mind to the family business. There is nobody else to do it, after all. Not since Archie and

Flora were taken from me. I did everything I could to keep them safe, but it was not enough. I have shrouded myself in grief for years now, haunting these rooms like a ghost, my features unrecognisable in the darkened windows. Most of the servants are gone now, for one woman alone does not need much looking after. I tend the gardens myself, a pastime I find soothing, watching life bloom beneath my fingertips, though a boy still comes to cut the grass and snip the hedges into shape. Even Sara is gone now, and, in truth, it was her death which was the final straw. I was convinced that she had been poisoned, but of course, the doctor did not listen to the ravings of an old woman, mad with grief. When did I become her, this madwoman who should not be listened to? Sara was a good woman, one I shall never see the like of again. I do miss her, especially on cold winter nights when the darkness comes so very early in the day and seems to last forever. But it is summer now, the days are long and the weather is fair, and my son is coming home. Perhaps he will be changed, now that he has a wife. Perhaps he will again be the boy I so desperately want him to be, and not the monster he has become.

15th August 1873

She is beautiful, my new daughter-in-law. Indeed, my first and only. She has hair the colour of wheat, shiny and long and oft pinned up in complicated dos. Her eyes are the blue of the sky, and though she is tall, she is slim and dainty with it, and so she does not appear to overshadow Cassius. Though I do not believe anyone could do so.

He has grown a moustache, one which makes him resemble his father so closely that, when he stepped down from the carriage this morning, I was transported back in time to when I first arrived at Helygen House as a new wife, clasping Edmund's arm. He is just as dashing as his father was, though at times his confidence spills over into cockiness. But this is not new for Cassius. He has always been very clear about what the world owes him.

I could not help the flash of fear I felt when she first took my hand in the drawing room, her gloved fingers gently clasping mine. For I saw the way my son looked at her, like a wolf sizing up a hare, waiting for the right time to strike. But what can I do? I am powerless in this house. It is no longer my home. It is theirs now, his. I am simply a guest. And yet I could not force myself to smile warmly at this new arrival, for I was so full of fear for her future. I simply nodded, averting my gaze from her wide, innocent eyes, and extricated my fingers from her grip.

'Welcome to Helygen House,' I said, unable to keep the stiffness from my voice. 'It is a pleasure to meet you, Ada.'

THIRTY-FIVE

ELIZA

1881

Head spinning, Eliza scooped up the letters, tucking them into her sleeve and hurrying out of the room. Ada Fox. Who was Ada Fox? Her mind was so full of chaos that she ran straight into a figure in the corridor, who reached out and grasped her by the upper arms.

'Steady,' Cassius said, his voice light, but his grip was firm, almost painful. 'Where are you going in such a hurry?'

She wished he would release her. The discovery of Ada Fox made her want to cry out, to push him away. 'I have just written a letter to Mama,' she said, trying to calm her racing heart. 'I wish to post it today.'

'Have you indeed?' Cassius said, and she looked up to see his eyes were dark as coal. 'And might you, perchance, have enquired about your dowry?'

Eliza's heart sank. 'It . . . it has not been paid?' she stammered, knowing the answer.

'I do believe your father said it would be sent within the month after we were wed, and yet here we are, and it has not appeared.'

'I will enquire,' she said, trying to move out of his grip. A pause, a fleeting moment where it seemed like he would not let her go, her stomach clenching in panic, and then she was free, moving around him towards the stairs.

'I will see you at dinner,' he called after her, and something in his tone made it sound like a threat.

She locked the bedroom door behind her and leaned against it, trying to take deep, calming breaths. Pressing one hand to the front of her dress, she reached into her sleeve with the other and pulled out the bundle of papers. Something was pressing in on her, some kind of foreboding, a feeling that she should not read what was contained within these letters, and yet she knew she must. She had to discover the truth. She had been living in Helygen House for almost two months now, and still she knew very little about her husband and his family. Cassius had been distracted lately, and she had believed it was due to the new business venture, but now she wondered what secrets he had been keeping from her. And what had Harriet said at breakfast? *He had thought you were unable.* Unable to conceive, to have children. But why would the discovery of her pregnancy cause him distress? Surely he would be happy, to have an heir to pass his legacy on to? Is that not what every man wanted?

Hands trembling, she read the words scribbled on the paper again, running a finger across the letters. Ada Fox. A sister? An aunt? Or a wife? Cassius was older than Eliza, almost thirty-two to her twenty years, but she had never really considered that he might have been married before. She took another deep breath before pushing off the door and making her way to the dressing table, where she laid out the sheets of paper. One by one she opened them, reading the same words over and over again. *Help me. They are trying to kill me.* The papers scattered as she tore through them, trying to find something else, something which would tell her who Ada Fox was and what had been happening to her. Her fingers trembled as she found something, this one a letter, addressed to a Mrs I. Stevens.

Mother, I beg of you, please send help. I should never have come. I should never have married him. I am not safe here.

Her stomach lurched as she recognised the address, a town she had visited often with her parents in her childhood. Had Cassius's first wife truly lived not ten miles away from Eliza? She knew her husband had attended university in Cambridge and had been visiting some old friends when they met, so perhaps there was a similarly simple explanation. Perhaps he had met Ada when he was still studying, then married her and brought her back to his ancestral home. There was nothing unusual in that, but it was clear now that Ada had been his wife, and Cassius had kept her a secret from her.

Please. I am not mad. They say I am mad, but I am not. Mrs Fox has been poisoning my food, I am certain of it now.

Eliza inhaled sharply, remembering the stomach pains and loose bowels she'd suffered from when she first arrived. Nerves, she had thought, too much rich food. But could Harriet have been poisoning her, like Ada seemed to believe? She shook her head. Surely not. Her mother-in-law was a cold fish, that much was true, but to poison her son's wives? No, it could not be true. Besides, she knew now that Eliza was with child and she would never harm her son's heir.

She shivered, reading on.

They no longer let me leave. I am trapped here, in this room, in this house. I long for the fresh air and the warmth of the sun on my skin, but they say I am ill and must stay abed. I am not ill. I know what I have seen, what he is hiding in there. I am not safe here. Mother, please come for me. Please. I fear for my life.

Eliza read the line again. *What he is hiding in there.* Cassius? What was he hiding, and where was it? *Is it still here?* Her eyes flitted around the bedroom, as if seeking possible hiding places. Helygen House was so large, there could be a thousand hiding places. *I could get lost here.* Her stomach clenched as she read the hastily scrawled words, the writing becoming more and more difficult to read.

Mother, why do you not come? Why do you not write? I am left here to suffer alone. Please, believe me. They will not stop until I am dead.
Mother, please.
Mother. MOTHER, PLEASE.

A loud bang sounded from above. Eliza jumped, dropping the papers. She watched them float to the floor, resting silently on the carpet beneath her feet. Her heart hammered in her chest as she lifted her gaze to the ceiling, as if she could see through the plaster into the room above. A bird, she told herself, or a servant putting things in storage for the winter. Another bang, this time on her bedroom door, making her jump again.

'Madam?' Mary's voice was muffled.

'Yes?' Eliza called breathlessly, one hand resting on her throat. Her gaze was drawn to the mirror and her own reflection there, her skin pale, her eyes wide. Ada's feverish writings had infected her, making her skittish.

'The mistress has asked you to join her for tea,' Mary said. 'In the dining room.'

'I will be there in a moment.' She listened to the maid's footsteps fade as she moved away from the door. Eliza stared at her reflection for a few seconds, willing herself to calm down. How could Ada have believed Cassius and his mother had wished her harm? She had not been well, Eliza told herself. She should not listen to the ramblings of a mad woman. And yet . . . She tried to dismiss Ada's words but they were starting to take hold of her, worming their way inside her and planting a seed of doubt. *What he is hiding . . .*

She glanced down at the papers she had dropped, bending to retrieve them. She squinted, trying to read the tiny writing scrawled in the top corner. *In the west wing.* What was in the west wing? It was closed off, unused, and had been for some time. Wasn't that what Cassius had said? She turned the paper over, and the breath caught in her throat. On the back of the sheet, words were scribbled in a different hand:

For the attention of Dr F. Brown, St Lawrence Hospital, Bodmin.

THIRTY-SIX

JOSIE

2019

I call the builders as I walk around the house towards the front door. The internal door has been locked since Flick came to stay and I intend to keep it that way, especially after what happened to Ivy last night. I need to keep a better grip on things. I check the lock multiple times a day now and have even placed one of Willow's toys in front of it, which would clatter across the floorboards if the door was opened. I'm leaving nothing to chance now.

I leave a message on Darren's voicemail to call me back with his availability, and, on a whim, send a message to Flick to ask her when she will be ready to start doing up The Hut. It's time to get things moving, before the slowness of Christmas grinds everything to a halt. It shouldn't take much longer than a few weeks for the builders to finish the first phase, then I can start ordering the bathroom suites and the kitchen units. It'll all need new flooring too, and I'm hoping the plumbing won't be too difficult to organise.

Despite the chill in the air, I feel a warmth inside that I haven't felt for a while. Excitement for the future, the feeling that making plans can give you. The feeling of looking forward instead of back. I try to grasp hold of it, clench it tightly between my fingers like a life raft. This is how we move on.

Willow is strapped to my chest again as I walk across the grounds, having left Ivy wrapped in a fluffy towel on her bed, gnawing on a fish chew. I need to speak to Alice about the renovation work and I want to ask her about what I found in the family bible, but something is giving me pause. It's as if Henry is beside me, a calm hand on my arm telling me to slow down, like he often did when he was alive. He was always so meticulous, often to the point of dithering, and it would sometimes infuriate me how he would agonise over the tiniest detail – which taps to have in the bathroom, which doormat in the hall – until I made the decision for us both. I suppose people would see me as bossy, though I suspect they'd never use that term if I were a man, but sometimes Henry needed a kick up the backside. And, sometimes, I needed a restraining hand, a word of caution. Something is telling me to listen to him now.

I find Alice in the dining room finishing a plate of scrambled eggs. I wonder, again, why she still uses this room. It could seat eighteen people, maybe more if we jiggled things around, which would be perfect for wedding breakfasts. I'll broach it with her again at some point, I decide, but not right now.

'Good morning,' she says, directing her smile at Willow, who turns her head towards the sound.

'Morning, Alice,' I say, hovering in the doorway. I suddenly feel out of place, not unwelcome exactly, but as if something is standing between us, keeping us at arm's length.

'Sit down, dear,' she says, raising one eyebrow. 'There's coffee in the pot.'

I go over to the sideboard instead and pour myself a cup before she can shout for Marie, then remember. 'Is Marie . . .?'

'She's fine. Back to full health and to work.' I open my mouth to speak but Alice raises a hand. 'Light duties only. No hoovering or heavy lifting, or anything like that.'

'She really ought to be resting,' I say, sitting down and adding a cube of sugar to my cup.

'She insisted on returning to work,' Alice says levelly. 'It was her choice.'

I don't mention that she, as Marie's boss, could have forced her to take extra leave, and given her full pay as well. Because if it's a choice between rest or money, is it really a choice at all?

'DS Fergus rang this morning,' I say instead, taking Willow out of the carrier and holding her in my arms. She stares up at the gallery wall, her tiny arms reaching out as if towards something. 'He said the bones are over a hundred years old, so there won't be an investigation.'

'Well, that's a relief!' Alice says with a short laugh. 'Do they know precisely how old they are?'

I shake my head. 'He didn't say so. There must not have been anything important going on here in the late 1800s.' She gives me a look. 'Historically speaking,' I add quickly. 'It's not like finding Richard the Third under a car park.'

'Indeed.'

'Although,' I continue, making shapes with my fingers in front of Willow's face. She grabs my thumb, fascinated by it. 'Something interesting did happen here then, didn't it?' Alice's face is unreadable as she sips her coffee. 'The fire? Henry never told me how it happened. Do you know?'

She brushes non-existent crumbs from the table. 'Oh, no. Not really.'

'Did anyone die?'

A pause. 'Why do you ask, Josie?'

I shrug. 'I'm just interested in Willow's heritage, that's all. In where she comes from.'

Alice sniffs. 'There isn't much to tell, really. My father inherited the estate when his father died in 1959, though he still lived in Australia and had never set foot on English soil, let alone visited Helygen House. It passed to my brother, George, when our father died in 1989. And then to Henry, when George died. The rest you know.'

'And before that? Did you know your grandparents?'

'My paternal grandfather died just before I was born and his wife soon after, so I never really knew them,' she says. 'My mother's parents lived in Adelaide, and we often spent

weekends and school holidays with them, but we never visited the UK as children.'

'When did George move here?'

'Oh, the early eighties, I believe. He was a . . . a homosex-
ual, you understand.' I almost laugh at the old-fashioned
term and try to hide it behind a cough. Alice flings me a
look before continuing. 'He had no children, so he left
everything to Henry.'

'Not to you?' I lean forward, my eyes on Alice's face. I
realise I am pushing the boundaries, pressing too hard. *Slow
down, Corbs*, Henry says, but I can't seem to help myself.
'Why was that? Why leave an estate to a toddler? It seems
so . . . bizarre.'

She avoids my gaze. 'It's just how it's done. Men inherit,
women don't. *Didn't*. But you've changed all of that, haven't
you?' She looks up, and I can't quite read the expression on
her face. 'You've changed so very much. And there's more
still to come, isn't there?'

THIRTY-SEVEN

HARRIET

18th September 1873

It is as I had feared. In the absence of a Fox in charge, the factories have been taken care of by the other directors of the company – or rather, they have been run into the ground by lazy, pompous men. Cassius was furious when he found out. He pretended that it was the men left in charge who he was angry with, but we all know it is me he blames. Everything had been left in trust until Cassius came of age, and I had no real power to do anything during that time. Women are only good for one thing, after all: producing an heir. And that is what he has decided he needs next.

'So this does not happen again,' he said pointedly at dinner tonight, after he had returned from his visit to the factory in Bodmin. With an heir and plenty of spares, he will not have to worry about any women messing things up for him. Ada and I will stay here, in Helygen House, quiet and meek and without fuss. What other choice do we have?

29th September 1873

Ada is unwell. This is the third time she has been kept abed by a stomach flu, though she bears it well and with good spirit. I have not yet seen her frown or look displeased. I ache to tell her that her sunny disposition will be her downfall.

Cassius had to call for the doctor today. He is a new one, closer to Cassius's age, and not someone I have engaged before. Ada was so unwell she could not even lift her head to drink. The new maid had to soak a cloth in water and press it to her lips. The doctor diagnosed a stomach ailment, caused or exacerbated by her excitement at being a new bride, apparently. The uterus can move around the body, he said, disturbing things. What things he did not quite explain. He prescribed plenty of rest and hearty foods, beef stew and vegetable soup. I will leave that in the capable hands of the cook, who is also new, from Germany. I am certain we will get used to her cooking in time. But I fear Ada will never get used to living at Helygen House. For her own sake, I hope she does not. I hope she disappears into the night and never looks back.

9th October 1873

Ada's parents joined us today. Her mother has been concerned about her daughter's ill health, but they seemed pleased that Ada was in much better spirits by the time they arrived. They are staying for a week, taking the opportunity to visit the sea and explore our beautiful county. It is strange having visitors again. I have had no one to stay in the years since Edmund died. Nobody wants a grieving widow at their soiree, after all.

Her mother, Iris, is so similar to Ada. A quiet beauty, ageing gracefully. Unlike myself, as Cassius likes to remind me. But her father is a rather rotund, loud man, with plenty of opinions and no care for those of others. No wonder his wife and daughter are so meek. He has beaten any life out of them.

I fear Cassius looks up to him. Though set in his ways, Edmund was never a harsh husband or father, but Ada's father can be quite cruel, and I see Cassius's eyes shining whenever this cruelty is dealt out. We three women sit in silence, even when we are taking tea alone while the men walk the estate or visit the factories. We sit in silence and drink our mint tea, our thoughts crowding the room until I fear the windows might shatter.

THIRTY-EIGHT

JOSIE

2019

I go back to the apartment and start tidying up the kitchen, which always seems to get into such a state. Flick rings just as I'm finishing the soup Halka set aside for my lunch. I keep my voice down, glancing at Willow in her Moses basket to check she's still sleeping.

'Hello, who's calling?' I say, putting on an accent.

She laughs. 'Yeah, yeah, tell me how bad a friend I am.'

'Well, now you mention it . . .'

'Has anyone ever told you that you're a twat?'

Now I laugh, too loudly. Willow stirs and I hold my breath until she closes her eyes again before whispering, 'You, all the time.'

We arrange for her to visit tomorrow, and to come armed with wallpaper and paint samples. I really need something to focus on, and until Darren calls me back about the stables, I'll just have to make do with The Hut. I do have other ideas bubbling away in the background, but I'm not sure how to orchestrate them yet. I feel so much closer to Henry when I'm thinking about our plans. This was his dream too, to open this beautiful estate up to others, for people to spend what is supposed to be the happiest day of their lives here with us. He was an old romantic really. He'd even fostered ideas about us renewing our vows here once everything was set up. He'd wanted to put a glass roof on the old, drained swimming pool, or completely renovate the ballroom, so people could get married here come rain or shine, but the cost would be astronomical.

'Someday,' I whisper to him as I load the dishwasher after I've eaten. We had so many dreams for this place, and now it's down to me to make it all happen. We used to lie in bed together, discussing what we would do if money were no object. A glass roof for the pool, a new ballroom, self-contained properties for holidaymakers. We wanted to open the main house up too, for weddings and private stays and tours. Henry wasn't very keen on the latter at first. He'd wanted to keep his family life and history private, and didn't like the idea of people poking around in his home. 'If you're going to do that,' he'd said, 'you may as well sell it to—'

'The National Trust, yes. I know.' I rolled my eyes at him, and he smiled in the way he did when he was probably going to change his mind.

The Foxes are hardly royalty or even gentry, but there is a rich history in this house, just waiting to be discovered. I know Henry had started to dig into his family history, but not how far he'd got or even where he kept his research. His laptop has been taken by the police, but . . .

I freeze, a dirty mug clutched between my fingers. Henry's phone. The CCTV is connected to an app on Henry's phone. Where is it? Did the police find it? I curse myself for not pressing DS Fergus more on the CCTV, but I had been too caught up in the bones and the family bible.

Dropping the mug back into the sink, I rush into Henry's office, tearing open drawers and shoving papers out of the way. Nothing. I jog upstairs and search his bedside table, finding only an old Kindle and a mess of charging cables, but no phone. I never bothered to download the CCTV app, an act I'm suddenly cursing myself for now. Is that why the police can't seem to access the footage? Surely there are ways around these things, but in truth, I have no idea how it all works. If I could just find his phone . . . I check coat pockets and open kitchen drawers, riffling through the detritus one collects over time, before going back into his office. The walls are lined with shelves, filled with books and a few medals from his running days. I could go through this room with a fine toothcomb, but the police must already have done that. If there was anything to find, they would have found it.

I exhale, slumping down in his chair and closing my eyes. No matter which way I turn, there always seems to be something blocking me. Something stopping me from finding out the truth. Opening my eyes, my gaze finds a torn piece of paper sticking out from beneath a notebook. Pinching the corner, I pull it out to see something written in Henry's untidy handwriting.

Lead, kindly light, amid the encircling gloom
Lead thou me on
The night is dark, and I am far from home
Lead thou me on
Keep thou my feet, I do not ask to see
The distant scene, one step enough for me

At the bottom of the verse is another sentence.

Hymn for christening? Corbs won't like it.

Laughter bubbles up in my throat at the same time as tears spill from my eyes. It's a hymn, something Henry must have found and written out. He'd mentioned having our daughter christened, but we'd never decided on it either way. As I read the words again, recognition suddenly slams into me. *The night is dark, and I am far from home.* Henry's note. What if what the police found hadn't been a suicide note at all, but part of a note to himself?

I feel the urge to go digging rise up inside me. Alice won't like it, but something's telling me that someone wants me to find out what happened. That Henry wants me to find out the truth. Why else would the family bible have been sent here? Even though it was addressed to Henry and not me.

Perhaps he'd stumbled across some papers during his renovation planning or his own research. Either way, I have to find out the truth about Henry's family history. It's Willow's future, after all.

While Willow naps, I open my laptop and google 'Clara Fox death'. Not much comes up, except for one article in the *Royal Cornwall Gazette*. I have to create an account, frustration building as I am told my email address is already in use, and several minutes pass until I can open the article.

2ⁿᵈ January 1862
New year's woes for Fox family
The eldest daughter of prominent factory owner Edmund
Fox was found dead in the early hours of this morning.
It is believed that a member of the family raised the
alarm during a new year's party, and the body of Clara
Fox was discovered on the rocks below the cliff
on the estate. An arrest has been made.

The article is frustratingly short. I scroll through the site, trying to find any further information, but there is nothing, not even who was arrested or whether they were convicted. I sit back. If Clara Fox was pushed off a cliff, what happened to the other children? How did they all die? I know infant mortality was much higher in the 1800s than it is now, but was it normal for a wealthy family to lose so many children?

I spend the rest of the afternoon online, searching for references to the Fox family. I discover that Edmund Fox had owned several factories in Cornwall, which all closed in the years after his death. His cause of death was easy to find – a fever, which also killed one of his children, Benjamin – and the factories were run by the other directors until his remaining son, Cassius, came of age. It seems as though they were mismanaged, and by the time Cassius took over there were none left, sold to pay off debts, though the figures mean very little to me, and I wonder if that was when Helygen House's financial troubles started.

I find several mentions of china clay, the names Fox and Dixon coming up a few times in reference to the clay pits in St Austell. I frown. St Austell is about fifteen miles from here, close enough for Cassius to have business there, I suppose, and it makes sense for him to have moved into the industry. The china clay industry was booming around that time – a quick Google search tells me that 120 million tonnes have been extracted from St Austell alone – and his father's factories had been involved in manufacturing parts for tin mines on the north coast. While tin and copper mining were decreasing, china clay was on the up, but it seems as if the Fox family has never been any good at holding on to money. From the scant information available, it looks as though Cassius's ventures failed.

Willow's cries snap me out of the hole I've dug myself into. I remember this feeling from university, when you'd be so deep in research that it took a while to bring yourself back to the present. I hurry up the stairs, stepping over Ivy who is stretched out across the bedroom door, and lift Willow from her cot.

'Hello, little one,' I whisper, settling down in the rocking chair to feed her. I remember that I should have called the midwife again and swear under my breath. Instead of chasing after Henry's ancestors, I should be focusing on his daughter. Our daughter. Although my body has been healing from the birth, it feels as if my mind has been going the other way, my memory becoming unreliable, my attention span shorter than usual. Perhaps it is the routine of being a new mum which is muddling my brain, letting the OCD seep back in. I gnaw on my bottom lip, trying to ignore the compulsion to touch my fingers together.

But, I remind myself crossly, I am still grieving. I shouldn't feel guilty for not being on top form. But I *do* need to get myself together. My mind has been playing tricks on me, and Flick's jumpiness the last time she was here didn't help. I hope she's more focused when she arrives tomorrow. I don't have time to go chasing after ghosts.

THIRTY-NINE

ELIZA

1881

The paper trembled between her fingers as she read the words.

Dear Dr F. Brown,

I am writing to request your assistance with a rather delicate matter. I hope I can rely on your absolute discretion.

My wife, Ada, has been increasingly unwell over the past few months. She has always had a sensitive constitution, and unfortunately she recently suffered the loss of a pregnancy. Since then, she has been prone to fits of hysterics. She has, I must confess, even begun to harm herself. I am increasingly worried about her health, and find myself in the embarrassing position of needing your help. Please attend Helygen House at your earliest convenience.

Yours respectfully,

Cassius Fox

Her stomach cramped and she ran into the bathroom, only just making it to the sink before she threw up, her husband's words swirling in her mind. *Worried about her mental health . . . Suffered the loss of a pregnancy . . .*

Had the letter never been sent? Or had Cassius written to the doctor again, or engaged him in another way? She ran the tap and splashed her face with water, rinsing her mouth and washing her hands. Her fingers gripped the edge of the sink, her eyes watching the water running down the plughole. A melody drifted towards her then, the sound of someone singing sweetly. It sounded like a child. She remembered the girl in the nursery, and fear rippled through her. It wasn't real, it couldn't be. She turned off the tap and the singing stopped, cut off like a hand across a mouth. She looked up, catching her own eye in the mirror, and noticed that the cabinet door was slightly ajar. She opened it, staring at spare bars of soap and razor blades, her mind slow like wading through mud, before closing it again with a snap. But now, it was not her own face she saw in the mirror. It was the face of a child, a girl of five or six, with long hair made dark by the water coating it. Droplets ran down her face as if she were standing beneath a raincloud, her thin nightdress clinging to her like a second skin. Her eyes were closed, her mouth open wide, a deep, dark hole from which words began to pour. 'Mother. Help me. Mother. MOTHER!'

The mirror cracked then shattered, glass falling into the sink below. Eliza gasped, staggering back until her legs hit the bath. Her heart was pounding in her chest as she stared at the broken mirror, one hand pressed against her cheek, the other against her stomach, attempting to reach the baby inside her. *The baby.* She took a deep breath, trying to centre herself, trying to calm herself down, but she couldn't control her trembling. She hurried from the bathroom on unsteady legs, tearing open the bedroom door to reveal Mary waiting on the landing. She jumped back as if startled.

'What is it, madam?' the maid asked as Eliza shut the door firmly behind her. The hallway was plunged into darkness, with all the doors closed and the only light coming from the window over the stairs. Why had someone not brightened this house up, torn down these dark wooden doors and installed more windows? She felt like she was half blind, constantly fumbling through the darkness. Perhaps she could do something with the place herself, revamp this wing to make it more open, more child friendly. Then she remembered the vision in the mirror and shuddered. *I'm losing my mind.*

'N-nothing,' she stammered, reaching out for the banister, the wood cold beneath her fingertips.

'I am to escort you, madam,' Mary said, fiddling with the hem of her apron. Eliza was confused for a moment before remembering that Harriet was waiting for her in the dining room.

'I am not an invalid,' Eliza snapped, trying to focus on her anger instead of the child's face in the mirror. *It isn't real. It isn't real.* Mary flushed and looked away, and Eliza regretted the venom in her voice almost immediately. 'Forgive me,' she said, fighting to keep her voice level. 'I am . . . not myself.'

'Is it the baby, madam?'

Eliza stared at the maid. 'How did you . . .?'

'My gran has the second sight,' Mary whispered. 'Says I do too. You are with child then, madam?' Eliza nodded dumbly, and Mary sniffed. 'There you are then. Gran says it's normal. What with the sickness and all, it can make you unwell.'

Eliza considered her words. She was not herself, that much was true. Perhaps the pregnancy *was* affecting her brain, and the crazed letters from Ada were not helping. Did she conjure that vision in the mirror, like she had the child in the nursery? Could it really all be because of the baby inside her?

'Thank you, Mary,' she murmured, indicating that the maid should lead the way. 'I appreciate your kindness. And I would also appreciate your discretion.'

Mary glanced back as she descended the stairs. 'Of course, madam. My lips are sealed.'

Downstairs, Eliza was surprised to find Cassius seated at the dining table beside his mother, a pot of tea in front of them. 'This is a nice surprise,' she said as she took her own seat, her hands trembling in her lap. 'I hadn't expected to see you until this evening, husband.'

'Mother has confirmed your news,' he said, his voice crisp. Eliza glanced at Harriet, who avoided her gaze. 'That you are with child?'

'Yes,' Eliza said, forcing herself to smile. 'I believe it will be a summer baby. I—'

'I was reliably informed,' Cassius said, cutting her off, 'that you were unable to have children. After . . . well, after what happened last year.'

Eliza felt the colour drain from her cheeks, her smile slipping away. 'Reliably informed . . . By whom?'

'Your father, of course.'

'And . . . and what did he tell you?'

Now Cassius glanced at his mother, who still did not speak. 'That you were . . . damaged. Irrevocably.'

'And you married me in spite of this?' Realisation dawned then and Eliza felt her stomach drop. 'No. You married me *because* of this. You do not want children?' Shock hit her like an icy wave. She and Cassius had never discussed starting a family, but she did not expect she would need to. It was the next logical step, after all. Marriage, children. Like lunch comes after breakfast, one day after another. It was the only path for her, for women like her. The right path. The respectable path. Cassius cleared his throat, avoiding her gaze. 'Is it because of Ada?' The words were out before she could stop them. She felt rather than saw Harriet jump beside her.

Cassius's face hardened, his eyes narrowing. 'What do you know of Ada?'

'N-nothing,' Eliza stammered, her heart hammering in her chest. 'I just . . . I just saw a mention of her, that's all, something in the writing desk when I was looking for an envelope for my letter to my mother.' She swallowed, hardly daring to ask the next question. 'Was she your wife? Before me?'

Cassius slammed a fist on the table, upsetting the sugar bowl. Cubes rolled across the wood, tiny specks scattering. Harriet seemed to shrink into herself, becoming a version of herself which Eliza had not seen before. She found she was more surprised by Harriet's reaction than Cassius's anger. Had she always suspected he had darkness lurking beneath the surface?

'Your father is a damned liar,' he hissed, pointing a finger at Eliza. 'And a cheat. Where is your dowry, Eliza?'

She remembered that she'd said she would mention it in her letter to home. 'I will add a note to Papa and send it today, I swear it.' She swallowed again, her eyes stinging with the threat of tears. 'There will be a perfectly reasonable excuse for the delay. But . . . well, is there such a great need for it? I thought the china clay business was going well.' Instantly she knew she had said the wrong thing. She had never seen her husband like this before, and she suddenly realised that he terrified her. Ada's words rang inside her head. *I am not safe here.*

Cassius stood, placing both fists on the table and leaning towards his wife. She cowered in her chair, suddenly desperate to be away from him, this man she had pledged to love and honour and obey. *Obey.* The word repeated in her mind. Would she obey him in everything? Would she be forced to?

'Choose your questions wisely, Eliza,' he said quietly, his eyes pinning her to the spot. 'You may not like the answers you receive.'

264

FORTY

JOSIE

2019

Flick arrives early the next day, finding me still in my pyja-
mas, Willow clamped to my left breast. I let her in, yawning,
and wave a hand at the kitchen. 'Excuse the mess, I've not
had a chance to tidy up the breakfast things yet.'

'You call a plate and a knife in the sink "a mess"?' Flick
says, raising an eyebrow. 'Have you had a cuppa yet?' Her
eyes find the mug on the side, still full of now-cold tea.
'Right, go and sit down. I'll put the kettle on.'

'But—'

'No buts. Sit down.' She opens her bag and slides out a
few sheets of paper. 'Look over these while I make the tea.'

I take the bundle and Willow, whose mouth is still
clamped firmly around my nipple, sending sparks of pain
through me, over to the sofa and sit down. Although it
hasn't been too bad, breastfeeding isn't as easy or enjoyable

as I'd hoped it might be. I don't know what I'd expected it to feel like, but the pain was a surprise, and these days, Willow seems determined to stay on until she has bled me dry. I have to forcibly remove her to swap breasts or when I feel she has had enough, her eyes glaring up at me as if to accuse me of starving her. But how do I know if she is getting enough milk? It's not as if I can measure it out, like you can with formula. Maybe she's still hungry.

I swap her to the right side, grimacing through the pain as I start to read the papers Flick gave me. The first sheet is a bullet point list of things she needs: paint, hooks, storage boxes. A smoke alarm, electric heater and units for a small kitchenette, complete with sink and coffee machine. The next page is a sketch of The Hut, marking out the kitchen, changing room and toilet.

'You've really thought this through,' I say when Flick comes over holding two steaming mugs of tea. 'It looks great.'

'I've had a lot of time to get it right,' she says, sitting down opposite me. 'I think it's the perfect space for the classes. So peaceful.' I fight the urge to make a face, remembering the way she was the last time she was here. I'd say *peaceful* is quite the opposite of how she felt. She looks at me as if she's read my mind. 'You know, last time I was here,' she says, the words coming slowly as if she is carefully choosing each one, 'it was weird, but I felt like I wasn't myself. Like I wasn't in control of my emotions.' She shrugs. 'Probably hormonal.'

'That isn't very feminist of you,' I say with a smile.

She laughs. 'You know what I'm like during the time of the month. Frustratingly cliché. Tears and chocolate and hot water bottles.'

'And seeing ghosts?' I venture and her smile slips.

'Yeah. That was weird, wasn't it?' Her eyes slide away from mine and I can tell she doesn't want to talk about it anymore. But it *was* weird. Flick has always been spiritual, in the sense that she believes that we go somewhere when we die, and that we can leave an imprint on people and objects after we're gone. Like Halka, I suppose, Flick probably believes that this house retains an essence of everyone who lived here. Even Henry. Maybe even me, someday. I try to take comfort in that, the idea that a part of Henry is here with us, as I gently remove Willow from my breast and begin to pat her on the back.

'She didn't want to let go,' Flick muses.

I sigh. 'It's like she's constantly hungry. I keep meaning to call the midwife about it actually.'

'Are you concerned?'

'I'm not sure. A bit, I suppose. She sleeps a lot too. I know, I know,' I add when Flick smiles, 'what new mum complains that their baby is sleeping too much? But I'm worried it *is* too much. That she's not getting what she needs because she's asleep all the time.'

Flick places a hand on my arm. 'I'm sure she's fine,' she says softly, 'but you should get in touch with your midwife if you're worried. Couldn't you book an appointment online or send an email?'

'That's a good idea. I left a message but didn't hear back. I'll have a look online later.' Willow burps and I feel a trickle run down my back at the precise moment that I remember I didn't put a towel over my shoulder. 'Bloody hell,' I mutter, standing. 'I need to get changed.' I look around for somewhere to put Willow, but her Moses basket isn't in sight. Did I take it upstairs yesterday? Why can't I remember where I put it?

'Here,' Flick says, reaching her arms out. 'Give her to me.' I hesitate, and I see a flicker of pain cross her face as she notices.

'I'm sorry,' I say quickly, passing Willow over. 'Thank you. I'll only be a minute.' I run up the stairs, holding on to the banister so I don't slip in my socks, and strip off my dirty top. The washing basket is full; I can't remember the last time I did a load. Jesus, what is wrong with me? *Get it together, Corbs,* Henry says, but his voice is missing its usual mirth. He sounds annoyed. Even the ghost of my dead husband is disappointed in me.

I change out of my clothes and run a brush through my hair before hurrying back downstairs. I almost trip over Ivy as she shoots past me into the living room, noticing first that the patio doors are open, and that Flick and Willow are nowhere in sight.

'Flick?' I call, my heart in my throat. Ivy hurtles out into the garden, her ears flapping as she picks up speed. I follow, quickening my pace until I'm jogging, the grass cold and damp beneath my socked feet. 'Flick!' I see Ivy round the willow tree ahead and start to run after her. How did Flick manage to get all the way down here so quickly? I look back at the house and feel my blood run cold as my eyes land on a window in the west wing. Someone is standing there, a baby in their arms. Willow. They are holding Willow.

I stop, almost slipping over on the muddy ground. I'm right next to the lake now, the water frozen in places, the wet spreading up my sock and the bottom of my leggings. It's freezing cold out here, barely above zero degrees, and I feel my body begin to tremble as I watch the figure in the window turn away.

'No!' I cry, at the same time as Ivy lets out a bark. I spin around to find Flick standing outside The Hut, holding Willow to her chest as Ivy growls at her. 'Ivy!' She doesn't turn around until I grab hold of her collar, and it's as if she's snapped out of a trance. She turns to me, licking her lips several times, her ears flattened against her skull. She whines and I reach out to comfort her, putting an arm around her neck. 'Silly girl,' I murmur, pressing my lips against her head. I look up at Flick, who is still staring at Ivy with wide eyes. 'Is everything okay? Why are you out here? It's freezing.' I straighten, holding my arms out for Willow. She hasn't even got a coat on. 'Flick?' I wave a hand in front of her face. 'Can you give her to me?'

She jumps as if startled, her eyes finally finding mine. 'S-sorry,' she stammers, passing Willow to me. I hold her close against my chest, her face nuzzling into my neck. 'I just wanted to show her The Hut.' She looks down at my feet. 'Oh. You haven't got any shoes on.'

'Neither have you,' I say, nodding towards her own bare feet. I frown at my friend. 'What's going on, Flick?' She doesn't answer, her eyes fixed on a point behind me, and I glance back towards the house, looking for the figure in the window, but they're all dark. 'Flick?'

'I know,' she says with a bark of laughter. 'I know, it must look mad. I'm not mad, though. I'm not.'

'I know you're not,' I say quickly. 'Let's get back to the house and warm up. My feet feel like they're going to fall off.'

'You do believe me, don't you, Josie?' Flick asks as we begin to walk back, Ivy just ahead of us like she's scouting the way.

I pause, not knowing what to say, or even what she's asking me to believe. She's giving off the same energy as when she tried to throw herself off Waterloo Bridge, all jerky movements and avoiding eye contact. Maybe the break-up with Jaz is taking its toll on her. Maybe being around a baby is too difficult at the moment. But how can I say that without destroying her confidence, along with our friendship?

'Of course,' I say, placing a hand on her shoulder. 'Let's have a cup of tea. I might even be able to rustle up some biscuits too, if you're lucky.'

FORTY-ONE

HARRIET

24th December 1873

Christmas. It used to be my favourite time of year, when the children would gather around the tree we had decorated together. Edmund had never decorated a tree until we were married; his mother always had the servants do theirs. But it was one of my favourite things to do when I was a girl, me, Mama and Alexandrina placing sparkling baubles on the branches, Papa lifting one of us to position the star at the top. We were supposed to take it in turns, but since Alexandrina was named for our queen, it was always my sister who was chosen.

Christmas Eve was the most magical of days throughout our marriage. Edmund would be home by luncheon and we would dine on roasted goose with sage and onion dressing, and plum pudding for afters, before getting into our coats and hats and going into the village. We did not often visit the village as a family, though we were of course well known and were customers of the butcher's, baker's and other shops, but on Christmas Eve we made the fifteen-minute journey on foot to visit The King's Head pub for a glass of mulled wine and to join in with the carol singing. All the village children would get together, standing in rows with the smallest at the front, and for a moment, it was forgotten that we were the Foxes, landowners and employers to many in the region, and our children were just the same as everyone else's, with pink cheeks and wide smiles.

I find myself lost in my memories more these days. I wonder if I can identify the moment it all began, a single event which set my son on this dark path, but there is nothing. Or rather, there are hundreds of moments, each one as small as a raindrop, and together they became a lake, high enough to drown us all.

Cassius was the only one who did not seem to enjoy visiting the village. I can see that now. He used to sneer at the other children when they tried to speak with him, mocking their too-small boots or their mittens with holes in. Edmund spoke sharply to him one year, telling him that he should be gracious towards those who have less than we do, and while I was proud of my husband for his ethics, I was concerned that Cassius did not hear the lesson that was intended. No, I fear that he took his father's words as justification for being cruel to the village children for being born into less fortunate families than ours. He has always been this way, though I did not always see it. I once saw him knock one of the farmer's boys into the lake and simply stand by while the poor child flailed, unable to swim, until Clara intervened. I should have seen it then. I should have known what my son would become, but instead I closed my eyes to it, and now we must all suffer. But I fear it will be Ada who suffers most of all.

18th February 1874

My worst fear has come true. Ada is with child.

I remember each time I realised that I was pregnant. I often knew early on, as if something was telling me that there was another life growing inside me. And although I feared the birth, as I am certain so many women do, I felt the most wondrous joy to feel the quickening. It was as if the child itself was communicating with me, telling me that they were there, ready to be loved. Edmund was overjoyed too. He had always wanted a large family. 'Helygen House should be filled with life and laughter,' he told me once, back when we were newly married and expecting Edgar. Edmund had only had his brother, who was ten years older than him and a virtual stranger, and so as our children came one after the other, we knew they would have each other, and we rejoiced.

Until they started to die.

I still cannot comprehend the reality of what has happened. Seven children born, so many children gone. Despite dear Edmund's wishes, Helygen House is no place for children now. And Ada will be bringing another life into this house. Will she be spared from the curse? I fear she will not. I fear both she and her baby are in great danger.

FORTY-TWO

JOSIE

2019

Once we've changed into dry socks, Flick and I spend the morning going over the plans for The Hut. It feels good to focus on something, to have a purpose other than being permanently attached to Willow. I love being a mother, but sometimes I wish I could go back, just for a few minutes, to the woman I was before I got pregnant. Before I lost my husband. But this is the best way for me to honour him, to carry out the work he envisioned. To make Helygen House sustainable, self-sufficient, even profitable. To protect his home and his family history, and to secure Willow's future. So we drink tea and eat biscuits and order things online, and soon enough Flick seems like her usual self again, laughing and joking, and I can almost forget my concerns about her mental health. And my own.

'Next time, we'll go into Truro,' I tell her as we're saying goodbye on the doorstep. 'Just you and me, brunch at Hub-box. Like old times.'

'Who will look after this little one?' Flick says in a higher pitched voice, reaching out to touch Willow's cheek.

'Alice will have her for me. She loves spending time with her.'

Flick looks up at me. 'You don't need to wrap me up in cotton wool, you know,' she says gently. 'I'm fine.'

I catch her gaze and hold it. 'Are you? You know you can talk to me any time. I'm here for you.'

She glances back at Willow, and I see the sadness hidden in her eyes. 'I'm fine,' she repeats, walking backwards off the front step towards her car. 'I'll see you soon.'

'Drive carefully!' I call after her. She lifts a hand and I turn back to Willow, who has started to cry. 'What are we going to do with Auntie Flick, eh?' I ask her, trying to disguise my anxiety. Flick is my best friend; if she called in the middle of the night, I would be there, no questions asked. But I'm starting to think that I'm not the best person for her to call. I'm starting to think that being around Willow is harder for Flick than any of us expected.

I make a sandwich for lunch, frowning at the bare shelves in the fridge. I really need to go shopping. I eat at the counter, Willow snoozing in her Moses basket while I do an online food shop. It takes a while for me to choose what to order, as everything seems to remind me of Henry. I haven't cooked a proper meal in longer than I care to admit, mostly because Henry and I used to cook together, flour on our noses, bits of cauliflower on the floor, potato peelings big enough to make chips with. It was fun, the two of us in the tiny kitchen in our flat, dancing around one another. And then we moved here, and we had more space than we knew what to do with, which just meant we made more mess. Cooking was always our thing. We were up for anything and did it all with love and laughter. Now, food is just food, and eating is something I have to do to survive. There is no joy in cooking without someone to enjoy it with.

I place the order and find myself back flicking through the newspaper archives. Fox is too broad a term, as it brings up every mention of the animal along with the family, so I type in *Cassius Fox* and *Helygen House* and finally come up with something.

Forthcoming marriages — Society papers announce that marriages will take place between Cassius Fox of Helygen House, Lostwithiel, and Ada Stevens, only daughter of Sir Walter Stevens of Panshanger, Hertford; and between Mr R. Adams and . . .

I go back to the line above. Ada Stevens. I've never heard the name before, but if Cassius was Alice's great-grandfather, could Ada have been her great-grandmother instead of Eliza? I check the date: 1873. It could fit, and there's nothing in the bible about what happened to Ada before Cassius married Eliza, but there are no births recorded after 1864. I know Alice said she'd never met her paternal grandparents, but did she know nothing about them? Is there something she doesn't know, or something she isn't telling me?

I wake in the middle of the night, heart racing, mind full of blurred images. The sheet beneath me is soaked in sweat, the duvet in a heap on the floor. It is pitch black but for the faint light coming through the window, the moon high and full outside shining in through the curtains, turning the bed to shimmer. My bare leg shines as I move it, and I focus on the paleness of my skin as I try to remember the dream which had woken me. I remember water, the sensation of being pulled beneath the surface, all sounds dulled but for the sea rushing in my ears. A shout, muffled, before I was pulled out, gasping, my leg radiating pain, my vision blurred with water, unable to see my assailant.

It feels like a memory, but it is not my memory. A fiction then? No. It feels real, as if it is a story someone has told me, an image conjured up by the recounting of an event so vivid that it has emblazoned itself on my mind.

I lie back, watching the shadows play across the ceiling. The digital clock reads 03.48. I feel exhausted yet wide awake, and I know I will not sleep again. Defeated, I drag myself out of bed and push my feet into slippers. The house is chilly, the heating switched off for the night, so I pull on a jumper – one of Henry's, I realise with a pang, as the sleeves trail down past my wrists – and pad into the kitchen to make a cup of tea.

Willow slept fitfully last night too. She went down at

around seven, was up at nine, half past eleven and two, and I feel as if I only managed a few minutes of sleep before the dream woke me again. She was fussing when I tried to feed her, turning her head from side to side, away from my breast. Her nappy was clean each time I checked, and she did not seem to want to be held. She wriggled in my arms, her hot little body pushing away from mine, her eyes screwed tight as if in pain. I sang and hushed and held her. I wrapped her in an extra blanket and took it off again, while Ivy paced the hallway outside, her tail low, her body tense. And still Willow cried.

I take my cup into the living room and sit down on the sofa, tucking my legs beneath me. A twinge of pain in my stomach reminds me that although my body is healing from the caesarean, I am not yet back to full strength. My mind returns to the mystery wife of Cassius, Ada Stevens, and I suddenly remember why it has been bothering me. There's a portrait of Eliza in the dining room, but there are none of Ada. I'm sure of it, and now I'm certain that the unreadable entry in the family bible is Cassius's marriage to her. But why would someone want to hide it, to erase Ada from history?

A scream tears my mind away from the past. Lights switch on outside, the patio suddenly illuminated, lighting up the living room. I stand at the glass, peering out, and see a figure running across the grass.

'Help!' they shout, waving their arms. 'There's someone in the lake! Somebody, help!'

FORTY-THREE

I stuff my feet into the first shoes I can find, dragging my arms into my coat and unlocking the patio door. Halka is hurrying towards me, her breath misting in the air before her.

'Halka? What's going on?' I ask, stepping out into the night air.

'Oh, Josie,' she says, her eyes filling with tears. 'I heard a noise outside, and noticed a car in the driveway when I looked out of the window.' I glance in the direction of the driveway, but it's too dark to see anything. 'I came out to check, and that's when I saw . . .' Halka trails off, her voice thick with emotion. 'Oh, Josie, I'm so sorry.'

I feel a sudden chill sweep over me. 'What? What is it?' But then a light goes on over the driveway and I see it. Flick's car. 'No.' I stagger across the patio, my legs too weak to hold me. 'No.'

'The ambulance is coming,' Halka says, reaching out to catch me before I fall. 'I got her out, but she . . .' She trails off, the air between us full of the words she cannot say. I don't need to ask. I know the answer. Flick is dead.

A feeling of déjà vu settles over me as I watch the paramedics wheel a stretcher across the grass. I feel numb, as if the cold has set in and turned my body to ice. Halka is inside the apartment with Willow and a cup of tea, and Alice is sitting beside me on the low wall, her feet encased in mismatched shoes. In other circumstances I might remark on the fact that she too is capable of disarray. That she too is human.

I look up to see DS Fergus making his way towards us and I feel Alice shift before rising to greet him a few feet away. They speak in low tones, their words too quiet for me to catch. My eyes are trained on the willow tree now, and the shape lying beneath it. A part of me wants to go to her, but I know I will never forget the image of my best friend lying dead. Just as I have never forgotten the image of my husband lying dead in our kitchen.

How could this have happened? I know Flick had been struggling recently, but she had been so excited to go through our plans for The Hut. She'd said she was fine, and I'd thought – or hoped – she was improving. But then I remember how she'd taken Willow down to the lake, the look in her eyes as if she had just been woken from a dream. Am I so blind not to notice when people close to me are suffering? Can I really not have seen it? But she'd left, I'd watched her go, watched her car drive out of the gates, so why had she come back? I groan, putting my head in my hands, my fingers digging into my scalp. There's so much I don't know, just like with Henry. Guilt washes over me, acid stinging the back of my throat.

'Josie.' I look up to see DS Fergus standing in front of me. 'Can we talk for a moment?' I nod, wiping my eyes on my sleeve. 'Your mother-in-law says your friend had been experiencing some . . . difficulties?'

I wring my hands together harder, squeezing until the knuckles click. 'Yes,' I manage. 'She's had a tough few years.'

'Can you tell me about it?'

I stare into the distance, unable to look at the officer's face anymore. I see that the stretcher has reached the lake and have to look away. 'She had a stillbirth,' I tell him, my voice catching. 'A few years ago. It hit her and her then-boyfriend hard. They broke up, she started drinking and . . . well, she tried to end her life. But she went to counselling and she'd been doing better, until she broke up with her girlfriend. I'd thought . . .' I look up again, catching the expression on his face. It's a mixture of sympathy and frustration. He must be sick of coming out here, I think, dealing with death.

'Were you expecting her to be here?'

'No. We've been working on The Hut together, but she left yesterday and I wasn't expecting her back for a while.'

'You saw her leave?'

I nod, getting to my feet, suddenly needing to be moving. 'I know she had her demons, but I just can't believe she'd do this. Could it . . . could it have been an accident?'

DS Fergus doesn't speak. He doesn't need to, his eyes tell

me everything I need to know. I feel myself deflate, grief bearing down on me like a physical weight. 'Do you know who her next of kin would be?' he asks gently.

I fish my phone out of my pocket and find Flick's mum's name with trembling fingers, and reel off the number. I wonder if I should call her, the mother of my best friend, but I can't face it. I can't face telling her that her daughter is dead.

DS Fergus tucks his notepad away. 'I'm sorry for your loss,' he says, his hand twitching as if he is going to reach out and touch me, but he stops himself and offers me a tight smile instead. I watch him walk away, my heart feeling as if it is tearing in two. I bury my face in my hands, my eyes burning with tears.

FORTY-FOUR

ELIZA

1881

A few weeks passed after she sent the letter to her parents, their silence making Eliza itch with nerves. She paused over the fourth letter to her mother, feeling hysteria bubble up inside her as she reread the words. They were false, every one of them, with no mention of Cassius's anger or her ever-growing fear. But what else could she do? Her parents would not have her back, not after last year, and especially not now. There was no such thing as a failed marriage in her circles. She simply had to get on with it.

She glanced up and caught her reflection in the window, the sky outside already dark, and for a second, she glimpsed a different woman looking back at her. Ada. She had found a photo of her hidden in a drawer in Cassius's study a few days before, had run a finger over her pretty face. Ada had been beautiful, with wide eyes framed by dark lashes, her dress fashionable and neat, her light hair tied back, curls framing her face. She had not looked like a madwoman – at least, not when that photo had been taken. What had happened to make Cassius write to the doctor for help? Had she been sent away? And was Eliza now mimicking the woman before her? Scrawling desperate pleas to her mother, pleas which went unanswered. *Stop being foolish*, she chided herself. *You are in no danger here.* But she had to know what had happened to Ada. The idea of her being carted off to an asylum left her breathless. Could Cassius truly have done such a thing? She could hardly believe it. She hardly dared to believe it.

She thought of his anger when he had discovered her pregnancy. She had not realised her father had told him about what happened the year before. She had hoped, prayed, that they would all be able to forget about it, to put it behind them and never speak of it again, but it seemed that her father had had different ideas. Perhaps he thought her husband had a right to know that his wife was damaged goods.

She put down her pen and sighed, pressing her fingers into her eyes. She had pushed the events of last year deep inside herself, desperately willing herself to forget, but he still came in the dead of night, forcing her to remember. Albert Hughes, member of parliament and acquaintance of Eliza's father, continued to haunt her dreams. The glint of his ring in the candlelight, the way he fondled his moustache before speaking. One of his hands on her hip, the other pressed against her mouth to stop her from crying out.

Though she would never say so out loud, Eliza's father had been a gambler. He still was, for all she knew. As he had steadily lost the majority of the family's wealth, he'd decided to put her education to good use, and so she had been employed as a governess to the Hughes children. She received bed and board and her wages were sent straight home to her father, who no doubt lost it all at the card table. Although she had envisioned a different life for herself, Eliza found that she enjoyed teaching the children, particularly Sophia, who was eight years old and seemed to excel in every subject. Sophia's brothers, both slightly older, had less patience for their education, and disliked being bested at spelling and arithmetic by their little sister. And yet it was the eldest boy who would inherit the family wealth, and the youngest who would go off to Oxford or Cambridge to study, and all Sophia had to look forward to was a good marriage and becoming a mother.

Now, Eliza felt again the unfairness of it all. Though they were ruled by a queen, England was not ready for women to rise beyond the limitations of their sex. They were still expected to rely on men to direct them. And Albert Hughes took very seriously his duty to direct the women of his household, ensuring complete obedience by whatever means necessary.

Eliza was thrown out of the house when the mistress discovered she was with child. It had been Sophia who had unwittingly given the game away, when she reported to her mother that their governess was regularly unwell in the morning. Perhaps it was not the first time a female member of staff had found herself in the family way; perhaps Albert Hughes had form for abusing the women who lived under his roof. But the mistress would not let Eliza speak, would not hear her explanation, and she was ejected from the house before the master could return. Not that she'd believed he would have helped her. No, to Albert Hughes, all women were at his disposal, their bodies his for the taking, and as Eliza walked the three miles back to her family home that day, she'd felt just as tainted as Mrs Hughes had said she was.

Her mother had taken one look at her and known the truth. 'So this is where your learning has got you,' she said, her eyes full of contempt, and Eliza had fled upstairs to her childhood bedroom, distraught. What was she to do? She was pregnant and unmarried. She would be cast out of society, out of her home. Where would she go? She considered going to her uncle, but her shame – and the thought of her mother's shame – had stopped her.

In the end, it was the maid who helped her. She had a friend, she said, who could deal with the situation, and so Eliza went with her to a dark, cramped house on the edge of town, where a woman with filthy fingernails gave her a vile concoction to drink. She laid on the hard table, her eyes following the progress of a spider crawling across the wooden ceiling while the woman lifted her skirts. When it came, the pain was hot and sharp, and even as tears streamed down her face, she knew she had made the right decision. Her mother had been furious with her, but her father had been relieved that there was no longer a baby to complicate things, so what on earth had possessed him to confide in Cassius?

She wiped her eyes, blinking away the tears, and finished her letter in the weak candlelight. They were in the dead of winter now, the lake frozen over, the ground hard and unyielding. The woodland was bare but for the evergreens, the huge pine trees standing resolute against the chill of the December air. The house too felt colder now. Harriet refused to have fires lit in the rooms they did not use, and even in the ones they did, the fire was laid only when they were occupied. Eliza had been shivering for the best part of an hour when she took tea with Harriet in her drawing room earlier, and the fire failed to warm the cavernous dining room at all during breakfast.

As she was sealing the envelope, Eliza felt her mouth flood with a metallic tang. She froze, her memories tangling in her mind. Could it . . .? Suddenly she was hunched over, acid burning her throat and splattering her shoes. Her stomach cramped violently and she gasped with the pain. She tried to straighten, to get up from the chair and call for help, but her throat started to close up, the pain gripping her so tightly she could do nothing more than try to breathe through it, to clench her teeth so hard she feared they may break, splinter like a china cup dashed against the wall. She moaned, low and long, shuddering as a familiar pain tore through her. She slid from the chair to her hands and knees, the rug coarse beneath her palms as she threw up again and again. Her forehead was slick with sweat, her muscles shaking as she fell, her cheek pressed against the rug, the acrid tang of blood filling her nostrils as she drifted in and out of consciousness.

Mary found her on the floor, her skirts soaked in blood. 'Madam!' She dropped to her knees beside her, hands fluttering over Eliza's body like a nervous bird. She glanced upwards, as if she was expecting a sign direct from the heavens, before pressing her fingers against her neck, feeling for a pulse. Eliza's lips were moving as if in prayer, her voice so low the maid was forced to put her ear close to Eliza's lips to hear her words.

'It is gone,' she murmured. 'It is gone. He killed it.'

FORTY-FIVE

JOSIE

2019

I try to bury myself in work. I cannot think about Flick. I cannot let myself fall into the pit of despair which is waiting for me, wondering whether she took her own life, wondering whether there was anything I could have done to stop her. I've been lost down this road for too long already; now, I fear I may never find my way back.

I call the builder again the next morning, leaving him another voicemail in the vain hope that he will call me back. Perhaps the discovery beneath the stables spooked the men, though surely it wasn't the first time he'd found something unexpected during a dig. England is covered in skeletons, houses built upon battlegrounds and burial grounds alike. And the bones were not recent, DS Fergus had said. The body may have been buried before the stables were even built. There may be nothing untoward about it whatsoever.

To my surprise, Darren calls back a few minutes later. 'Listen, maid,' he says in his thick accent. 'I thought you'd given us the sack.'

'What gave you that impression?'

'We were told not to come back. That you weren't going ahead with it after all.'

'Who told you that?' I ask, but I know the answer.

Alice is on her laptop when I enter the drawing room, which she closes with a snap when she sees me marching towards her.

'Why did you tell the builders not to come back?' I demand, placing the Moses basket on the floor. 'You had no right, Alice.'

She watches me coolly, one eyebrow arched. 'Hadn't I? Is this not my home too?'

'No, it isn't,' I hiss, unable to control my anger. 'Henry might have said you can live here, but you can bloody well leave if you're going to start meddling.' I exhale sharply through my nose, trying to get my emotions under control. 'There'll be no house for you to live in if we don't start making money, Alice. You know that. I—'

'How dare you.' Her eyes flash as she gets to her feet, her words silencing me. 'How dare you threaten me in my own house.'

'This isn't your house,' I shout back, before glancing at Willow. Despite the noise, my daughter is still sleeping. 'This is Willow's house,' I say, lowering my voice. 'Henry left it to her. And you said yourself that Henry . . . did what he did because he was worried about money.' Even as I say the words, I know they do not ring true, and anger flares again as I remember the hymn Henry had written out, how quick Alice had been to believe that what she had found was part of a suicide note. 'But you were lying about that as well, weren't you? I know you're not telling me the truth, Alice. What are you trying to hide?'

She smirks then. 'People close to you seem to have a habit of killing themselves, don't they?'

I flinch at the venom in her voice. 'You have no idea what you're talking about.'

'No, *you* have no idea what you're talking about. You don't have a clue, Josie. You're so self-obsessed, you can't see what's right in front of you.' She exhales loudly through her nose. 'You really didn't know Henry at all.'

'What does that mean?' I take a step closer, my fury threatening to bubble over. 'What are you saying, Alice?'

She moves closer too, so our faces are inches apart. 'I'm saying that you should think carefully about your next move, Josie. You are far, far out of your depth.'

I am trembling when I go back to the apartment, my whole body shaking with rage. I have never seen this side of my mother-in-law before, and in truth, I felt more than a flicker of fear at the coldness in her eyes. She has never been the warmest person, but she seemed to love Henry dearly, the same way she loves Willow. I know something must have happened before Henry's death, something she isn't telling me, but what?

And Flick. My eyes fill with tears as Alice's words echo inside my head. She was right about that, at least. I've been so buried in my grief and the renovation and Willow, that I didn't see what was right in front of me. How could I have let this happen? How could I have let Flick down so badly?

Oh, Henry. What am I going to do? I beg silently, but he doesn't reply. Both he and Flick are gone, and I have to find a way to carry on without them.

Willow and I spend a few days in the apartment, avoiding Alice and Helygen House. I avoid the lake too, walking through the wild field instead of the gardens, Ivy at my side. Alice doesn't visit either, though I see her sometimes marching across the grounds, wrapped up in her thick winter coat. Sometimes she glances back at the house as if she is looking for someone, her eyes always on the first-floor windows. I've watched her from the nursery, stepping back when her eyes have found me in the window, though I know the distance is too great for her to have seen me properly. Perhaps she is seeing something – or someone – else entirely.

We are halfway into December, and soon it will be Christmas, I realise with a jolt. What a strange celebration it will be this year, if you could even call it that. The day will be observed, for the sake of normalcy if nothing else, but it will be tinged with sadness, Henry's absence stronger than ever. And where will Alice and I be by then? Seated beside one another at the table, or still at each other's throats?

I glance over at Willow, whose eyes are staring up at the mobile which dangles above her, her tiny hands stretching up towards the plastic stars. No, I think, feeling something like defiance flare through me. This will be Willow's first Christmas. I will not let it be overshadowed by grief, or Alice's poison. I can't let what happened to Flick pull me back under. Willow still needs me.

FORTY-SIX

HARRIET

1st July 1874

The baby is gone.

3rd August 1874

Ada has not left her bedroom in over a week. The baby was buried beneath the old stables, for he was born without having drawn a single breath and had not been baptised, and Cassius refused to lay him to rest in the family cemetery. It was this act, I believe, which destroyed her.

Though she was ordered to stay abed by the doctor, I found her wandering the house at night, fingers trailing along the bookshelves, laughing softly to herself. Sometimes I got to her in time, gently taking her by the shoulders and guiding her back to bed, but often the tears would come, and the screams, and then Cassius would be thundering down the stairs, his hands gripping Ada's thin forearms so tightly I feared they would snap.

Once, when he found her climbing the stairs to the west wing, I knew his patience had run out. He dragged her back down the corridor, eyes blazing, teeth gritted as she flailed against him, her nails raking across his cheek as she twisted in his grip.

'Enough is enough,' he snarled as he threw her bodily into the bedroom and locked the door. I jumped as her body slammed against it, fists pounding on the wood as she screamed to be let out.

'Cassius,' I said, watching as he ran a hand over his face. 'Could she not . . . Would her parents not allow her to go home?'

'They cannot afford to keep her,' he snapped. 'Her father is bankrupt.'

I was stunned. I'd had no idea Ada's family had been in financial difficulty. Cassius was supposed to be being primed to take over the business, since the Stevens had no living heirs, so did that mean . . .?

Cassius, as if seeing this realisation pass over me, nodded. 'No dowry, and no inheritance. The swine.'

Which meant no money to save our failing factories. No other source of income to save us from ruin. And now there was nobody in this world who would take responsibility for Ada. Nobody who would miss her. Fear flashed through me and I decided to try again, my own guilt forcing me to speak up on her behalf as she sobbed behind the locked door.

'Why don't you go away for a while?' I suggested, my fear making me bold. 'Just you, alone. Visit some friends on the continent perhaps. You work so hard; you could do with a break.'

Cassius's eyes hardened at my attempt at flattery. 'The only one leaving here, Mother, is her.' He kicked the door with his heel, making it shudder, and Ada fell silent. And I knew that she was lost.

20th September 1874

She is gone.

FORTY-SEVEN

JOSIE

2019

The day before the winter solstice, I decide to go into Truro to do some Christmas shopping. Willow has been sleeping less recently and waking more often in the night, and although it also means that I have been sleeping less, I feel better seeing her interacting with the world a bit more. But Truro so close to Christmas will be busy, and I hesitate at the front door, wondering whether I should be taking her with me. The alternative is to leave her with Alice, and that, if I'm honest with myself, is what makes me hesitate. I'm being ridiculous; Alice is her grandmother, she adores Willow. But I can't help feeling that she is hiding something from me. That she is deliberately keeping me in the dark, and something is telling me not to leave my daughter alone with her.

In the end, the decision is made for me. I'm carrying Willow across the driveway when a car pulls in. I watch as

Halka gets out of the driver's seat, followed by two little girls who emerge from the back, giggling. I put up a hand and call good morning.

'Morning, Josie,' Halka says with a smile. 'Come on, girls, I want to introduce you.' She leads them across the drive, gravel crunching beneath their boots. 'These are my brother's children, Bela and Lida. His wife has a hospital appointment and school has finished for the holidays, so I said I would take them.'

'Are you working today?' I ask, smiling at the two girls beside her. One of them smiles back, but the other hides her face behind Halka's skirt, her eyes peeking round at me.

'No, Alice said I can take the day off.' Something flits across her face and she glances at the girls. 'I was going to take them to the storage room, it is comfortable and has a TV, but –'

'Marie,' we say in unison, our eyes meeting. She seems to be healing physically, but her eyes are puffy and ringed with red as if she spends every night crying. If I've learned anything from what happened to Flick, it's that the last thing Marie needs is to be around children right now.

'Why don't you use the apartment?' I suggest. I riffle through my bag and pull out Henry's keys, pausing to smile sadly at the keyring before holding them out to Halka.

She takes them, her eyes reflecting my own sadness. 'But, Josie, I can't—'

'You can. I've said so.' I smile. 'Make yourself at home. There's food in the fridge, for once.'

She laughs before glancing again at the girls. 'Are you sure?' I nod, opening the car door and sliding the car seat in. 'Where are you going today?'

'Oh, just into Truro. I thought I'd do some Christmas shopping.' I wrestle with the seat belt and Willow lets out a frustrated wail as I lean across her. My fingers get caught in the contraption and I swear under my breath.

'That is no place for a baby,' Halka says. 'Why don't I watch her for you?'

'Oh, you don't have to do that, Halka. You've got enough on your plate.'

'Ah, what's one more?' She smiles, gesturing at the children behind her, who are gazing up at Willow. 'It looks as if they're already keen to make a new friend.'

I smile, considering. I wouldn't mind going shopping alone. It would be quicker, and, truth be told, I'd quite like some time on my own, maybe grab a coffee and read a book in peace. 'Do you really not mind?' I ask hopefully, trying to ignore the flicker of guilt.

Halka shakes her head. 'Really. I would love to spend some time with little Willow. And Ivy, of course. The girls would like it too, wouldn't you?' They both nod in unison and I smile at them.

'All right. Thanks so much, Halka.' I turn back to unclip the car seat. 'I won't be long, a few hours max.'

'Take your time,' she says, giving me a knowing look. 'Make sure you find me the best present. I am fond of diamonds, you know. And chocolate.'

'Chocolate-covered diamonds coming right up.' I kiss Willow on the cheek and hand Halka the car seat. 'Be good, little one. Thanks again, really. Call me if you have any problems.'

'We won't.' She lowers the car seat so Bela and Lida can see Willow properly. 'My two big girls and my little girl,' she says proudly before turning back to me. 'Off you go then! You're losing daylight.'

I get into the car, waving as Halka leads the way towards the apartment. Ivy will be in her element with those two girls to play with. She's always adored children, though as a puppy she often forgot how big she was and barrelled into a few in her excitement. She's much calmer now, thank God, and she'll love being fussed over today.

I open Spotify and plug in my phone before setting off, my fingers drumming on the steering wheel as I turn onto the main road towards the A30. The journey will take about forty minutes, so I turn the music up and sing along to Kaleida, my heart feeling lighter than it has in months. I feel as though I've left the grief and guilt back at Helygen House, though I know it will be waiting for me when I return.

I find a parking space in the multi-storey and make my way towards the shops. It's still early, the sky a dull grey, the lights strung up between the buildings still twinkling, and the streets are full of shop and office workers hurrying past, takeaway cups in hand. It's the Friday before Christmas, and here, standing beneath the lights, I can almost feel normal. I make my way through town, buying a bath set for

Alice, and a box of chocolates each for Marie and Halka. I throw in a pair of fluffy socks too, as Marie is always complaining that her feet are cold, and find a beautiful scarf Halka will love. Willow is harder to buy for – there's really too much choice for a child so young – but I settle on a couple of soft toys and a rattle with a little fox on the top. I pause at a shop window, pain gripping my heart as I take in the display of festive, ethical teas and a little teapot shaped like an elephant. Flick would have loved something like that. I should send a card to her mum, some flowers or a plant, but I know nothing will heal the pain of losing a loved one. I take a deep breath, closing my eyes for a moment and letting the grief fill me. I let Flick down, and now I have to find a way to live with this pain.

I force myself to move on and go into Waterstones, picking up a few children's books for Willow before browsing the fiction aisles. I've always been a crime lover myself, but since Henry died I can't see myself picking up a novel where someone dies under suspicious circumstances, so I wander around the historical fiction aisle, recognising titles from Henry's collection. He was always an avid reader, and he read more widely than I did too, picking up whatever took his fancy. I'm drawn to a book with a beautiful cover, and as I read the blurb, it strikes me that this is exactly the kind of book I would have bought him for Christmas. I take it with me to the till then up to the café, laying it on the table beside my hot chocolate and opening the front cover. I read for a while, absorbed in the story, enjoying the feeling of being close to Henry and relishing the fact that I'm alone. When I pick up my bags and head outside, the air is still crisp, though the streets are a little busier now. I've been out for more than two hours, and Willow is due a feed soon. I hope she hasn't been too unsettled for Halka.

On the way back, I get stuck behind a car loaded with bikes on the back and tut. Tourists don't quite flood Cornwall over Christmas like they do during the summer, but it's almost guaranteed that the roads will get busier as they drive too slowly, not confident on the narrow roads. Still, it's better than them crashing, I suppose. I breathe out as I drive up the lane towards Helygen House. I'm suddenly desperate to get home. It's the first time I've been away from Willow since she was born, and it's only now that I realise just how much my world has shrunk. I park on the edge of the drive, closer to the apartment front door, and open the boot to unload the shopping bags. I stopped at the supermarket to pick up some food as well, including some cream cakes to thank Halka for today, and know I won't be able to take it all in at once. I glance up to see her hurrying towards me.

'Ah, perfect timing,' I say, holding out a bag for her to carry, but I falter at the look on her face. Dread pools in my stomach. 'What's wrong?'

She swallows, her eyes wide and tearful. 'Oh, Josie. It's Willow. She's gone.'

FORTY-EIGHT

ELIZA

1881

It is gone. He killed it.

Mary had run to fetch Cook, and together they'd dragged Eliza up the stairs to the bathroom, where they washed away the remnants of her child. They'd dressed her like a doll, slipping a clean nightgown over her head and helping her into bed, where she had stayed ever since, staring up at the ceiling for what felt like forever. And still Cassius had not come to see her.

She knew he had not wanted the child, and might even be glad of its passing, but did he feel so little for her? His wife, whom he had pledged to love and honour? She thought of Ada, and realised that those vows meant nothing to Cassius, just as her baby had meant nothing. Her baby was gone. Killed, poisoned within her womb, and now all she could do was lie in bed, waiting for them to come for her. For Cassius to come and finish the job.

She was left alone, trays of food and cups of tea brought in by Mary and taken away again, untouched. She drank water from the tap in the bathroom, her eyes avoiding the place where the mirror once hung above the sink. Once, she almost tried the bedroom door, but the fear that it would be locked stayed her hand. She did not know what she would do if she found she was locked in. *Just like Ada had been.*

She kept a candle burning through the night, her eyes fixed on the shadows in the corners of the room. She fought against fatigue, only allowing her eyes to close when the sun rose and the room was bathed in light, for she was afraid of what might be hiding beneath the bed, behind her eyelids. She dreamed of her lost child, watching in horror as it morphed into the girl she'd seen in the nursery, in the mirror. Day and night, the girl whispered into her ear, her voice slowly maturing until she turned into a woman. *Ada*, Eliza thought deliriously. *Ada is telling me to run.* But how could she? There was nowhere to run to.

One morning, Harriet bustled into the room just as Eliza was falling asleep. She wrinkled her nose as she crossed the room and threw open the window before turning to her daughter-in-law, disdain written across her face.

'Enough of this now,' she said briskly. 'You must get up. You will be joining us for breakfast this morning.'

'Us?' Eliza sat up slowly. 'Will Cassius be there?'

Harriet frowned. 'No, Eliza. But you must—'

'I *must* speak with my husband,' Eliza hissed. Harriet looked surprised, but Eliza knew she had to speak to him, to find out the truth, no matter how much it terrified her. She had to find out what he was going to do with her.

'I am sorry for your loss, Eliza,' Harriet said. 'But you must know that—'

A wave of fury tore through Eliza and she sat up, her hair falling into her face. '*My* loss?' Her hand went to her stomach, feeling its emptiness. 'My child is dead, and it was *your* son's doing.' Something flashed across Harriet's face. Guilt? Fear? Or was it understanding, from one mother to another? Eliza did not know, and she did not care. Her mother-in-law was not her friend. No one here was. 'What has he done to me, Harriet?' she whispered, her throat tight with tears. 'What has your son done to me?'

Harriet was silent, her eyes fixed on a spot above the bed, while Eliza struggled to draw breath. Did she know? Did Harriet know what her son had done? Or was she in on it too? *Never underestimate a mother's love,* she thought, something scrabbling at the edge of her mind, a memory waiting to be recovered. But what?

'Mary will be in to draw you a bath,' her mother-in-law said finally, avoiding Eliza's gaze. 'I will see you downstairs in an hour.'

'Are you not even going to acknowledge it?' Eliza whispered. 'Are you going to pretend that my child was not murdered? And what of Ada? What did he do to Ada, Harriet? You have to tell me. You must—'

'Be careful, Eliza,' Harriet hissed, her eyes flickering to the empty doorway. 'You do not know what he is capable of.' And then she was gone, leaving Eliza alone. The door opened again a moment later and Mary crept in, her eyes darting around the room as if she was looking for something – or someone. With the door open, Eliza heard something from downstairs. Shoes clicking across the tiles, a male voice. Cassius.

Eliza pulled back the sheets and slid to the edge of the bed. The floorboards were cold beneath her feet as she moved slowly across them, her muscles weak. It felt like years had passed since she'd last risen from her bed.

Mary caught her in the doorway, her grip surprisingly strong. 'Madam, I am to draw you a bath.'

Eliza pushed her hands away. 'I will speak with my husband.'

'Let's get you dressed first, madam.' Mary's eyes were pleading. 'Please, madam. It's for the best.'

Eliza ignored her, shoving past the maid and running down the hallway. She almost slipped on a patch of water at the top of the stairs, her fingers reaching out to grip the banister. 'Cassius!' she called as she descended the stairs. 'Cassius!'

'Madam!' Mary shouted from behind her. 'Madam, wait!'

At the bottom of the stairs, Eliza glanced left to see the drawing room was empty. She turned right instead, following the voices. She could hear Cassius, she was sure of it, but the dining room too was empty. Where were the voices coming from? She turned back, stopped, one hand pressed against the panelled wall as she listened. The ticking of the clock behind her was suddenly too loud. A noise came from the kitchen, the sound of a metal pot clanging against the sink. Cassius would not be in there, would he? Then she heard him again, noticed the door to his study was standing open. She crept closer, listening. She could hear two voices now, another man with her husband. Fear prickled across her skin as she tried to determine who it was.

'It is a sorry state of affairs, Mr Fox,' the unfamiliar voice said. 'But you are doing the right thing.'

'I am concerned for her, Doctor,' Cassius said. 'I cannot bear to see her so unwell. She is . . . Well, I cannot help but think of Ada.'

Ada. Eliza pressed a hand against her mouth to catch the sob that escaped her lips. *They are trying to kill me.* History was repeating itself, the second wife sentenced to the same fate as the first.

'You are quite right, Mr Fox,' the doctor replied. 'If she has indeed been poisoning herself with . . . Well, your wife needs help. Which she will receive, under my care in Bodmin.' Some shuffling then, the sound of a briefcase snapping closed. 'I will return tonight with my attendants. Can you have a case packed for your wife by then?'

'Yes, of course. Thank you, Doctor Brown.'

Doctor Brown. The hospital in Bodmin. No. *No.* Eliza shook her head, trying to make sense of the words. She was not unwell. She did not need to go to hospital. What was Cassius doing? And why had the doctor said she had been poisoning herself?

'It is probably best if your maid serves Mrs Fox her evening meal in her room,' Doctor Brown said. 'We do not want to give her another opportunity to harm herself.'

She looked up at the sound of footsteps, catching sight of herself in a mirror in the hall. Her hair was dishevelled, her nightdress dirty and rumpled. She had dark circles beneath her eyes and her lips were cracked and peeling. *The face of a madwoman,* she thought, backing away from her reflection and into the shadows of the hall. *The face of a madwoman who poisons herself and kills her own child.*

She watched as Cassius opened the study door and saw the doctor out. She watched him pause in front of the mirror, running a hand through his hair, pushing it back so it sat neatly against his scalp. He offered himself a small smile before slipping back into his study. Eliza felt a wave of fury wash over her. How dare he. How *dare* he do this to her. She hadn't done anything wrong. Hadn't she tried to be a good wife to him? He hadn't even given her a chance. She would not go. But how could she fight him, and the doctor too? She had to hide, run upstairs and gather her belongings if she could, and escape before they returned tonight.

Then she heard it, the sound she had heard over and over in her dreams since she arrived at Helygen House. A baby crying. She knew then where she needed to go, the realisation hitting her like a blow. *In the west wing.* She followed the cries back up the stairs. Mary was nowhere in sight, and so Eliza was unseen as she crept towards the nursery. She shivered as she passed the room, hurrying as fast as she could towards the staircase at the end. She had never gone down here before. She'd heeded the warnings not to go exploring, but what did she have to lose now? It was empty, Cassius said, unused. Too draughty, the floorboards rotten, unsafe to be opened up until it was repaired. But something was telling Eliza that he had lied to her. Something was drawing her this way now, a force driving her on, Ada's scrawls echoing in her mind. *What he is hiding . . . In the west wing.* Is that where Ada was now? Had he been keeping her locked up for all this time?

She paused at the end, staring at the narrow staircase. Up or down? The west wing must be small, barely large enough to be called a wing, for the ballroom took up most of the ground floor on that side, the glass roof extending out to the side, and where she stood now must have been above the kitchens. She went up, her bare feet slapping against the wood, her breath misting in the air before her, like a ghost leading the way. The stairs opened up into a wide corridor, with only one door at the end. Was there a child up here? Perhaps this was what she had heard before, on those dark nights. The sound hadn't been coming from the nursery at all, but from up here, locked away. Ada's child? She could hear the baby crying louder now, and the thought of reaching it filled her mind, urging her on.

The door at the end opened at her touch, as if a servant was waiting on the other side to welcome her in, but she could not see anyone. The room was too dark and she blinked, willing her eyes to adjust. 'Hello?' she whispered. 'Is anyone here?'

The cry came again, so loud she jumped. The baby must be in the room with her, but it was still too dark to see. Then a match flared and she turned towards the corner of the room, where she saw a woman lighting a candle, a baby cradled in her arms. Her features were suddenly illuminated, her long bright hair hanging over one shoulder, her thin nightdress trailing down to the floor.

'Who are you?' Eliza asked, her throat tight with fear. 'Ada? Is it you, Ada?'

The woman tilted her head as if considering her question, but before she could speak, there was a burst of movement in the corridor behind Eliza, and she turned to find Harriet in the doorway, her eyes wide with terror. 'Eliza! What are you doing up here? You can't—'

'Who are you?' Eliza asked the woman again, her heart beating so loud she could hardly hear her own words above it. 'Are you Ada Fox?'

The woman shook her head, a high giggle emanating from her lips. 'I'm Flora,' she said, and Eliza felt the ground tilt beneath her.

FORTY-NINE

HARRIET

14th December 1880

News arrived this morning, from the hospital. The news Cassius has been waiting for since they dragged Ada out of the house all those years ago. She fought them, her eyes full of a ferocity I'd had no idea she possessed, but the doctor had brought three strong men with him and her efforts were wasted. I have written to her a number of times since that day but a reply has never come, and I always wondered if the doctor was in league with Cassius and whether he knew of his true, dark nature. And although it is perfectly legal and even reasonable for a husband to send his wife to an asylum when he has tired of her, it has meant that Cassius could not remarry while Ada still lived. Until now.

He grinned when he read the letter over breakfast, surprising me by handing me the slip of paper. He never lets

311

me read his correspondence, and will always read my own if he gets to it first. He caught Mary slipping me a letter once and terrified the poor girl, and it made me wonder about Sara, what he had been doing to her for all those years. He has never admitted it, but I know he killed her. Poison, his weapon of choice. He had been practising for so long, after all.

The letter was brief. I skimmed the words before finding the reason for Cassius's joy.

I regret to inform you that your wife, Ada Fox, has passed away. My sincere condolences for your loss.

Ada is dead. Pneumonia, the letter said. I felt a sense of grief settle over me then. She had only been in her twenties, with her whole life ahead of her. And, I confess, guilt settled over me too. For my own part in this sorry mess. For not being able to protect her. The tea had worked, yes, but it had not been enough to save her.

'I will be leaving in the new year,' Cassius told me when I handed the letter back, smiling that wolfish smile that he had been born with. Where did he come from, this beast masquerading as a son? 'I will visit the continent again before joining friends in London, and then I will return.'

By the look on his face, I knew what he planned to do. Now Ada is gone, he will be looking for a new wife. Whoever she is, I must warn her to stay away. I will not let her down.

12th July 1881

Dearest Mama,

I write to you with good news and an invitation to my wedding, though I suspect you will not attend. Indeed, I urge you to consider your health, as the journey to London is a long and unpleasant one. So I shall tell you about her, my bride-to-be, who you will meet when we return to Helygen House after our honeymoon.

Her name is Elizabeth, and she is the daughter of a rather savvy businessman. He owns a factory here in Hertfordshire, close to where I am staying with friends, which makes a matchless range of soaps. Cleanliness is next to godliness, he likes to say, though I see very little of the latter in him. Regardless, he seems a good sort and has no heir, so I expect the factory will come to me in time, and he assures me that Eliza will come with a rather handsome dowry. I happened to run into Dickie in France back in May, and he suggested a new venture for us to embark upon at home in Cornwall, so I intend to use the dowry to join him and improve our fortunes. Especially now I will have someone to pass it all down to.

After the wedding, we intend to take the train from Cowbridge, near Eliza's home, into London, and then a short tour of the south coast before returning to Cornwall. She looks forward to meeting you, dearest Mama, and settling in at Helygen House. I am sure you will make her feel most at home.

Your loving son,
Cassius

FIFTY

JOSIE

2019

I gape at Halka as her words slowly register. Gone? How can my daughter be gone?

'Josie,' she says, coming towards me and placing her hands on my arms. 'Did you hear me?' I nod slowly. It is as if I am in a stupor, my mind failing to grasp the reality of what is happening. 'I was only gone for a moment,' she continues, tears streaming down her face. 'I went into the kitchen to make some sandwiches for the girls, and when I came back . . .'

Halka's terror seems to infect me, worming its way inside and turning my body to ice. The bags fall from my hands, the rattle I bought for Willow tumbling onto the cold ground. I watch it roll a few times, coming to rest against the car tyre. This cannot be real. This is a dream, and I know I will wake up in just a moment. I will wake up and none of this will have happened. Henry will be alive, Flick too, and everything will be well. I hear Halka say she's calling the police, that she has taken the girls to the main house and cannot find Alice, but something flickers in the corner of my eye and I turn to see a shadow passing across one of the windows at the front of the house. My gaze follows it as if entranced, then a bark echoes across the garden and I look up to see Ivy bounding towards me, and suddenly I am back, gasping for air. Willow. Willow is gone. Willow is *gone*.

Ivy barks at me again and starts to run. I follow her, my heart pounding in time with my feet. The grass is slippery beneath me, the morning frost melting in the weak December sunlight, and I skid as I follow Ivy down towards the icy lake. I try to think rationally, try to tell myself that Willow is with Alice, that she is safe with her. But what if someone took her? Halka said she'd only been gone a few minutes, had been only a few metres away in the kitchen. Wouldn't she have heard someone come in behind her? None of it makes sense, but my mind is too chaotic to try to puzzle it out. All I can think about is getting my daughter back.

The winter air is freezing, numbing my cheeks, and the damp scent of the lake is almost overwhelming. Has it always smelled like this? I'd never noticed it before, how potent it was. Insidious.

As I get closer, I notice that the door to The Hut is open, framed by the weeping branches of the willow tree. Ivy stops outside, sitting in the mud and turning towards me. I pause beneath the willow, my pulse rushing in my ears. Is someone inside?

'Alice?' I shout, one hand on the trunk. Silence. Ivy barks once more, the noise seeming to echo off the water, and then I hear it. A baby crying. 'Willow!' Her name tears from my throat, and before I know it I am climbing the steps to The Hut and pushing open the door, my footsteps loud on the wooden floor.

A woman steps out of the shadows, Willow in her arms. I gasp with relief at the sight of her, before confusion and fear settle over me once again. I stare at the woman, recognition slowly dawning.

'India?' My mouth opens and closes as I take in Henry's sister, the power of speech suddenly deserting me. Why is she here? And why does she have my daughter? Wordlessly I hold out my arms, silently begging her to give me my daughter, and to my surprise she crosses the room and places Willow in my arms, resting a hand on top of her head before moving away again.

'I'm sorry to have frightened you,' she says, her eyes wide. 'I should have called first.'

I seem to deflate, the adrenaline suddenly leaving my body. I lean against the wall, head spinning. 'What are you doing here?' I demand, holding Willow close against me. She is wrapped up against the chill, and she seems unharmed as she turns her head towards India, curious and unafraid.

'I've been here for a while,' India says, her eyes soft as she watches Willow wriggle to look at her. 'Ever since I heard about Henry.'

I frown at her in confusion. 'But why didn't you come to the funeral? Why didn't you tell us you were here?'

India smiles sadly. 'I'm afraid I wasn't welcome. *She* made sure of that.'

'Who?' I blink, struggling to keep up. 'Alice?'

She nods. 'Alice. Dearest Mama.' The smile slips from her face. 'I suppose she's got you under her spell?' She tilts her head, considering me. 'No, perhaps not.'

The look in her eyes sends a shiver through me. 'I have no idea what you're talking about. Whatever has gone on between you and Alice, it's not—'

'No, it isn't your business,' she says sharply. 'But it was Henry's business.'

'What has Henry got to do with anything?'

'Oh, Josie. Haven't you figured it out yet?' India chuckles softly. 'Even after I sent you the family bible? Henry always said you were sharp.'

I stare at her, trying to untangle the knot of her words. 'You sent me the bible? But why?'

'You needed to know,' she says, lifting a shoulder. 'For Willow's sake, if nothing else. It's too late for Henry, after all.'

'Stop talking in riddles,' I snap, and she smiles again.

'You've got fire. I like that. You're going to need it here.' She tilts her head again. 'Though, perhaps not anymore.' She turns, and I follow her gaze towards the door behind her, which Flick had earmarked as a new toilet and changing area. India pushes the door open with her foot, revealing a shape slumped against the wall. Alice.

My knees almost buckle as I take in the sight of her. The right side of her head is matted with blood and her eyes are closed, her mouth slack. 'Is she . . .?'

'Dead?' India makes a noise in the back of her throat. 'Sadly not.'

I turn back to her, my mouth open in shock. 'Did you do this? Why?'

'Because she's a liar,' India says angrily, her eyes flashing. 'And because she murdered my brother.'

I feel my legs go numb, the breath leaving my body in a whoosh, as if I have just been punched. I try to hold Willow securely against me as I process India's words. 'Alice . . . murdered Henry?'

India smiles, but there is no warmth in it. 'Did you believe it to be an accident?' she asks. I shake my head. 'Or suicide?'

'No,' I whisper. 'I didn't believe that he would have done that.'

'And you were right.' India aims a kick at Alice's leg, her foot lashing out so violently that I flinch away. '*She* killed him. Shot him in the head, and made it look like suicide.'

I feel my stomach clench, acid burning the back of my throat. 'But why?' It comes out as a wail. My whole body is trembling, my head swimming. How could she do this? How could Alice murder her own son?

'What did she try to pass off as a suicide note?' India says, tapping her chin with a finger. 'Oh yes. *The night is dark, and I am far from home.*'

I repeat the words silently. *The night is dark, and I am far from home.* I remember Henry's note about Willow's christening, and the torn section along the top. She must have found it in his office and thought it fit. But why? Then I remember the same words on Eliza's gravestone. *Lead Thou me on.*

'It's a hymn,' I murmur. ' "Lead, Kindly Light". It's written on her great-grandmother's grave.'

'Yes,' India says. 'She believed Henry had lost his way, but really he'd just escaped from her clutches.' She sneers at her mother. 'I suppose she thought it was poetic.'

'She said it was about money,' I say slowly, staring down at my mother-in-law. 'Debts. He was hiding things from me – us, she said.'

'She was right about that,' India says. 'Henry *was* hiding something. But it wasn't anything to do with money.' She kicks her mother again and this time Alice groans, her eyelids flickering. I stare at her, my mind feeling as if I am wading through mud. I can't believe Alice would do that, that Alice would kill her own son. India smiles again, as if she is reading my mind. 'It's true, Josie. She killed Henry because he discovered her secret. Because he was going to expose her.'

Alice moans again, her eyes opening and finding mine, her mouth moving as if she is trying to speak.

Panic flashes through me at India's words. 'What secret?' I demand, directing my words at Alice. 'What did Henry discover?'

FIFTY-ONE

ELIZA

1881

'Flora?' Eliza stared at Harriet in confusion. Who was Flora? Then it struck her: the lost girl. The twins, Archie and Flora. Cassius's sister. She staggered, one hand going out to steady herself against the wall. The baby cried again and Eliza stared at it in horror. 'Whose baby is that?' she asked, her voice a whisper.

Flora giggled like a girl much younger than her years. 'He's mine, silly.' Something shifted behind her and Eliza's hand moved to cover her mouth, suppressing a cry. A girl, aged five or six, was peeking out from behind Flora's skirts. The girl from the nursery. The ghost. Flora laid a hand on her head. 'And so is she,' she said with a smile.

'These are your children? But who . . .?' Eliza turned to Harriet as if for answers, but the older woman was staring at her daughter, her shoulders slumped as if in defeat. Or was it relief? 'Who is the father?' The truth suddenly hit her and acid burned at the back of her throat. 'Cassius,' she breathed.

'Cassius,' Flora repeated, drawing out the syllables, her eyes clouding over. She glanced at her mother as if for comfort, but Harriet was still frozen in place, a statue of terror. 'Is he coming here, Mama? You said he would not come for a while.' Her voice rose. 'Mama?'

Blinking, Harriet reached out and took Flora's arm. 'Hush, child. Do not worry.' But Eliza could see the terror in her mother-in-law's eyes, and she realised then what she had always feared: Harriet knew.

How could she let her son do this to her, his own sister? Eliza felt anger bubble up as she took in Flora's dirty feet, her daughter's tangled hair. It was cold and damp in here, so Cassius had been telling the truth about the state of the west wing after all. It was uninhabitable, for all but Flora and her children. For *his* children.

'How long has she been up here?' Eliza hissed at Harriet. Her mother-in-law did not reply, would not even look at her. One hand clutched at her chest, her fingers tight against the cloth of her dress, while the other gripped her daughter's arm in what looked like a mixture of comfort and terror. Eliza turned to Flora, who had hooked a finger into the baby's mouth. 'How long have you been here, Flora?' she asked, trying to keep her voice light.

Flora giggled again. 'Forever,' she said in her high, singsong voice, reminding Eliza again of a child. 'I live here.'

'Harriet.' Eliza's voice was like a whip and now her mother-in-law jumped, finally turning to look at her. 'What is going on? Why is . . . What has he done?' These last words came out as a whisper.

The woman's mouth opened and closed a few times, as if she was gasping for breath. 'I . . . I cannot . . .'

'No,' a voice said from the doorway. 'Perhaps it is best if you don't, Mother.'

Eliza turned, her heart hammering in her chest. Cassius stepped into the room, bringing another candle with him, the light turning his features into a monstrous mask. 'Cassius,' she breathed. 'What is—'

'I told you,' he said, his voice low and menacing, 'to be careful with the questions you ask. You might not like the answers.'

Eliza's stomach clenched, the words bubbling up her throat before she could stop them. 'What have you been doing, Cassius?' she demanded. But she knew. She only had to take one look at the children to know what had been going on. At the fear in Flora's eyes. At the shame on Harriet's face. At the smile on his lips. Cassius had no need of children with her because he already had children. Eliza's child would not have been pure enough. Only an heir with Fox blood on both sides would be enough for him and Helygen House.

Cassius ignored her, turning his anger on his mother. 'This is your fault. You've never understood. You've never loved me as a mother should.'

Harriet straightened, her eyes flashing with her own anger. 'And you've never loved anyone at all, except for yourself.'

To Eliza's surprise, Cassius laughed. 'All these years. You've always known what was going on here. It's why you sent the servants away, and why you live in your widow's weeds and accept no callers. It's why you poison my wives.'

Eliza's mouth fell open. 'You?' she whispered. 'But how . . .?' Then it hit her, the taste of metal flooding into her mouth as if she had bitten her tongue. The concoction, served in china cups and disguised as mint tea, had been the same as the one she had drunk out of desperation to end her first pregnancy. It was not Cassius who had been poisoning her, but Harriet.

The colour had drained from Harriet's face. 'I . . . I did not . . .'

'You see? It is as much your secret as mine,' Cassius interrupted. He glanced at Flora, his eyes glittering. 'Well, there's no need to keep it anymore, is there, Mama? After all, I have a son now.'

A noise came from Flora that sounded like a strangled sob. Her demeanour had suddenly changed to someone in fear for their life. She pushed the girl behind her, clutching the baby tight to her chest as she backed into the corner of the room, as if she was trying to hide in the shadows. She was scared of him, had probably always been scared of him, and who could blame her? How long had he kept her locked away up here? And Harriet had known. Had she let her daughter out of this prison whenever Cassius was away? But why hadn't she freed her completely, taken her away before Cassius returned? Harriet's eyes were full of fear, and Eliza realised that her mother-in-law had been just as terrified of her son as Flora was.

Eliza felt her body start to tremble, this time with rage. She wanted to hurt Cassius, to gouge out his eyes and tear at his skin with her nails. She hadn't felt this way since Albert Hughes, since she'd felt his clammy hand clamp across her mouth, his fingers digging at her skin. Since she drank what the woman gave her and felt the life of her rapist's child bleed out of her. She felt the fury of those things fill her once again. The shame she felt when Mrs Hughes threw her out of the house. The disgust in her mother's eyes every time she looked at her afterwards. The way she avoided looking at herself in the mirror for months, lest she allow herself to believe she was to blame for what happened. The terror of Ada, echoing down through the years, filling her with fury. The child Harriet murdered. Time seemed to slow down. Cassius was advancing towards Flora, who was cowering in the corner, trying to shield her children with her body. Eliza took a step backwards, towards the mantelpiece behind her. The windows were boarded up but for one, the candles too small to illuminate the large room, but now her eyes had adjusted to the dark, she could see a bed on the other side of the room, with two cots lined up beside it. There was a wardrobe lurking in the corner, and a child's rocking horse in front. Her eyes scanned the shelf above the mantel, which contained a few books and a box of matches, and beneath, leaning against the fireplace, was what she was looking for.

She picked up the poker slowly, weighing it in her hands. She only had one chance to get this right, she knew. He had been hurting Flora for years, and now he was going to hurt her, kill her or worse, throw her into an asylum to rot, like he had done to Ada. *In the west wing.* Ada must have discovered the truth, and she had paid dearly for it. Eliza needed to make it count, for all of them. For Flora, for Ada. Even Harriet. She turned back, raising the poker above her head and with a cry of fury, brought it down on Cassius's head. He crumpled to the floor and she hit him again, the poker vibrating in her hands as it connected with his skull.

'Eliza!' Harriet cried, but she did not move to help her son. Instead, she was wrapping her arms around Flora, murmuring into her ear as Eliza hit him again and again, until his face was unrecognisable. She stared down at the body on the floor, watching the blood pool around his head. The baby let out a shriek, snapping Eliza out of her reverie to find the two women staring at her, their eyes wide.

'I'm sorry your children had to see that,' she said, her voice oddly formal. Flora gave something like a snort, and in it Eliza recognised that they had seen much, much worse than this. What horrors must they have experienced, and been witness to? 'Are there just the two?' she asked, stepping forward and blocking the little girl's view of Cassius. 'Are there any more children?'

'There were,' Flora said, her voice young and dreamlike. 'They went away.'

'Away?' Eliza glanced at Harriet, who was staring down at the body of her son with a mixture of revulsion and relief.

'They died,' Harriet said, her voice barely above a whisper. 'He only needed two.'

Eliza stared at her as the truth hit her like a blow. 'He killed them?'

Harriet nodded. 'Just like he killed mine.'

And mine, Eliza thought but didn't say. *What kind of house is this? A graveyard for children.* Though it had been Harriet who had given her the tea which had killed her baby – pennyroyal, she knew now, finally recognising the taste – Eliza realised that it was Cassius who had been behind it all, in one way or another. And it had been going on for decades.

'But he was so young,' Eliza murmured, her eyes stinging with tears at the horror of it all. 'How could he have killed his siblings when he was still a child himself?'

'Maisie was the first,' Harriet said, her eyes taking on a faraway look. Eliza remembered the portrait hanging in the dining room, the young girl with the soft curls standing beside a dog. 'She drowned in the lake.'

'An accident?'

Harriet pursed her lips. 'He watched her drown. My maid Sara told me later, after it became too much for her. He'd forced her to keep it quiet for so long, she'd been terrified for her life. But it was too late by then.'

Eliza pressed a hand against her chest. Her heart was pounding so hard, she was beginning to feel light-headed.

'Clara was pushed from a cliff,' Harriet continued. 'The farmer's boy took the blame, though he escaped before he could be tried. Benjamin was poisoned, along with his father.' She closed her eyes and inhaled slowly, as if trying to breathe through the pain. 'Then Archie too, smothered in his sleep.'

'But not Flora?' Eliza asked. 'Why did he kill the others and not her?'

'Oh, he tried,' Harriet said, her voice bitter as she stared down at her son. 'He tried to smother them both, but Flora survived. Someone must have interrupted him. He saw something in her after that, he said.' Her voice was bitter, the look in her eyes suggesting that her daughter might have been better off dying alongside her twin brother.

A noise made Eliza turn, fearing that she would find Cassius on his feet, ready to pounce on her. But the man was still, the floor stained with his blood, and beside him, the candle he had brought with him. It must have been knocked over when she hit him, and rolled across the floor to rest against the edge of a sheet pooled against the wall. Before Eliza could react, the sheet ignited.

'Come on!' she cried, reaching a hand towards Flora. 'You have to go!'

Harriet grabbed the arm of the small girl and pulled her towards the door, Flora following behind with the baby in her arms. 'Eliza!' Harriet called, but Eliza was looking for something to throw onto the flames. She could not stamp on them with her bare feet, and she could see nothing in the room to help. *The house, it will burn.*

Flames were dancing along the wall now, licking up towards the ceiling. *How fast it moves,* she thought, feeling a sense of calm settle over her as she felt the heat on her face. *How quickly it destroys all in its path.* She glanced down at Cassius again. He was on his front, the back of his head caved in, the one visible eye covered in blood. And she felt nothing but regret that he had not been stopped sooner.

'Eliza!' Harriet cried again. The fire was creeping across the room now, stretching out towards the body lying on the floor. She wanted to see it take hold, see his body burned to ashes. She backed away, urging the other women to take the children and run. Their feet pounded down the stairs while she stood in the doorway.

'This ends now,' she whispered as the fire swallowed her husband whole.

FIFTY-TWO

ALICE

2019

She was not expecting him to be at home.

Henry had told her that he would be out all day, running errands before a meeting with the bank manager, trying to kickstart his hare-brained scheme of 'monetising' the estate. She had never heard such rubbish in all her life. Yoga classes and retreats and sodding *yurts*. People invading her house, her *home*, the home she had fought so hard to get into. The home she had made so many sacrifices for. And now he was going to take it all away.

She was just about to go upstairs – she'd had a headache building for most of the day – when the internal door to the apartment opened. Expecting Josie, Alice was surprised to see Henry moving through the narrow corridor. His eyes widened when he saw her.

'What are you doing?' they asked in unison. Though

Henry gave a short laugh, the air between them crackled, and Alice knew that something was about to happen. Something that would change her life forever.

'What is that?' she asked, nodding towards the bundle of papers in his hand. He moved his arm as if to hide them behind his body, reminding her of the child he once was, hiding a stolen biscuit behind his back.

'Oh, nothing. Just papers. For the renovations.'

'Did the meeting at the bank go well?' she asked, hoping it had not.

Henry shuffled from foot to foot. 'Yes, it did. We've got the go-ahead.'

She sniffed, pressing a finger to the throbbing behind her left eyebrow. 'So you're serious then? All of these wild plans of yours. You're really going ahead with them?'

'They're not wild, Mother,' he said, somewhat sullenly. 'It's going to work. You have to trust us.'

'I trusted you not to tear my home away from me.' Her words were sharp; she saw them fly across the space between them and slice into her son. He shifted and a sheet of paper drifted to the floor beside his feet.

'You know that's not what we're doing,' he said with a sigh. 'The estate is huge, there will still be plenty of space for you.'

'Ah, yes, the "huge estate" line. Why on earth did you marry a socialist, Henry?' She saw a flicker of a smile then, and it angered her more than usual. 'I won't go quietly, you know.'

'You're not going anywhere, Mum. You can stay here. We're starting with the stables and The Hut.'

A flash of fear went through her, the pain of another woman, another time, echoing through the years. 'The stables? What are you doing there?'

'We're turning it into accommodation.' Annoyance flickered over his face. 'You know this. We've told you everything, shown you the plans. And you agreed.'

'I did nothing of the sort!' she said, aiming for indignant, but instead sounding sullen. 'I was bullied into it, by you and that wife of yours.'

'She has a name,' Henry said, his voice low. In that moment, he reminded her of his father, the expressions he must have learned from him at a young age, despite her attempts to scrub away his memory. She should have staged it better, had him poison himself or something more dramatic than the brakes failing on his car. But she had never been an expert murderess, only a necessary one. She realised then that Henry had been more guarded with her of late, his patience shorter, and she wondered if it was simply their disagreements over the renovations, or if there was something else at play. If he knew something he shouldn't. Then she remembered the missing family bible, and nausea rose. Had he found it, and the diaries too? No, he couldn't have done. He would have said something. *And he wouldn't still be digging. He would know to leave well alone.*

'You'll be a father soon,' she said, trying a different tack.

'Surely you'll have other, more important things to be worrying about.'

'Everything will be underway by then,' he said, his voice short. 'The builders have already been booked to start work on the stables later in the year.'

'You can't!' Her words came out as a screech, echoing off the walls. Henry raised an eyebrow at her as she tried to compose herself. 'You can't do this, Henry. I won't allow it.'

'I don't think you have much say in the matter,' he snapped, the venom in his voice surprising her. 'Because I am the owner of this estate, am I not?'

The way he said it, the look in his eyes as he spoke those words, sparked fear in her heart. She knew then that he knew the truth, or at least suspected, and she told herself to back off, to go upstairs and end this conversation now, before something was said that couldn't be taken back. But something kept her rooted to the spot, pushing the words up her throat and out of her mouth.

'What does that mean, Henry?' And then it all came tumbling down.

FIFTY-THREE

JOSIE

2019

I stare at India as she tells me about Henry's argument with
his mother a few days before he died. 'How do you know all
of this?' I demand. 'I thought you and Henry weren't that
close.'

A shadow passes over her face. 'We drifted apart, after I
got married and started travelling. But he came to me when
he discovered what our mother had been hiding. You see,
she always wanted a son.' India spits the word out as if it carries a bad taste. 'A daughter was never good enough for her.'

'*Girls cannot inherit,*' I murmur, echoing Alice's words
when I told her about Henry's will.

India nods. 'She's never been what you'd call a feminist,
but that line of thinking belongs back in the 1800s. Which
is where this all began.' I think of the family bible, the line
scratched out between 1865 and 1881. *Ada.* 'Like my dear

Mama here, her great-grandfather was concerned about having a male heir to inherit Helygen House,' India continues. 'Only, he went a step further. His first wife Ada was sent to an asylum after he poisoned her, causing her to lose her baby and then her mind, where she later died. He was a big fan of arsenic; he'd started using it on his siblings when he was younger. And then there was his second wife.'

'Eliza,' I murmur, remembering. 'They had two children? Alice's grandfather and his sister?'

India laughs softly. 'Cassius did, but not with Eliza. Nor with Ada.'

I stare at her. 'Then who . . .?'

'Flora. His sister.'

The world tilts as I remember where I've seen that name before. *13th October 1864: Archie Fox & Flora Fox b., twins.*

'Her twin died,' India says, as if reading my mind. 'Their mother, Harriet, believed Cassius killed him, as he killed the rest of her children. All except Flora.'

Alice moves then, pushing against the floor with her feet, but she doesn't have enough strength to pull herself up. I stare at her, open-mouthed, as I try to piece everything together. 'So Alice's great-grandfather was –'

'A rapist. An abuser. And, thanks to him, we are all inbred.' I flinch at the term and look down at Willow in horror. 'But not her,' India adds, speaking more gently. 'That's what Henry found out.' She lays a hand on my arm. 'Henry wasn't a Fox, Josie. At least, not by blood.'

All the breath leaves my body as I absorb India's words.

Henry wasn't a Fox? I feel my legs give way and I crumple to the ground, Willow held tightly against my chest. I try to take deep breaths, but the air catches in my throat and I feel as if I'm drowning.

'She stole him, from a hospital. It sounds insane, I know, but it's true,' India says. 'After I was born, she had to have an emergency hysterectomy. She would have died without it, apparently.' India glares at her mother in a way that tells me she wishes she had.

My mind is whirling, my heart pounding in my ears. 'But why steal a child? And how did she get away with it, bringing a child home without going through a pregnancy?'

'I didn't . . .' Alice whispers. 'He wasn't supposed to find out.'

'And neither was our father,' India says. 'Or rather, my father. She killed him, you know, when he discovered the truth about Henry.' She glares at her mother. 'But what isn't clear is how Henry found out.'

I keep my eyes on Alice, try to read the emotion written across her face. Fear, pain. Desperation. 'The DNA test,' I say suddenly, remembering.

India looks at me. 'What DNA test?'

I lean my head back against the wall, trying to calm my racing heart. Slowly this story is coming together, piece by piece. 'The one which tells you about your ancestry,' I tell her. 'Henry was looking into the family history. For the house, our idea to open some of it up to the public. But I didn't know he'd decided to go ahead with it until the test arrived. It wasn't something we were planning to do for a while yet.' I turn to India. 'We need to call the police. We need to tell them what's happened.' I glance at Alice again, trying to smother my concern at her injuries. She doesn't deserve my sympathy. Not after what she did to Henry.

India shakes her head. 'Do you think she's going to tell them the truth?'

'But we have evidence. The DNA test results must be logged online somewhere. And maybe the company connected him with living relatives, his birth parents perhaps. Maybe . . .' I trail off as I consider the magnitude of Henry's discovery. And he hadn't told me about it. Willow wriggles in my arms and I suddenly know the reason why. He would have wrestled with it, wanting to discover the truth, but desperate not to uproot our family, to change the course of our daughter's future irrevocably. So he'd confronted Alice himself, and he'd paid the price.

I feel myself slump against the wall. 'How could you do it?' I whisper, watching as a single tear tracks down Alice's cheek. I hold Willow close, closing my eyes as pain shoots through me.

'Now I'm the only one who carries the Fox family secret,' India says bitterly. Her eyes are sparkling with rage. 'Me and my daughters. The daughters of Flora.'

Flora. Cassius's sister. Alice's great-grandmother. Nausea rises and I try to take a deep breath. 'How did you find out about that?'

'Didn't you find Harriet's diaries?' she asks. I shake my

head. 'Henry sent them to my in-laws' house not long before he died, for safekeeping. I sent them to you here, before I sent the bible.'

We both look at Alice. I'd thought the post had been erratic for a while, but now I realise that she must have been taking it. Such a tangled web she has woven here. Willow fidgets in my arms and I stand up slowly, leaning against the wall for support.

'If you'd read them,' India says, 'you'd know what happened. Before and after the fire. That's how Henry found out about it all.'

'The fire? In the west wing?'

'It was set when Eliza discovered what Cassius had been doing. They all got out, except for him.'

'Cassius died in the fire?'

India nods. 'Harriet infers that Eliza killed him. She didn't seem too upset about it, though. Seems she knew what Cassius had been doing to Flora and hadn't been able to stop him.' She makes a face which mirrors my own emotions. How could you let your son rape and imprison your daughter?

I shudder. 'What happened to them?'

'John, my great-grandfather, was a baby when the fire started, less than a year old. Harriet took them all to Australia, Flora and the two children, though Flora died during the crossing and the girl, Arabella, was living in New Zealand with a Māori woman when she died in her late sixties. Harriet died just before the First World War broke out.'

'And Eliza? What happened to — ?' Sudden movement makes me stop. I turn my head just in time to see Alice get to her feet and hurl herself towards India. I stumble back, my arm moving protectively over Willow, and watch in horror as the two women fall through the door towards the water beyond.

FIFTY-FOUR

The water in the lake is high, almost to their knees as they wrestle one another, arms locked like the antlers of deer. I suddenly have a vision of Flick, thrashing beneath the water, and my stomach lurches. 'Stop!' I cry, but the wind has picked up and my words are lost to it. I hesitate for a moment before turning and rushing back through The Hut and out of the other door. The grass is wet but the water isn't as high on this side. I remember Henry telling me that this is why the building was on stilts, because the lake grows during the autumn and winter, stretching out like a membrane towards Helygen House.

Willow is quiet as I rush around the side of the building, one hand on the back of her head, holding her close. 'Don't worry. You're safe,' I tell her, though I'm not sure who I'm trying to convince. When I round the corner, I see India is on her knees, Alice above her. The water is lapping at India's chest now, and her eyes are wide with terror. 'Alice!' I cry. 'Stop!' Her head jerks at the sound of my voice and for a second our eyes meet, and I see a terrifying mixture of fear and fury. She turns back to her daughter, but that pause is enough for India to get to her feet. She throws herself at Alice and they go down, both of their heads beneath the water.

'No!' I scream. I pace up and down the edge of the lake, my heart in my throat. There's nowhere to safely leave Willow so I can go in after them, and what if something happens to me? I have to protect her. I need to call for help. I run back around The Hut, then up the incline towards Little Hel. I slip on the wet grass and almost fall, letting out a cry, but I manage to stay upright and keep moving.

I'm shivering by the time I open the door and slip inside. I look around for my phone but I can't see it. The coffee table is empty but for a remote control and a candle Halka must have left burning. I realise with a jolt that my phone must still be in the car. I frantically pat my pockets, trying to hold Willow still against my chest, but they are empty. I move towards the kitchen and breathe a sigh of relief when I see Henry's keys lying on the counter. I try not to think about what is happening outside, try to concentrate on getting to the car, where I can lock the doors and call the police, but my feet are slippery on the tiles and I almost fall over when I hear the front door opening. I look up to find Alice standing in the hallway. She is soaked, her hair hanging in dark, tangled clumps, blood crusting the side of her head, and she picks up a large knife from the block as she moves through the kitchen towards me. The keys fall to the floor, clattering against the tiles.

'Sit down,' she orders, and I move backwards until I am beside the sofa, my daughter held against my chest. 'Put her down.'

I shake my head. There's no way I'll ever be parted from Willow again. I move past the coffee table, the rush of air causing the candle to flicker. 'What are you doing?' I whisper. I am still shaking, my whole body trembling with cold and fear. 'Where's India? Alice, you can't—'

'I am *sick* of people telling me what I can and cannot do,' she cries, lifting the knife and pointing it at me. 'My father, my husband, my brother. My son.' Her eyes fill with tears. 'Why does nobody trust me? Why does nobody believe that *I* know what's best?'

'Is stealing a baby from a hospital "what's best"?' I spit before I can stop myself. I think of that poor mother, whose newborn disappeared from a place they were supposed to be safe. She must have been beside herself. I stare at my mother-in-law, trying to reconcile the woman I know with these cruel acts. 'Is killing your son "what's best"? How could you do that, Alice?'

'Who are *you* to question me?' Alice sneers, taking a step forward. I can see the whites of her eyes, manic like a cornered dog. 'You are not part of this family, Josie. You have no idea what it was like.'

'Tell me then,' I say hurriedly, trying to turn so my body is blocking Willow from Alice whilst keeping my eyes on her. 'Tell me what happened to you.' She blinks as if she doesn't understand the question. 'You said you grew up in Australia, then came back to England so you could claim Helygen House. But your younger brother inherited instead. That must have been difficult, being passed over like that.'

Alice glares at me. 'What would you know about it? You know nothing of our lives, of this house.'

'I know it's poison,' I say, trying to keep my voice even. 'I know it has made you do things you should never have done. Would never have done otherwise. You are not this person, Alice. This isn't you.'

'Am I not?' she scoffs, then her face crumples. 'I killed him. And I regret it, Josie. You have to believe that. I have regretted it every day since. But he knew the truth.'

Anger flares inside me. 'So your reputation was more important than your son's life? You killed him to protect the family secrets?'

'I killed him to protect the house!' Alice shouts, glaring at me again. 'Henry didn't understand either. You poisoned his mind. He would never have reacted the way he did if he hadn't met you.'

I stare at her in disbelief. 'I'm pretty sure Henry knew right from wrong before he met me. You're not to blame for what happened in the past, but protecting that legacy, what you did to hide the truth of what happened all those years ago, was wrong.' I take a deep breath, trying to control my emotions. Alice is unpredictable, I remind myself. She killed her own son; she won't think twice about killing me. 'You weren't to blame for what happened back then, Alice,' I repeat, my voice softer now. 'You're just another one of Cassius's victims. Henry saw that too, I know he did. He would have wanted to help you.'

'How could telling the world the truth possibly *help* me?'

she cries. 'Everyone who lives at Helygen House has to protect the family legacy. That's how it works. And Henry was going to destroy everything.' She looks around the room, her eyes wide. 'This was where they lived, you know. Cassius and Eliza. Your bedroom is their old room.' My face must show the horror I feel, for she smiles. 'You've felt it too, haven't you?'

A shiver passes over me as I remember the nightmares, the baby crying in the night, the wet footprints on the floor. The way Flick behaved when she was here. 'Flick . . . She said she saw something when she was here.'

Alice nods. 'She certainly did, but not in that way. She came to me, asking about the painting of Eliza. Almost a hundred and forty years, and not one single person had ever mentioned her black hair.' She snorts, waving a hand at her own fair hair, the hair India and even Henry share. 'Flick wanted to do a family tree as a gift to Willow,' she says, her eyes meeting mine, and I stare at her in horror as the truth hits me like a blow. Flick figured it out, and Alice killed her for it. I feel myself begin to tremble. 'I panicked. She was digging where she shouldn't have been. Just like those builders.' She straightens, tilting her chin in defiance. 'She should have stayed out of it. You all should have stayed out of it.'

I think of Flick lying beneath the willow tree, how I didn't go to her, how I couldn't bring myself to see her face. She deserved so much better than that. She deserved a better friend, one who didn't abandon her in her hour of need. One who didn't so readily accept that she had taken her own life. *I'm so sorry*, I tell her silently, tears stinging my eyes. *It's all my fault.*

'If you hadn't brought her here . . .' Alice says, as if reading my thoughts.

I feel my hands bunch into fists, nails digging into my palms. I can't let my grief take over now. I have to focus. 'You're right. We should never have come here. We should have left you and Helygen House to rot.'

Alice gives a bark of laughter, making me jump. 'Henry would never have agreed to it. He was always going to come home, to me. Unlike his ungrateful sister.' I glance towards the French doors, wondering where India is. Whether Alice drowned her like she did Flick. 'Cassius killed all of his siblings, except Flora,' Alice says. She has an almost dreamlike expression on her face now. 'They say I look like her, you know. My great-grandmother.' Willow makes a snuffling noise and I take a step back, holding her tightly. Flick, India and Henry deserved better, but I can't save them now. I have to focus on Willow. 'The fair hair, the grey eyes. The Fox features,' Alice continues. Her eyes suddenly snap back into focus, fixing me to the spot. 'Henry had them too. It was meant to be, when I saw him in the hospital. He was supposed to be mine.'

I think of his face, the features Willow has inherited, and feel something harden inside me. 'Except he wasn't,' I say, moving back again. We have been circling one another like wolves, the sofa and coffee table between us, and now I can see the car keys lying beneath the island. If I'm quick, maybe I can grab them and run. 'He was never yours, Alice. You only wanted him so you could have this house, and I think a part of him knew it. That's why he left it to Willow.'

'She has no right to it!' Alice shouts.

'Neither did Henry,' I shoot back. 'You had the opportunity to change things when you took over here. You could have created a new legacy, rewritten history in a way which would change the future. You could've been the one to break the cycle. But you're weak, Alice. You always have been.'

Her eyes narrow at my words and she takes a step forward. 'I should never have let you move in here,' she says, her voice low. 'I should never have let him marry someone like *you*.'

'You're right,' I say, inching further away from her. 'Because *I* will be the one to break the cycle. I will tear the roots of Helygen House and put an end to it all.' Moving as quickly as I can, I twist and drop to the floor, reaching out to grab the keys and trying not to drop Willow. Alice lurches forward, her leg hitting the coffee table, and as I regain my footing, the candle topples over onto the floor. Before either of us can react, the rug bursts into flames, and fire begins to lick at the bottom of the sofa.

I back away, the kitchen tiles cold beneath my feet. Alice is still standing in the middle of the living room, as if mesmerised by the fire. 'Alice!' I cry before I can stop myself. 'Get out!'

She looks up, that dreamlike expression in her eyes again. 'Tear the roots,' she says, the knife falling from her hand as the flames engulf her.

FIFTY-FIVE

ELIZA

1939

She watched the house burn that night, the grass beneath her feet freezing in the December air. But she did not feel the cold. She was warmed through, knowing that Flora and her children were going to get far away from this house, and that Cassius would never return.

Eliza moves slowly through the corridor now, her right hand tightly clasping her stick, her left trailing along the panelling as it has done every day for the past fifty years. It is July, and soon Germany will invade Poland, but Eliza will not live to see it. She will not live to see the American soldiers who will make Helygen House their base, or hear the stories they will tell one another of the small fair-haired child who haunts them in the night. She has already lived through one war which killed many, and a flu which killed even more, and now she is ready to go. Almost.

In the dining room, she allows Mary to help her into her chair. She wonders what will become of the girl – woman now, she reminds herself – when she is gone. She will leave her a sum, which she knows John will not object to. Though he inherited the estate in 1881 as an eight-month-old baby, Flora's son has never once visited and only corresponds with Eliza occasionally, though his sister, Arabella, writes more often. She has taken up the mantel since her grandmother passed away and Eliza is glad to know her, even if it is from a distance.

Eliza was heartbroken to hear of Flora's death on the crossing to Australia. For her to have finally escaped her prison, a lifetime of horror and abuse, only to die from dysentery on a ship a thousand miles from home, was a pain unlike anything Eliza has ever known. She secretly wondered if they should have stayed, all of them, together in Helygen House, but she knew that the children had to get away. The remaining members of the Fox family are on the other side of the world now, living new lives on the south coast of Australia, and it is up to Eliza to break the cycle.

Now John is married with two grown-up children and his first grandchild on the way, and a steady business which has something to do with importing or exporting – Eliza has always failed to understand it. Arabella remains single, though Eliza suspects that the Māori woman she often refers to as her 'partner' in her letters is more than just someone she runs her coffee shop with. Eliza has no feelings on that one way or the other. She only wishes them happiness, after their wretched start in life. Sometimes she longs to see Australia, to sip a drink on the veranda of Arabella's coffee shop and to feel the white sand between her toes. But it is too late for that now.

'Tea, Eliza?' Mary says, holding the teapot aloft. They had done away with the airs and graces long ago, becoming companions and then friends instead of mistress and servant. When Eliza urged Mary to leave with the rest, to find someone nice to marry and get away from this house, Mary had refused. She felt at home in Helygen House, she said, and Eliza had understood. She too felt at home here, since it had been cleansed of Cassius's evil.

'I still see them,' Mary would say, her eyes wide not with fear but wonder. 'All the Foxes that have gone before. We have to set them free.'

Eliza had waved away the notion of holding a séance or inviting a priest to cleanse the house, but now that the end is near, she finds herself wondering if she should do something to rid the house of its ghosts. She wonders if it is possible to set them free. She wonders if they even exist at all. Since realising that the ghost she saw in the nursery had in fact been Arabella escaped from her prison, Eliza has no fear of ghosts, not even that of Cassius. She has never seen him, except for in her dreams. And yet . . .

'Mary,' she says now, watching her friend pour them both cups of tea. 'Do you still know how to . . .?'

'Yes,' Mary says quickly. 'I've been waiting for you to ask. To give your permission.'

Eliza smiles at that. 'It is your house as much as mine. You could have done it without me ever knowing.'

'But where's the fun in that?' Mary grins, reminding Eliza of the young girl she had been when she'd first arrived at Helygen House, with her red curls and bright eyes. Now her hair has faded to grey, as Eliza's has, though it still curls wildly down her back.

They finish breakfast in companionable silence. Eliza feels at peace, now she knows what Mary will do. It feels right somehow, as if it is the final piece of a puzzle slotting into place. Even if it does nothing, if there are no ghosts in Helygen House and never had been, the curse will die with her. She will take it with her to the grave.

After breakfast, Eliza makes her way to the sitting room, bringing out the diaries Arabella sent to her when Harriet died. She has read the words so many times over the years, reliving Harriet's horror as she realised what her son had been doing to her other children. Maisie drowned, Clara pushed from the cliff, Archie smothered. And her husband, poisoned alongside little Benjamin. So much tragedy. Eliza's memory is not what it used to be, but Harriet's grief has been seared into her mind. This too will die with her, the painful knowledge of what Cassius Fox brought upon his family. For the curse originated with him, she believes. It did not come from God. It was manmade, created by the evil notions of a boy who turned into a man, and who had always been a monster.

But who had made him into a monster? Despite everything,

Eliza cannot believe that a child could be born evil. Perhaps Harriet's guilt had been founded after all, in a way. Perhaps she had played a part in what her son became. She will never forget the way Harriet treated her, the cups of pennyroyal tea she had given her, though she understands now the reasons for it. She had been trying to warn her, to force her from Helygen House, just as she had done with Ada before her, and to stop any more children from being born into that hell. But there could have been another way, and Eliza can never forget that it was Harriet who killed her unborn child. This is the sole act for which she could never forgive Harriet, even on her deathbed over two decades ago.

'And not even now,' she murmurs to the portrait of a young Harriet hanging in the sitting room. 'But I will take it to my grave. That is the best I can do.'

A week later, Mary holds the séance. Though she says it is not a true séance, Eliza has no other word for it, and so this is the word she uses. They sit in the dining room, hands held across the wide table, the faces of the Fox forebears staring down at them, while Mary speaks to the ghosts. Eliza thinks of Cassius, and the night the west wing burned down. She has never felt any guilt for watching him burn that night. The locals had come running when they saw the house was on fire, armed with pickaxes to smash through the ice coating the lake, but it did not yield and Eliza had not moved to help. *Let it burn*, she thought, *let it burn with him inside it.*

Though the fire destroyed the west wing, it did not touch

the rest of the house. Mary has always been adamant that that was the spirits' doing, that they had joined up to protect the house, a notion Eliza has never challenged her on for she has no alternative explanation and has never sought one. Mary has always been one to search for deeper meanings, but upon discovering the dark secrets of Helygen House, Eliza has never wanted to know more than what she can see with her own two eyes.

The candles flicker as Mary speaks, a draught coming from an open window. The house has been stuffy this summer, the heat almost unbearable, and Eliza has been glad of the new fashions women can wear now. She shed her Victorian garb as soon as she could, as if she were stepping into a new life as well as a new era. Her skirts were no use in the gardens, forever getting caught on thorns and trailing in the mud, so she altered a pair of Cassius's trousers for herself. By that point, only Mary remained in the house, the other servants having fled either from the fire or their new mistress's bizarre ways, and so Eliza could do as she pleased, which is precisely what she did.

They have lived a quiet life, a simple life, and though the shadow of the past has always loomed over them, Eliza thinks now that the past fifty years have been far happier than her first twenty on this earth. With Cassius gone and a small allowance giving her the means to sustain herself without having to find another suitor, Eliza has achieved what she never dreamed possible: freedom. This is what she will give to the generations to come. Even if John and

Arabella never return to England, if their descendants stay in Australia and shun Helygen House forever, Eliza will have done what she was supposed to do.

Mary looks up, smiles. 'They're gone,' she whispers, and Eliza feels herself exhale. Now, she is free.

EPILOGUE

JOSIE

Four years later

Time and tide wait for no man. It was something my dad used to say, his eyes creasing as he smiled at me from his sickbed. And he was right. Time rushes on, and we find ourselves moving with it, life continuing whether you are ready or not. Now, four years later, Willow and I are returning to Helygen House.

Sometimes I wonder how we got here, how time has managed to keep marching on despite everything that happened. We have been living in a cottage in St Agnes rented from the woman who owns the local bakery, where I work three mornings a week, apron dusty with flour and fingers sticky with dough. It has given me a sense of normality, a routine so comfortable it is easy to forget the horror of what happened. Here we are far enough away from Helygen House to put it out of my mind, yet close enough to still feel its pull.

I watched the house burn that night. The fire moved quickly, swallowing Helygen House whole. The police arrived in a rush of blue lights and noise, and then there were firefighters carrying heavy hoses across the grass and an ambulance pulling up in the driveway. I was moved back, a blanket wrapped around me, fingers reaching towards Willow. I slapped them away, holding her tight against my chest. Nobody would take her from me again.

Paramedics dragged India from the lake, miraculously alive, though they did not know then if she would make it. I felt a heavy shroud of grief settle on my shoulders as I watched them carry her towards the ambulance. Henry, Flick, Alice, India. My father. I have lost so much, so many people close to me gone. There is no one left, no one except Willow. She is turning into such a sweet little girl. Though she is still a quiet child, forever with her head in a book, sounding out the words to Ivy, who rarely leaves her side, her confidence is growing too, and she loves nothing more than visiting the shops in the village, saying hello to everyone she meets. St Agnes can be busy in the summer, full of tourists staying at the hotel or in holiday homes, but outside of the peak season it is calm and quiet, wrapping us up in its comforting arms. We spend most days on the beach or walking across the headland, exploring the crumbling tin mines. And while we have grown and rested and rebuilt ourselves, Helygen House has been rebuilt too. The house had been completely destroyed by the fire, so it has been torn down and a new, smaller building now sits in its place.

Today we are going to officially open The Helygen Centre, which will provide food, education and leisure facilities for underprivileged children. There will be a free childcare facility on site for the children of local workers, and a hot meal will be provided for every child who needs one, including during the school holidays when free school meals are not available. The owner of a national charity reached out to us when he heard of our plans for the estate. They had been focusing on inner city children for a time, but now they are expanding to cover rural areas and we will be the first to offer these facilities in Cornwall. Fruit and vegetables will be grown in the newly cleared fields, sold locally or donated to foodbanks. We are healing, and trying to make our small corner of the world a tiny bit better.

I think now of DS Fergus, and how he had said my name that night, how in that word was everything: an admission, recognition, vindication. Regret. I exhaled, feeling everything at the same time, and managed to lower myself slowly to the grass as blackness rushed up to meet me.

He was standing by my bedside when I woke a few hours later. The unfamiliar hospital room swam into focus and I sat up, desperately searching for Willow.

'She's here,' he said, indicating a translucent cot beside my bed. 'They checked her over but she's completely fine.'

I reached over and snatched my daughter up, holding her tight against my chest. I never wanted to be parted from her again.

'Your mother-in-law . . .' DS Fergus cleared his throat. 'Alice Fox died in the fire.'

'And India?' I asked, barely registering his words. I knew Alice was dead. I watched the flames engulf her, our eyes meeting for a second before she fell. I watched her burn, and I felt nothing but fury at what she had done.

'She's in the ICU. She has hypothermia and a nasty gash on her head, but the doctors seem hopeful she'll make a full recovery. The paramedics got to her just in time.'

'Flick.' Her name burst from my lips. Willow fidgeted in my arms and I relaxed my grip a fraction. 'Alice killed her. It wasn't suicide.'

DS Fergus narrowed his eyes for a second. 'Are you sure?'

'She confessed, just before she died. And . . .' The words died in my throat as grief threatened to overwhelm me. 'Henry.' His name came out as a gasp, a strangled sob.

'Alice killed her son?' DS Fergus asked. I nodded, unable to speak. 'I'm going to need you to come down to the station at some point. Make a full statement. When you're ready, of course,' he added, glancing at Willow, who was sleeping soundly against my chest. I felt something strengthen inside me then, resolve straightening my spine as I stared down at my daughter. *I will keep you safe*, I told her silently. *I will not let this family's dark past determine your future.*

As I drive through the gates to the estate, Willow and Ivy in the back of the car, a feeling of trepidation washes over me. I have only seen architects' drawings and photographs in the years since the fire; this is the first time we have returned, and I wonder if I am doing the right thing. Should I have left the estate to rot? Should the fire have been the end of it all? I shake myself. No. Now Helygen House will stand for something good. It will be a place of respite, of fun and laughter, of growth and hope. It will be Henry's home, his lasting mark upon the world.

I park up and turn to look at my daughter. I have a sudden memory of her as a newborn, so tiny in her car seat, so vulnerable. Now she is kicking her legs, peering through the windscreen at the place she was born in. She still has no idea what happened, what tragedy has surrounded her short life. 'Are you ready?' I ask her, and she grins. I get out of the car and open the back door, clipping Ivy's lead to her harness before freeing Willow from her seat. She clambers out by herself, ignoring my offers of help, and we stand on the driveway for a few moments, peering up at the building before us.

I can't seem to stop my mind going down dark paths, memories of the last time I was here flashing before my eyes. I squeeze them shut, trying to focus on my breathing as my mind turns to India. She spent a week recovering in hospital before moving up to Sheffield with her in-laws. She wants nothing to do with the house or the estate, and I can't say I blame her. But she gave her blessing for me to do what I thought was best, so I raised money by selling off some of the land and turning the stables into a workshop, where a local woman runs pottery and painting classes. There's also a small, self-contained annexe where artists can stay for up to six months for a small contribution, working on their art. The Hut has been turned into a yoga studio, with classes seven days a week, though it has the new name of Felicity's Place. My friend lost so much and felt so much pain, and she died because she asked the wrong questions, noticed the wrong things. Though the investigation remains open, Alice will never face justice for what she did and I will never forgive myself for what happened to my friend, but this is one small way I can honour Flick's memory.

I feel a tug on my jeans and look down to find Willow peering up at me. 'Are you okay, sweetie?' I ask, crouching down beside her. 'Are you ready to go in?'

'Together, Mummy,' she says, reaching out and clasping my hand in hers. Her fingers are warm against my skin, and I try to take my strength from her. In all the years he has been gone, Henry has truly never left me, and standing here now, I can almost feel the letter from his biological parents burning a hole in my pocket. But there will be plenty of time for that. For now, I want to enjoy the feeling of Henry standing beside us; not his ghost, but his memory. His legacy. He would be proud of Willow, his beautiful, intelligent, wonderful daughter, who carries him onwards, the best parts of him handed down to her.

I smile down at her, my throat tight with emotion. 'Together.'

ACKNOWLEDGEMENTS

When I was younger, someone once told me not to let my past dictate my future. It was something I've held onto in the years since, the belief that things really can change, and that, although we cannot alter the past, we can learn and move on from it. It was this which first sparked the idea for the Fox family and the dark secrets contained within Helygen House.

Helygen means 'willow tree' in Cornish. The Cornish language is a revived one which I have enjoyed exploring, so my thanks to organisations such as Kowethas an Yeth Kernewek and Speak Cornish for their incredible online resources and work on encouraging the use of the Cornish language. Helygen House is fictional, and the pronunciation of its name is purposefully different to the real Heligan Estate, but it was inspired by some of the beautiful estates across the UK I have enjoyed visiting over the years (thanks to the wonderful National Trust!). My thanks in particular to Jill Campbell at Knebworth House for her detailed knowledge of the history of both the estate and its occupants, and for taking the time to answer my questions.

However, writing this book in lockdown meant I very much relied on online resources, which gave me the perfect excuse to scroll through endless interior accounts on Instagram in the name of research. In no particular order, thanks to Samantha (@making_walford_magical), Heather (@theforeverhomeproject_), Tash (@woodsintothewoods), Becki (@aplaceinthecountry_), Christina (@houseofhorspool), Jo (@theelmsrenovation and @househistorian), and Fiona (@seasidevictorianhome) for sharing their beautiful homes with the world and answering my (sometimes slightly odd) questions. Special mention to Katie from @beechhouse53 for the fascinating deed reads and history of Beech House. Never underestimate the kindness of strangers on the internet, nor how inspiring a good floorplan can be.

My thanks also to the British Newspaper Archive and the various articles, blogs, and books I read as part of my research, as well as *Downton Abbey* for reminding me that there is usually a gap between a burial and the installation of a headstone, which called for a last-minute change. Any historical errors are entirely my own. Shoutout to Kaleida and their song *Tear the Roots*, which I listened to on repeat whilst writing this book.

There are several references to miscarriage in this novel, so I wanted to take a moment to acknowledge everyone who has experienced such loss, and apologise for any triggering moments in this book. Thanks to my sister, Nicole, whose childbirth experience was very similar to Josie's, and who talked me through life with a newborn.

Although this isn't my first rodeo, it is my first historical suspense novel as Victoria Hawthorne, and I'm grateful for the chance to branch out into this genre. This is the novel which got me my wonderful agent, Emily Glenister, whose passion and enthusiasm is second to none – other than my fabulous editor, Florence Hare. Huge thanks to everyone at Quercus for believing in this book and giving it the perfect home. I am so privileged to be working with such a fantastic team. Thanks also to my amazing beta readers Chloe Osborne, Michaela Balfour, Wendy Robey, and Josephine Bilton for their very early feedback.

Being an author can be a solitary job, but thankfully the writing community is such a kind and welcoming one. Thanks to the whole PSAA gang and Savvy Writers for being so supportive, and especially to Lesley Sanderson, Ruth Heald, and Rona Halsall for their sometimes-daily encouragement and the opportunity to vent whenever needed.

As ever, my thanks to the Cornish contingent, Amy Fergus (I made you a DS in this one!) and Rachel Allen, for their continued friendship and patience when I asked for their knowledge of the local area and their opinion on how to pronounce Helygen (result: mixed). To my wife, who always reads the earliest, dirtiest drafts of my books and is now waiting for the audiobook to come out so she can listen to the final version. To the reason all of my fictional dogs will live forever – the best golden retrievers in the world, Vixen, Chloe, Toffee, and the real Ivy, who will find a muddy puddle wherever she goes. And to *that* registrar whose words have now been immortalised – I hope you read this and are suitably embarrassed.